TROUBLE WITH A TWIST

IRENE BAHRD

Cover design by Irene Bahrd
Edited by H.M. Darling
Formatted by Irene Bahrd

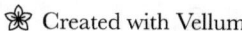

For all my neurospicy readers.

And… for Lakshmi who has been simping over Jason since Mine with Extra Lime.

Enjoy!

CONTENT WARNINGS

By reading this book, you may experience the following side effects:

- Wet panties
- Wanting to leave your significant other in search of your own Jason.
- Forcing your partner to wear gray sweatpants and lean against doorframes for the ultimate book boyfriend experience.
- Finding yourself eating waffles and playing Taylor Swift on Sundays.
- Always choosing "10."

You're welcome.

All joking aside, this is a slow-to-medium burn, age gap, friends-to-lovers **romantic comedy** with on-page explicit content. It is intended for mature audiences.

Additionally, there are scenes with:

- Handcuffs
- Brief general discussions about BDSM and kinks
- Orgasm control
- Sexytime in public

Author Note: While this book is technically an interconnected standalone, it is recommended that you read *Mine with Extra Lime* or *Royally on the Rocks* first for the best reading experience.

Your new bestie, Charlotte, is autistic and has ADHD. In this book, she has an on-page meltdown and a few instances where she dissociates. There is discussion of on- and off-page sensory overload/experiences in a few chapters. Charlotte and Jason both go to therapy in this book (on-page), but please note, any advice provided by the fictional therapists is just that, fiction.

If you or someone you know feels they can benefit from therapy, please research your options and/or speak to a medical professional. Though there were two sensitivity readers for this book, everyone's experience with ADHD and autism is different. Charlotte is **fictional**, but it was important to highlight both the beauty and some of the struggles that neurodivergent people have in their day-to-day lives.

Additionally, it was important to the sensitivity readers and author that Jason *not* treat Charlotte as an equal for the first part of the book. You'll see scenes where he is borderline controlling. Don't worry, he figures it out and makes big changes! Unfortunately, neurodivergent people and people with disabilities can experience this in their romantic and non-romantic relationships. The greatest way you can support neurodivergent people in your life is to **listen**. The author, being neurospicy herself, wanted these voices to be heard.

Representation matters!!!

PLAYLIST

"Clumsy" — Fergie
"Dandelions" — Ruth B.
"Bejeweled" — Taylor Swift
"Dark Horse" — Katy Perry [feat. Juicy J]
"You Belong With Me" — Taylor Swift
"Here With Me" — marshmello & CHVRCHES
"Levitating" — Dua Lipa
"Shake It Off" — Taylor Swift
"Made You Look" — Meghan Trainor
"Just A Girl" — No Doubt
"All Of The Girls You Loved Before" — Taylor Swift
"Paper Rings" — Taylor Swift

PROLOGUE — CHARLOTTE

"*Happy Birthday!*" The shouts could be heard from a mile away.

Emma's boyfriend, Dylan, has been planning her birthday surprise for months and asked that I fly in for it. I love my step-sister, so obviously my answer was yes. While Emma and I didn't grow up together, we've become great friends, and I'm so happy that she's recon-nected with Dylan after sixteen years apart. He invited all of her friends to come for her birthday... and their engagement—she doesn't know about the latter, yet.

"You guys! What is this?" Emma exclaims as she makes her way over to greet all of us.

Her ex-husband, Jason, and their son, Aiden, hug her first. Jason's smile is kind and a little sheepish as he greets her. "Hey, Em. Dylan told me about a surprise he had for you. We wanted to be sure the boys were here for it. I know this is your first birthday since the divorce, but I hope you don't mind me being here with them to celebrate with you."

"Of course not! Thank you. I don't know what's going on, but I'm glad you're here." Emma has an unconventional friendship with her ex-husband. According to her, they just didn't work out and were better off friends. They co-parent their three boys beautifully and I wish I saw more of it with divorced families.

Aiden's still clinging to Emma's side. "Mommy, these pants are itchy." I can't blame the little guy; the pants aren't the best sensory experience.

Emma glances down, then around to everyone. A wide smile spreads across her face as she finally realizes we're all wearing matching white and black buffalo plaid pants.

"Okay, everyone! Mimosas are ready!" Riley calls from the kitchen.

Jason takes Aiden to get changed and all of the adults head to the kitchen for drinks; the rest of the kids are in the living room playing, reading, and laughing.

Emma startles me mid-sip when she spots me. "Char! I don't know what this is all about, but thank you for coming." She wraps me in a tight hug and I appreciate the added pressure.

"I'm actually moving back!" I tell her. "I just need to find a place. Tyler said I could stay with him for a few days until I figure out something permanent. I wanted to surprise you for your birthday."

I was offered a position moderating focus groups here in California. It was a no-brainer to accept it. My job in New York was fizzling out and I'm excited to live closer to family and my best friend, Eddie. Edmund lived in New York with me before he moved out here a couple years ago. To everyone else, he goes by Tyler, but he'll always be Eddie to me.

"You're moving back? Are you serious?" She squeezes tighter, making me chuckle. "You know, Jason mentioned his noisy neighbor was moving, maybe it's vacant?"

"Oh my gosh, that would be amazing! Finding an apartment has been brutal. I'll have to chat with him while I'm here."

"Thanks for coming. We'll have to get drinks after all of whatever Dylan has planned is over." Emma keeps me wrapped in her arms and I savor the squeezes. She begins to say something else, but is interrupted by Aiden bringing over a small present.

"Mommy, this one says it's for 'my love'—*ew, bleh*—from Dylan, can I open it?" Damn, I love this kid.

Dylan doesn't take it from him. Instead, he tells Aiden, "If your mom is okay with it, you can unwrap it, but I need her to open it. It's her birthday gift."

Aiden nods and rips the wrapping paper to shreds before handing what's inside to Emma. It's a small velvet box and I can't help my smile.

It's finally happening!

The room is quiet; we've all been waiting for this moment. Emma scans the room, finding all eyes on her. She blushes, and when she turns back to Dylan, he's on one knee.

"E, before you open it, I want you to know that we can take as long as you need for us to figure it out. There's one thing that I have no doubt about, though—I want to spend every day of the rest of my life with you. Nearly seventeen years ago, you were my first love, but you're also my last. I've always been yours, beautiful. I can't go another day without asking: Will you spend the rest of your life as mine? Make me the luckiest man in the world and marry me?"

Emma cups his cheek and whispers, "Yes." She kisses him and we all cheer and clap. There isn't a dry eye here —she's found her happily ever after.

Our friend, Ethan, calls from across the room. "Open it! I picked it out."

Melanie smacks his arm. "You did not!" It's playful, and if I didn't know any better, I'd say there's something going on between them.

A few minutes later, Lily and I are laughing in the kitchen at Ethan and how painfully obvious it is that he's interested in Melanie. He looks at her like Dylan looks at my sister, with hearts in his eyes.

My giggles subside when I spot Jason. I'm hoping Emma is right and there's a vacancy in his building. I don't know why I'm so nervous to approach him. Oh, right, I'm only 5'6" and this beast of a man is almost a whole foot taller than me at 6'5". I'm not normally intimidated by tall men, but he also has a whole rugged mountain man thing going that I normally find incredibly attractive.

Why does he have to be my step-sister's ex?

"Hi, Jason." My voice is meeker than I'd like. I can't help it, the moment his eyes meet mine my stomach flips. I've never noticed before, he has the most beautiful dark blue eyes.

"Hey, sweetheart, how've you been?" he asks as he sips his beer. My breath catches at him calling me that. He doesn't mean anything by it, but it still gives me butterflies.

"Oh, I'm good. I'm actually moving back. Got a job in the city."

His pupils dilate and I'm not sure what to make of it. As a market researcher, I am normally great at reading respondents in a focus group; it's data driven. In my personal life, there are usually big, complicated feelings. I can't figure out what he's thinking. Jason could be anything from upset to turned on—I'm going with upset. I shouldn't indulge in the fantasy of an ex-baseball player, who used to be married to Emma, wanting me like that.

"*Anyway*, Emma mentioned your next door neighbor is moving? I'm actually looking for a place."

He sputters a cough. "Oh, I don't think you want to live there."

"Why not? It's a great location and I'd get to see more of my nephews with you living next door."

Jason mumbles something into the beer bottle.

"Sorry, didn't catch that."

"Nothing," he grumbles. "I'll help you find somewhere else to live."

"Let me see your phone," I demand with a forced smile. I've been masking all day and it's starting to slip. Plastering on a smile and hiding how you're feeling is exhausting for neurospicy folks like myself. I've found smiling helps disarm people, even if it's fake. Jason hands his phone to me and I send myself a text before handing it back to him. "Now you have my number and I have yours."

"Great," he grunts with a small smile, but it doesn't reach his eyes.

"Are you sure you don't want to be neighbors? I'm a lot of fun, you know," I tease, hoping to make light of it.

He shakes his head and I swear I hear him say "*or a whole lotta trouble*" under his breath.

1

JASON
TWO YEARS LATER

"You are *not* driving up the mountain by yourself, sweetheart. There was a big storm last week and the roads aren't safe. I'll take you in my truck." If anything happened to Charlotte, I'd never forgive myself.

"Don't be such a grump," she groans. "It'll be *fine!* I've driven up there a few times in worse conditions."

"Absolutely not. I'm driving. End of discussion." My eyes narrow and she mirrors my expression. "That's not going to work on me, babygirl. You can't break me."

"Damn it!" Charlotte huffs with a roll of her eyes. "Okay, you can drive me. Let me call the resort to make sure I can reserve the two bedroom cabin. It shouldn't be an issue, they love me there. One second, I'll confirm it."

I shake my head. "I'm not staying with you. I'll get my own."

"Don't be ridiculous. I'll get one with two rooms, Jay. It's not like we're going to have a 'one bed trope' situation." I don't bother asking what the hell she's talking about. She types on her phone for a minute while I take out a few mugs from her cabinets for coffee. She startles me when she hears back from the resort. "*Fuck*, sorry, they're completely booked. They only have a one bedroom available, but there's a pull out couch." Char shows her phone to me.

"If I stay with you, I'll take the couch. I don't mind. But I'm driving you whether you like it or not."

"You're not taking the couch! Your legs will dangle off the end of it. We can share a bed."

Oh, my sweet Charlotte, there is no way in hell I'm sharing a bed with you.

Charlotte is fucking stunning with delicious curves I could sink my teeth into. I love a girl with something to hang onto…

Fuck. I need to stop thinking about her like that.

Over the years, Char's become one of my best friends. Except, I've also fallen in love with her and don't want to betray her trust by admitting my feelings. While she's a big flirt, I don't put any stock in it. It's who she is as a person; she isn't interested in me that way. All it would take to lose having her in my life is her slinging her leg over me in the middle of the night, finding my morning wood… Or worse, having one too many drinks and finally telling her how I feel. There is absolutely no way I can stay in the same bed with her.

"Done! Reservation confirmed. If you won't share a bed with me, I'll take the couch. It's the least I can do if you're driving," Charlotte insists, never looking up from her phone.

I place my hand over the screen to get her attention. "Doesn't Dylan have a cabin? Maybe I can stay there? I'll text him and stay there; you keep your cabin."

A few minutes later, my backup plan saves the day. Dylan's friend, Matt, and his girlfriend were supposed to be there for the weekend, but they changed their plans and are headed to Montreal. The cabin is vacant.

Shit, that was a close one.

"Well, babygirl, looks like no one needs to sleep on a couch. Dylan's is available."

"I want Dylan's cabin then! I'll make you a deal, if I get his cabin, you get to pick the movie tonight." Charlotte's figured out she has me wrapped around her finger and I'll never say no to her.

"You can pick the movie, too, sweetheart." I tuck her hair behind her ear. Where most women's breath would hitch at the subtle touch, Charlotte doesn't flinch. She only smiles up at me. But, fuck, I'd do just about anything for her smiles.

The drive up to the cabins is worse than I expected; the roads are slick and the traffic is fucking brutal. These past few years, I've gotten used to Charlotte's topic jumping and storytelling. I'm grateful for it. Her excited chatter helps pass the time while we're stuck behind a lumber truck currently peaking my anxiety. *Final Destination 2* did a number on me and I never recovered.

We check in at the resort to pick up keys for both cabins. The front desk attendant, Tamra, is typing away at the computer a little too long for my liking. Her brow furrows; something's wrong.

"I'm so sorry, Ms. Wentworth, it appears your reservation was canceled."

"That's not possible, I confirmed yesterday." Charlotte checks her email on her phone. I peer over her shoulder and, sure enough, it's a cancellation email. The buttons to confirm or cancel are next to each other; it could've happened to anyone. She mutters to herself, "How did this happen?"

I wrap my arm around her shoulder. "Don't worry about it, sweetheart. We have Dylan's cabin and it has three or four bedrooms."

"I apologize for the mix up," Tamra says as she pulls the keys. "Here are the keys for the Alexander's family cabin and a voucher for our on-site restaurant."

"Oh, that's not necessary. It's my fault," Charlotte sighs, defeated.

"Ms. Wentworth, I insist. We hope you enjoy your stay with us this weekend. If you need anything else, please don't hesitate to ask. Also, your meeting with our marketing manager is confirmed for 2 p.m. in her office." Tamra pulls out a map and circles the office for Charlotte. "Two lefts and a right from here."

Charlotte takes the map, voucher, and keys. "Thank you, Tamra. I'm sorry for the confusion. I'll be back after lunch to meet with Kelly. Thank you so much for your help."

We walk away, and once out of earshot of Tamra, I stop Char to tell her, "Hey, it's okay." She still looks slightly heartbroken over her innocent mistake as she nods. "You're going to have a great focus group later and look"—I pull out the voucher and wave it like a winning lotto ticket—"lunch is on me!" Thankfully, it earns me a small smile. "Come on, no more moping, babygirl. It could've happened to anyone. Let's get something to eat and settle in at the cabin."

"I got it! They're giving me the contract," Charlotte squeals.

"I knew you would." I wrap her in a tight hug, resisting the urge to kiss the top of her head. "I'm so proud of you, you deserve it." As I pull back, she clings to me. "Hey, is everything okay?"

She takes a deep breath, letting it out slowly. "Yeah. *Holy crap*, you smell good." Her voice shakes ever so slightly. No one else would ever have noticed it, but I do.

"Don't change the subject, Char. What's wrong?"

"Sorry, just a little overwhelmed. It's the biggest job I've ever landed."

I give in, pressing a kiss to the top of her head. *She's* the one that always smells good, like coconut and vanilla. "You've got this. They hired you because you're the best."

Charlotte finally pulls back. "Thank you for coming up here with me." Her infectious joy is back and I'm so glad things have turned around since this morning. She's usually so full of life; it breaks my heart when she gets lost in her head.

"What time is your group?"

She glances at her watch. "I have one in an hour, so I need to get going. They added one more right after. I should be done around 7 p.m."

"I'll come up to the main lodge when you're done, and we'll go out on the town to celebrate," I insist.

"You're on! I'll see you later." She grabs her bag and practically skips out the door.

For dinner, Charlotte is craving tacos and I find the closest Mexican restaurant with good reviews. After her first bite, she moans, the sound shooting straight to my cock. "These have to be the best tacos I've ever had!"

I shake my head. "They're good, but there's an amazing taqueria in San Diego I need to take you to sometime. *Those* are the best tacos."

"You want to take me to San Diego?" Charlotte asks with a furrowed brow.

"Sure." I shrug and take a bite of my taco. "Pick a weekend and we'll go."

"Maybe this summer? There's a lot going on with this new contract, Mel being back from Paris all mopey she can't see Ethan, and Eddie's throwing a tantrum every four minutes about his coworker he's obsessed with but won't admit it." The fact that she wants to be here for her friends is endearing and I'm thankful neither of them take advantage of Charlotte's big heart. Though disappointment settles in my gut that I'll have to wait months to take her on vacation.

"Summer's good. I'll have the boys, but I'm sure I can get away for a weekend."

Eyes wide, Charlotte sets down her taco. "What? No, we can bring them. I love my nephews! We can take them to the beach; Aiden would love it."

Just like that, I'm snapped back to reality. Charlotte's not mine, and we could never be together. I've been getting a little too comfortable having her in my life lately, and shouldn't be suggesting vacations or enjoying alone time with her like this.

I clear my throat and change the subject. "So, where are we headed next?"

"There's a tequila bar across the street. What do you say we do a tasting and then maybe go dancing?"

"If that's what you want, let's go." I don't dance, but as always, I'll do anything she asks. I finish my taco and signal to the waiter for the check.

"Really? Are you going to lurk at the bar and make sure no man comes within ten feet of me?" She narrows her eyes and I can't help but laugh.

"You bet, sweetheart."

"I think we've had enough to drink, Char," I grunt. She's been dancing for hours and I've consumed my body weight in tequila.

"One more shot! Then I have a brilliant idea, Jay. It would be *so* funny!" Char wraps her arms around my neck and pulls me to her until our faces are mere inches apart. *Shit, I know this look.* She almost kissed me at Emma's wedding a year ago; this feels awfully similar.

I lean in beside her ear and whisper, "We can't do this, babygirl."

She gasps and releases her arms. "Oh, sorry, I didn't realize I was—"

"Come on, ready to head out?"

Charlotte narrows her eyes at me then signals to the bartender. "Another round, please?"

"*One* more, then we're leaving. What was the brilliant idea you had, anyway?"

"Emma would be *so* mad." She smothers her giggles with her fingers to her lips. "So would Eddie and Ethan. How do they all start with an E? You know, I'm glad your name starts with a Jay. Did I ever tell you—"

"Char. Focus, sweetheart. Your idea?" I remind her gently.

"Right, wouldn't it be hilarious if we pretended to get married? Like Ethan was fake engaged? We go to one of those chapels and have Elvis fake marry us! Then, we send the pic to everyone. Can you imagine the look on their faces?" Charlotte bursts into laughter.

She's officially cut off.

As soon as the shots arrive, I finish both, toss down sixty bucks, and grab Charlotte's hand. "Time to go, Char."

I wake up to my head pounding, holding a perfect, soft body in my arms. I'm wrapped in a familiar coconut scent that reminds me of...

Oh fuck!

I open my eyes to confirm that, yes, I am indeed in bed with a nearly naked Charlotte. I'm only wearing my boxer briefs; this is *not* happening. I pull away to try and figure out what the fuck happened. The last thing I remember, we were leaving the bar.

"Char, get up, sweetheart." I've never jumped out of bed so fast in my life. I find my shirt on the chair and yank it on. She hasn't stirred so I try again, squeezing her shoulder, "Charlotte, you've gotta get up."

She groans. "It's so early. And bright. And loud." Pulling the covers over her head she gasps, "Why am I only wearing my bra and underwear?" She lowers the comforter and covers herself. "Oh no. *No, no, no.* We didn't... I didn't... Fuck, Jay! Did we have sex?" She reaches under the covers and breathes a sigh of relief. "Nope, no sex. Oof, that was a close one."

"How do you know? I don't remember anything after that last round of drinks."

Quirking an eyebrow at me, she explains, "A woman knows when she's been pounded the night before."

I groan and tie my hair up in a messy top knot. "Then what the fuck happened?"

"I don't know, but why is there confetti in your beard?"

I check the mirror hung above the vanity in confusion. Sure enough, there's silver glitter in my beard. I try to dust it off but this stuff isn't coming out for a week.

Grabbing her clothes from the chair and bringing them over to her, I ask, "Are you sure you don't remember anything?"

She shakes her head. "No, but whatever it was must've been fun!"

2

CHARLOTTE

Last night was so fucking weird. I can normally handle my liquor—so can Jason. It doesn't make sense that both of us woke up without a memory of the night before. He called the bar and asked if we could review the footage. Turns out, someone slipped something into my drink when I was out dancing, and again before Jason drank both shots. We were both drugged. I feel violated and a little heartbroken. I was so lucky Jason was there with me. If he wasn't, who knows what could've happened to me.

Melanie and I were supposed to have lunch today, but since Jason and I slept in, we rescheduled for dinner. She made reservations at a steakhouse I've been dying to try and invited Emma, Lily, and Riley to join us. Unfortunately, Riley can't make it, she's at a work conference in Montreal. I could definitely use girlfriend time after everything that happened in the last twenty-four hours.

"How was the focus group?" Emma asks. I can't meet her eyes after I woke up in my underwear with her ex-husband. Even if it was an accident, I still feel guilty.

"Oh, it was good," I reply, idly circling the rim of my glass with my finger.

She probes further, "The contract is for the year, right?"

"Um, yeah." I look up briefly to appease her, then back to my glass.

"Hey, what's wrong?" Melanie asks, resting her hand on mine. "I thought you'd be more excited about it."

I smother everything I'm feeling and put on my well-rehearsed smile. "It's fine, really. Just didn't sleep well last night."

Mel knows me well enough to see through what I'm doing. She squeezes my hand once and narrows her eyes. "If you say so."

Lily thankfully changes the subject. "So, how was Paris? Andrew and I are planning a trip, but you know how it is with kids. Getting away isn't easy."

"It was amazing," I reply at the same time Melanie says, "Beautiful," and Emma swoons, "Incredible."

We laugh and tell Lily all about our trip last week. I haven't had a chance to properly thank Sage for coordinating Ethan and Melanie's wedding. She flew me to Paris on Ethan's dime to see one of my best friends get married. With Eddie having his panties in a twist about

Sage, I've avoided reaching out. I hate conflict almost as much as I hate tags in my shirts.

As dinner wraps up, Emma and Lily rush off to the restroom, leaving Mel and I alone for a few minutes.

"Okay, spill. What's going on with you?"

I freeze for a moment before replying, "I... I don't know what you're talking about. I'm great. Fantastic, actually."

"Fucking liar," she chuckles. "It's Jason, isn't it?"

"Oh, come on! You, too? Ethan's been teasing me about him for years. Nothing's happened!" *It can't happen.*

She smirks. "*Yet.* You can tell me! I promise I won't tell Ethan or Em. Did you grip his manbun as he went down on you? I bet you did. Gotta hold onto something when you're grinding yourself against his mouth."

"Fuck, Mel." I glance around with wide eyes. "Keep your voice down! No, I didn't, and I never will. Please, drop it. I don't know if you're joking or not, but either way, it's not funny. Should I start teasing you about your forest frolicking?"

"Sure," she says confidently, sipping her wine. "Maybe you should take that man in the woods and let him break you with his ax—"

"Mel!"

"What?" She shrugs. "Would you prefer a baseball analogy? He should hit that grand slam already so he can slide into your home pl—"

"Stop!" I'm unable to stop a laugh from escaping. "That's worse than the lumberjack one." I'm in a fit of giggles from one too many martinis at Melanie's ridiculous suggestions. Emma and Lily come back to the table as I insist, "Please no more baseball, I don't think my ribs could take it."

"Baseball? That reminds me, do we want to go in on a suite for next season?" Emma asks, and Lily, Mel, and I groan. "Oh, come on! It'll be fun!" I'm just grateful she didn't catch on to what I was talking about with Melanie.

Mel rolls her eyes. "That's your thing with Dylan. I don't mind going to a game or two, but I'll pass. Ethan wouldn't want to go, either. Except maybe to get a bigger suite next to yours." We all laugh. Ethan and Dylan have had a faux rivalry for years, always one-upping each other.

"Andrew might; I'll ask him," Lily replies with a half-shrug.

"What about you, Char?" Emma asks expectantly. I feel an obligation to say yes; the guilt of last night is eating away at me, even if nothing happened.

"Sure. Sounds like fun." I attempt to sound excited but I'm sure it falls flat.

"Great! Jason's in too." I still at Emma's words. "I'll set it up."

Fuck.

When I get home, I take a long shower with hopes it'll help me forget about everything. The water is scalding, but part of me feels it's a well-deserved punishment for last night. I unwrap one of the lavender shower bombs Ethan got me for Christmas last year and put my Taylor Swift playlist on my smart speaker.

While I'm singing along obnoxiously loud to "Wildest Dreams," there's a knock at my bathroom door, making me jump. Exactly four people have a key to my place—Mel, Emma, Eddie, and... Jason.

Please don't be Jay.

"Char, you okay?"

Fuck. My. Life.

Turning down the music, I shout loud enough for him to hear through the door and the sound of the water running, "Yeah. I'll be out in a second."

I shut off my music and the shower, grab a towel, and dry off. My mirror is clouded with steam and I use my hand to wipe it away. After a deep breath and a quick pep talk, I open the door with a towel wrapped around my chest, hoping he's in the living room.

He's not.

The last time he saw me this undressed, we were in bed together. Everything after the bar last night is a blur, no matter how desperately I've tried to remember. I've been avoiding Jason all day, afraid we may have crossed a line that should *never* have been crossed. While my pussy is confident we didn't have sex, who knows if we did anything else.

"Hey." My voice is an octave higher than normal, hope-fully he doesn't notice.

"Rough day?" Jason quirks an eyebrow.

"No, *pfft.*" I wave him off. "Why?"

"You only blast sad Taylor when you've had a bad day, sweetheart. What's wrong?"

"*You're what's wrong, Jason.*" I want to scream. Instead, I lie. "I'm fine." I slip past him into my bedroom and pull out a pair of black and white plaid pajama pants and a black tee from my dresser. I look back at him, and snap, "Do you mind?"

"I'll be in the living room," he grumbles and turns to leave. The temptation to drop my towel enters my mind, but I need to think with my head and not my bored cunt. Tonight will be a fun game of "don't think about my hot neighbor while fucking myself."

In the time I dressed and blow fried my hair , Jason left, unprompted, and changed into his matching pair of black and white buffalo plaid pants. Buffalo plaid is reserved for celebration or pulling yourself out of a funk. If he only knew *he* is the reason I'm in such a bad mood.

I plop myself on my couch with the remote. "All right, Jay, what'll it be? *Bridget Jones* or *The Devil Wears Prada?*"

"Whatever you want, sweetheart."

JASON

Things have been tense between Charlotte and I since we woke up together in the cabin. I knew something was wrong when I heard Taylor Swift blasted from the other side of our shared wall; I just wish I could fix this awkwardness between us. Since then, she's been avoiding me for two weeks without explanation. Now, she's on a plane to Paris to visit Ethan with Melanie, putting a whole ocean between us. I wish she would've asked me to join her; she hates flying.

After a long day of training with our new bullpen coach, I check my mail and head up to my apartment. Sifting through the mail, there are a few bills, junk mail, and paperwork from Nevada. It appears to be legal documents, but I'm not sure what for, and I open it first.

Marriage Certificate
Doc 28372947372
This is to certify that the undersigned…

Fuck! No, this isn't happening.

… join in wedlock Charlotte Anne Wentworth of San
Francisco, California, date of birth February 17, 1993,
and Jason David Kelly of San Francisco, California,
date of birth May 13, 1981.

This can't be real, but the signatures and the certificate
look real. I set down the paper and begin pacing my
living room. My heart races, trying to think of some
explanation for this. Am I being pranked? Is this Ethan's
doing? He's been meddling for years, but this is taking it
too far.

The date of the marriage certificate is the same as the
night we can't remember.

What the fuck is going on? I'm married? To Charlotte?

I frantically read it over and over again. There must be a
mistake. I grab my phone and look up the chapel listed
on the certificate. They open in twenty minutes. *Shit.*

"*Wouldn't it be hilarious if we pretended to get married?*" Her
words echo in my ears. Did we actually do it?

Twenty minutes later, I call the chapel and they pick up
on the second ring. "Lover's Lane Chapel, this is Diane.
How may I help you?"

"Hi, yes, I just received a marriage certificate in the mail
that states I was married there two weeks ago. I'm
wondering if you can confirm the details."

There's the clack of typing on a computer in the background. "Of course. Do you happen to have it in front of you? What is the document number?" I read it to her. "Ah, yes. It shows here you married Charlotte Wentworth. It appears everything is in order. Is there anything else I can help you with?"

No, everything is not in order, Diane.

"So… I'm married? Are you sure?"

She chuckles. "Yes, sir. Now that I think about it, I remember you two! You mentioned you've been friends for years. That is truly the key to a successful marriage; marrying your best friend. Congratulations to you both. I do see a note here that you didn't pick up your rings because they needed to be sized. My apologies, we were unable to reach you at the number you provided. Would you like us to mail them to you?"

My heart won't stop racing, unsure what to make of all this. "That won't be necessary. Thank you, Diane. I appreciate your help today."

We hang up and I feel stuck. I can't call Charlotte until I figure this out. I definitely can't tell Dylan or Emma. Melanie is a lawyer, but I don't trust she won't immediately tell Charlotte. I search "dissolve a marriage without a spouse knowing" but come up empty.

What the fuck am I going to do?

JASON
FOUR MONTHS LATER

"Looks like we're on our own! Eddie is with Sage, probably doing despicable things to her. *Lucky bitch*."

An involuntary growl erupts from my chest, but I clear my throat to cover it up. Here I am, in London with my wife—who doesn't know she's my wife—and she's talking about how she needs to get I'm in hell. Even if we weren't married, the thought of her being with another man makes me irrationally jealous. It shouldn't, but it fucking does. I have nothing to worry about with Edmund, but Char has mentioned a few times how she's sexually frustrated. It's only a matter of time before she meets someone and I'm no longer in the picture.

Charlotte hasn't been with anyone recently and I haven't so much as looked at another woman since she moved to California. Especially once I found out we are married. It feels… wrong, even if the marriage is only on paper. I wish it was the same for her.

I try to lighten the mood and change the subject. "All right, sweetheart, what do you want to do, since we have time to kill?"

She's lost in thought for a moment, then asks, "Sorry, what?"

"We have time to kill, and—"

"*Shh.* You can't say unalivey things in the airport!"

Fuck, she's adorable.

"Fine." I roll my eyes and sigh. "What do you want to do while we wait for your friends?"

"Let's go do some tourist shit!"

I nod and take her hand to guide her out of the airport. It's something I do to help her stay grounded in busy spaces. While it isn't intended to be romantic, I enjoy it all the same.

"There's a subway system here that is similar to BART and I'm sure we can navigate it easily. Or would you rather take a cab?" I offer.

"It's called the Underground." I can't help but smile at her miserable attempt to deadpan.

"Let's take the *Underground*, then. I've never been here, and if you're up for it, I'd like to have the full British experience. Complete with fish and chips for lunch."

"Lead the way!" She smiles brightly at me, and it dawns

on me she hasn't smiled at me like this in a long time. Fuck, I've missed it.

We take the train to Piccadilly Circus. When we get off, there are advertisements for a few different tours. She sighs in disappointment. "A magical castle tour? Damn it! I wish Ethan or Aiden were here. They would have loved it!"

"Aiden did it with Emma and Dylan when Harriet was touring schools for college. If you want to, we can," I offer.

"Really?"

"Of course, sweetheart, let's do it."

After the tour, lunch, and a visit to the National Gallery in Trafalgar Square, Charlotte checks her phone for any messages from Edmund. I peer over her shoulder.

EDDIE

> Ten minutes from London. Where are you?

> We can meet you somewhere. Or, if you're ready to leave, I can charter the plane to Delasnia.

> Did you finally shack up with Jason?

> And you say I'm a bad influence.

When she notices I'm reading them, she clutches the phone to her chest. "Excuse you, *Sir*. What do you think you're doing? These are private."

Quirking an eyebrow, I stifle a groan. "Shacking up?"

"Jay, it's a joke. I know I suck at jokes, but you know he's kidding, right?"

"You're my w— friend. Best friend, actually. I'm not exactly appreciating the joke, considering you confide in Edmund and Melanie more than me." Not for the first time, I wish things were different—different circumstances, different people. Maybe then…

Why couldn't she be anyone other than my ex's step-sister?

"Will you shush? You're not supposed to know that Eddie is Tyler, and Tyler is Eddie. Talk about trust… You know something no one but Sage and his family knows!"

I know a lot more than that, babygirl.

She sighs. "Can you be cool for ten seconds? I'm supposed to bring you in front of an ascending King and his Queen Consort and you're complaining about my friends?"

"Sorry, this whole thing is fucking weird. I'm not quite sure why we are even here. They love each other but aren't together?"

She recaps why things have become complicated with Sage and Edmund, but I still don't get it. Edmund is a prince who has been hiding out in America for years. He even changed his name to Tyler to keep his identity a secret. His brother is adopted, so he's come up with a plan to change the laws. In order to become King, he must be married. That's about as far as I got with her explanation, but I'm still stuck on why he's marrying a woman he's in love with but pissed off about it.

"You said he loves Sage?"

Her hand flies to her face in exasperation. "I mean, yeah, he's fucking obsessed with her. But neither of them want to get married. It makes sense for him. Personally, I don't get it. I want to get married one day. You know, do the whole 'forever' thing. But, it's not my life, it's theirs."

"You're already married." *Shit.* I clear my throat and immediately add, "To your work, I mean."

"I'm not married to my work," she insists, a little hurt by the suggestion.

I change the subject before I slip up again. "Come on, sweetheart, we need to get going if we want to meet up with your friends."

"I want to see Buckingham Palace," she whines, though it's all an act.

"Call Tyler… *Edmund*… I'm still not sure what name I should call him, but you should at least text him first. *Then*, I'll take you to Buckingham Palace."

"Fuck you and your first/then statements! You think I'm not onto you? You don't need to coddle me, I'm not Aiden." The hurt is evident on her face.

I'm such a fucking asshole.

I didn't realize I was doing it, but I was absolutely using first/then language. It's something Emma and I normally do with Aiden to help him stay focused, but I never intended to do it with Charlotte.

She recoils from her own harsh words I absolutely deserved, mumbling, "I'm sorry, Jason, I—"

"No, *I'm* sorry. You're right. I shouldn't have phrased it that way. You want Buckingham Palace? Please text Edmund so he knows where we are and isn't chasing us all over London. We should give him a time and location." I take a deep breath. "I know you're excited; I am too. I want to experience London with you, but your friend is here. You owe him a heads up of where we are going, babygirl."

"Fine. One second…"

Charlotte types out a few messages but Edmund calls her.

"Hello?"

Edmund says something I can't hear. Her eyes lock with mine when she replies, "I don't think he'll let you pay, Eddie." I smirk and chuckle to myself—there is no way in hell that I'll let him pay for anything on my watch with Charlotte here.

They hang up. I take Charlotte's hand as we head to Buckingham Palace. She puts her earbuds in, listening to an audiobook to help her drown out the noise of the busy London streets.

Waiting to cross the street, her eyes are wide. I'm pretty sure she's listening to a romance book and got to the *fun* part. I turn to face her and take out one of her earbuds so she can hear me. "Do I even want to know what you're listening to?"

She bites her lip. Damn it, it's fucking cute. *What I would give to...*

"Um, no. You don't," she replies sheepishly.

I put the earbud back in her ear and we cross the street to do a tour of Buckingham Palace. This is going to be the longest vacation of my life.

"She sort of explained it to me, but I don't get it. Why are you getting divorced after being married for six weeks?" I ask Sage. We found a small pub after the tour to meet up with her and Edmund, and I still can't wrap my head around it.

"I don't want to get married in the first place, but I know Edmund doesn't want the crown, so I'm helping him," she explains. "Their backwards laws prohibit his mother from changing anything. It's only temporary."

"You two are obviously happy together, why not stay married? I was married to Emma for years, but in the end we were better off being friends. We weren't in love. You? You're in love." I still don't get what's going on with Edmund and Sage. At this point, I'm not sure I want to. The way he looks at her, he's fucking obsessed with this woman.

Edmund offers, "I've done enough weddings to know that while love is important, friendship is the key to a successful marriage or relationship. If you're in love with your *best* friend, you should marry them."

I already did, Edmund.

At his words, Charlotte chokes on her martini. I offer her my water, but still notice Edmund has a shit-eating grin. He rests his arm behind Sage's chair, leaning in to whisper something to her.

"Sorry. Went down the wrong way," Charlotte explains through her coughs.

I rub her back and ask, "You okay, sweetheart?"

"I think so. Sorry, what were you guys talking about?" Charlotte asks.

Crap, I hope he doesn't say it again...

"How you should marry your best friend," Sage offers, mirroring Edmund's knowing smirk. I narrow my eyes at both of them.

"You have no room to talk since neither of you want to get married," Charlotte grumbles defensively.

"You're right, but I'm sure when you two get married it'll be amazing."

Fucking hell, Sage. Really?

"Oh, we're not…" Charlotte turns to me with a thick gulp, then back to Sage. "With my track record, I'll probably end up single forever. Marriage isn't something I'm thinking about, especially considering I'm not even in a relationship."

Sage's eyes widen. "Sorry, I just assumed—"

Charlotte insists, "It's fine. Anyway, I was thinking, since you aren't doing an engagement or bachelorette party, we should do a buffalo plaid party."

I chuckle and shake my head. "You'll need Em for that, babygirl. Or at least Ethan and Mel."

"What's a buffalo plaid party?" Sage quirks her brow.

"Something my sister—"

"Step-sister," I correct.

Char glares at me. "Something my *step-sister* does back home." She turns back to Sage, and continues, "We'll watch a cheesy romance movie, make a charcuterie board, drink too much wine, and we all wear buffalo plaid pajama pants. We do it when someone is sad or celebrating, and this is definitely a celebration."

"Sounds like my kind of party, I'm in," Sage replies and takes a sip of her whiskey. "My friends are in town, I'm sure they'd want to come."

"Great, let's do it the day before the wedding, when Ethan and Mel fly in. I'll text them and let them know to bring their pjs." Char then asks me, "Did you pack yours?"

"No, but I'm sure we can pick up a pair in town before we head to Delasnia."

"Do you guys want to stay here for the night?" Eddie asks.

"Sure," Char replies, then giggles to herself. "So long as there is more than one bed." Sage and Eddie laugh, but I freeze.

There sure as fuck better be more than one bed.

Eddie pulls out his phone and types something. After a moment, he announces, "It's settled. I'll book us a couple rooms, *with multiple beds*, and we'll head to Delasnia in the morning."

5

CHARLOTTE

"Oh, come on, Jay! We're going to be stuck in Delasnia for a week, where there's nothing to do. Let's go out on the town while we're here!"

This is the most time we've spent together since the cabin incident, and I'm hoping a night out will help reset us. He's been avoiding me for months, so now that we're here, I want to make the most of it. Things have been good between us in London, but before our trip was weeks of awkward glances and stilted conversations. I want to go back to the way things were before the cabin incident.

Jason reluctantly agrees to my suggestion. Sage and Edmund are probably humping like rabbits. Not wanting to interrupt them, we head out, just the two of us.

I need to get over my little crush I have on him. To assist in my denial, I'm hoping to get lucky tonight—not with Jason. I put on a dress that I could probably only pull off in my early twenties, and take extra time to ensure my hair is perfectly curled and makeup is flawless. Admiring myself in the mirror, I can't help my smile.

Damn, I look good!

Jason said he would meet me downstairs at the hotel bar while I got ready. When I head down, he's talking with a gorgeous redhead. I breathe a sigh of relief. This is perfect! He'll hook up with someone, I'll hook up with someone, and *voila!* Everything will go back to normal.

"Hey, Jay," I say, tapping on his shoulder.

He swivels in his seat and his expression is undeniable—even he knows I look good. Except, he hops out of his stool, grabs me by the wrist and begins walking us toward the elevator. The bartender is calling after him, but he doesn't stop.

"What the hell, Jason?" I try to pull back, but he's stronger. I yank a second time and he stops, turning toward me. I try again, "What the actual fuck are you doing?"

"You're *not* going out like that, sweetheart." He glances down at his grip on my wrist and releases it as if I burned him. "I'm serious, Char. You look…" He groans, a deep rumble coming from his chest. "Do you want every man out there to hit on you?"

"Yes. That was the plan. I haven't had sex in—"

Jason growls, like a fucking dog, and I blink in surprise. "I don't care when you last had sex; you're not going out like that." His expression softens to something between worry and anger. "You remember what happened last time we went out?"

"Are you seriously blaming me? Fucking unbelievable." I cross my arms.

"No," he barks. "Being drugged was the least of it."

"What are you talking about?" I pause for a second to consider what he's so concerned about. "Do you mean waking up with me? That won't happen again. I'm going home with someone else tonight."

"The fuck you are. No wi— *friend* of mine is going home with another man in a strange city."

"You're not my boyfriend, Jay," I groan. "I don't have to explain to you that women and men have needs. If I want to go have sex, I'm going to have sex!" My voice carries, catching the attention of a few people walking by. Not wanting to cause any more of a scene than we already have, I lower my voice and add, "It's not like I'm going to have an orgasm or anything. I just want to feel a man's hands on me."

Jason frowns and asks, "What do you mean you're not going to have an orgasm? Why the fuck would you want to have sex if you're not going to come? That's kind of the point."

The questions take me by surprise. I shouldn't tell him the truth, but this conversation is already inappropriate enough, and we're still in the hotel lobby. "It doesn't matter."

"Oh, it absolutely does. Why would you go home with a stranger without the intention of finishing?"

Casting my eyes down, I fidget with my handbag. I blow out a deep breath and stupidly admit, "I don't have orgasms during sex." He lifts my chin with his thumb and forefinger. I finally meet his gaze. "It's normal for women to not come from sex, but for me... I can't come unless there's an emotional connection there. I don't need to be in love, but if I don't feel *something* for them, I don't come."

"You're demisexual?"

"I don't know. Maybe? Or I'm just broken. I shouldn't be talking to you about this." *Especially since I have feelings for you.*

Jason rakes a hand through his hair, loosening his bun. "You're right, we shouldn't be talking." He takes my hand and continues walking toward the elevators.

"Whoa, wait. I'm not changing, I'm going out tonight." I channel my inner Taylor—she wouldn't put up with this shit. "I want to walk into a bar. I want all eyes on me. I want someone to touch me. I don't have a man, but I have a fucking buzzkill of a best friend."

When we reach the elevators, he presses the button, and it opens instantly. Jason pulls me in and, as someone walks up, he stops them, "This one's full." Only when the doors close does he let go of my hand.

"Fuck it," he mutters, shaking his head.

"What?"

"Never?" He blurts out. I don't respond, so he asks again, "*Never?*"

"Never, what? What is going on with you?"

"Don't make me say it," he grits out.

My arms wide, I ask again, "What?"

Jay backs me up against the wall of the elevator, making me gasp. He rests his forehead against mine and squeezes his eyes shut. "You're my best friend, Char. I'm going to suggest something once. If you say no, you have to pretend we never had this conversation. I can't lose you."

My voice trembles as I whisper, "Okay…"

"What if…" He shakes his head. "No. It's not worth it."

"You're not making any sense. What's not worth it? You have to spell it out for me here, I'm so lost."

What's going on with him today?

Jason opens his eyes. In them, there's a swirl of emotions I can't place. "I can't risk it, sweetheart."

"Risk what?" He's so close, I could tilt my head *just so* and kiss him. *No. This is Jason.* He's not into me, as he made abundantly clear when I tried to kiss him at Emma's wedding.

"This." He slides his hand up my hip and my breath hitches.

What is happening? Is he into this?

"If you're going to suggest that we have sex, *just once,* then my answer won't be no," I rush out.

He pauses, then moves his lips to my ear, his beard tickling my neck. "You tell me you've never come from sex… I want it to be me."

"You want to have sex… with *me?* What if you can't do it? Things will be awkward as fuck." *As if they weren't already.*

Jason groans. "I'm not worried about you coming, babygirl. I wouldn't suggest it if I wasn't up for the challenge. I'm worried about what happens after. I don't want to lose you if we sleep together."

I've wanted him for so long. This might be my only chance to be with him with no strings attached. "What if tomorrow it's as if it never happened? It'll just be this one time, and we'll never speak of it again." I jump at the elevator door opening to our floor.

Taking my hand, he doesn't say another word, leading us to our room. He slips the keycard into the door and pauses. "Are you sure about this?" Jason looks at me expectantly. "You promise nothing changes?"

"Nothing changes," I confirm. He nods and opens the door. I add, "To be clear, you can't kiss me, Jay. It would blur the lines. Just sex." The silence after the door shuts is deafening. I stop and start talking at least five times, unable to make sense of what might happen.

"If that's what you want. I'll never do anything you don't want to do. You say stop at any point and we stop." He stuffs his hands in his pockets. "Now, let's start at the top. You said you don't come from sex, do you come by yourself?"

"Yes," I reply without hesitation.

He takes his bottom lip between his teeth, nodding slightly. "Show me."

"I'm not going to masturbate in front of you."

"Yes, you are, but you don't finish until my cock is deep inside you." His voice is commanding, sending shivers through me. He takes off his shoes and pulls his shirt over his head, tossing it to the ground. I'm stunned into silence. I've seen him shirtless dozens of times, but not like this. Not when he *wants* me to see him. I can't stop staring. *Am I allowed to stare?* "Take it off," he demands, gesturing to the dress he was so offended by.

Someone's bossy... Fuck, why am I so attracted to this?

"Oh, um, sure."

I'm used to guys who let me take the lead in the bedroom; I have no idea what's going on here or how I should act. Jason's never spoken to me like this before. He's always so sweet and unassuming. A gentle giant. I'm so turned on seeing this side of him. I know this is only a one time offer, but I plan to enjoy every last minute of it.

I make a show of slipping out of my dress as he sits in the side chair, facing the bed. I leave my underwear and bra on; he's never seen me fully naked before—there's no point in starting now.

"All of it, sweetheart."

Damn it.

With a galloping heart, I comply, and stand before him fully naked. I'm comfortable in my own skin… when that skin is covered in clothes. I'm a curvy girl and don't love being naked in front of other people. I'm especially nervous with Jason.

"Fuck, Char. You're so fucking beautiful. Come here."

I swallow thickly and my stomach dips. "You can't say things like that to me."

"Too bad, I already did," he chuckles. His laughter dies almost immediately. "What are those?"

I follow his line of sight to a constellation of fresh bruises on my thigh. "Those?"

"Yes, Char," he growls. "Who did that to you?"

A laugh bubbles up and I can't help it escaping me. "You know I'm a bit accident prone. I bump into everything."

Jason breathes out a sigh of relief. "Since I'm not going on a manhunt tonight to murder someone…" His jaw ticks. "On the bed. I told you I want to see you touch yourself."

"Why? If I wanted to get off, I would just do it when you're not around." Maybe this wasn't the best idea. I didn't sign up for masturbating in front of my best friend…

"I need to see what you like. Now, be a good girl and go lie down."

I burst out laughing. "I don't have a praise kink, Jay."

"Noted. Lay down, close your eyes, and touch yourself," he demands, still smirking. My eyes linger on his lips for a moment too long.

"No. *You* can touch me," I insist, desperately trying to maintain some kind of control over this situation. "You're the one who thinks you have a magic dick."

"Fine." He stands, unbuckles his belt and pulls down his pants, and… *Fuck. He's huge.* I must be gaping at his monster cock when his voice pulls me from my fascination. "Eyes up here, babygirl."

"Oh, right. Sorry."

"Apologize again and I'll take you over my knee to teach you a lesson."

My hand covers my face and I can't help laughing. "This isn't going to work. I don't do the whole punishment thing, either. What next? You gonna tie me up? Gah, what is it with you guys? Not every woman wants a Dom in the bedroom."

The thought of being tied up isn't the worst idea though...

He removes my hand from my face. "Sweetheart, I'm just trying to figure out what you're into. I want to experiment and see what will send you over the edge, but my number one priority is your pleasure, not mine. I don't come unless you do." Tucking my hair behind my ear, my breath hitches. The simple touch gives me butterflies, something that's never happened before. He notices. "Is this okay? I won't kiss you here." His thumb grazes my bottom lip. "But can I kiss you everywhere else?" I nod and he lifts me, wrapping my legs around his waist. "Come on, babygirl. Let's have some fun."

6

JASON

I walk toward the kitchen. There's a small counter, and set Charlotte on top of it, then take out the ice cream sundae makings that we bought earlier.

"I'm perfectly capable of walking, you know." Her eyes widen at the syrup and whipped cream. "Oh no, you are not putting any of that near my pussy. No, nope. Try again."

"Maybe another time, but we're going to have ice cream first." Sugar relaxes her. She's nervous about all of this; I should be, but I'm not. I've been fantasizing about my face between her legs for the last two years.

"There won't be another time, this is just tonight, remember?"

I set everything on the counter and stand between her legs, pulling her close until her already wet pussy is against me. "Sex may only be tonight, but you never said anything about touching you or eating ice cream off your perfect tits tomorrow."

"Fucking hell, Jay. Do we need to draw up a contract? No sexytime after tonight! If you're going to make this weird, I'm out."

Brushing a kiss to her neck, I whisper against her skin, "If you only want tonight, then that's all it'll be. But once I've had you, I won't be able to help thinking about how amazing it felt sinking myself inside you. I'll keep my hands to myself after this, only because you want me to."

She whimpers a sigh and, fuck it, the ice cream can wait. I lift her off the counter to take her back into the bedroom. "What about the ice cream?"

I keep one arm wrapped around her to put the ice cream back in the freezer. She takes advantage of my other hand preoccupied and slides down my body. I shut the freezer and bend to toss her over my shoulder, but she slips out of my hold.

"Really? It's going to be like that? Where's my ice cream, Jay?" She laughs as she runs to the other side of the kitchen.

"If I only get tonight, you think I want to waste time eating ice cream?" I quirk an eyebrow at her.

She narrows her eyes. "Ice cream, or no sex." Unable to contain her laughter, she then groans, "Fuck, I can't talk to you when we're just standing here naked. Your massive cock is distracting me, but I'm standing my ground. Ice cream. Make it happen."

"You're fucking adorable." I shake my head and chuckle. I grab a bowl and retrieve the ice cream from the freezer. She watches me intently as I take out the smallest, teaspoon size scoop of ice cream and place it in the bowl. "There you go."

"Two *regular* scoops."

My eyes never leave hers as I scoop two regular scoops into the bowl for her. Eye contact makes her nervous, she normally looks away. Right now, she can't keep her eyes off me. It gives me hope I shouldn't have; I don't want one night with her. I want *her*.

I slide the bowl over to her after drizzling chocolate sauce and topping with whipped cream. She grabs a spoon from the drawer and eats excruciatingly slow. My eyes linger too long on her mouth, then shamelessly roam the rest of her naked, fucking gorgeous body. I brace myself on the counter and stare down my best friend… my wife… who is twelve years younger than me… and also my ex-wife's sister. *Step-sister*, but that's semantics at this point. My beautiful wife is eating ice cream with me, naked in the kitchen…

Fuck the rest of the baggage, she's mine.

"Penny for your thoughts? Starting to doubt the power of your schlong?" she taunts.

Her voice pulls me from my thoughts. I shake my head, and huff a small laugh. "Not at all. Finish your ice cream, I'm patiently waiting for *my* dessert."

Charlotte snorts as she breaks out in a fit of giggles. "Seriously? What am I going to do with you?"

"All right, that's enough from your smart mouth." I can't wipe the smile off my face. "You have one minute, then I want you spread out on that bed for me."

"Yes, *Sir*."

"Careful, babygirl. No honorifics."

"Honorifics?" She pauses, considering it. A moment later, it clicks that what she said is a bit too much of a turn on for me. "*Ohh.* Got it. I didn't mean anything by it, but I'm saving that one for a rainy day." She winks. "But I'm sure as fuck not going to call you Daddy, so you better never ask."

I chuckle. "Please don't." *But if you slip up and call me 'Sir' again, I definitely wouldn't mind…* "Thirty seconds."

"Oh shit!" Charlotte shovels a mouthful of ice cream. "Shit! Brain freeze!" She winces and I cup her cheeks, pressing a kiss to her forehead. I set her bowl into the sink, and she lifts her chin with entirely too much faux confidence, I can't help but smile. "Okay, let's do this."

Of course she has to go and be her adorable, chaotic self. It's too fucking endearing. She runs into the bedroom with a skip in her step and leaps onto the bed.

"All right, do your worst. Just don't get offended if I don't come."

"I'm not worried, sweetheart. Lay down." She lays her head back and I spread her legs wide for me, making her gasp. "Say stop and I will stop whatever I'm doing immediately. If you can't get your words out, you tap three times on any part of my body, okay?"

"What the hell are you going to do to me that'll require a safe word or tap out?"

"I'm going to let your body tell me." With a featherlight touch, I slide my hands from her knees down her thighs and back up again.

"Stop."

I freeze; it could be a sensory issue. "Too much?" She nods. "Do you need firm pressure or a light touch?"

Charlotte replies without hesitation, "Firm."

"Got it. Can I touch you?"

"You already are…"

She takes everything literally, so I rephrase, "I'm going to slide my fingers in this wet cunt and play with your clit before I replace my hand with my mouth. Is that okay?"

"Yes," she confirms.

I lean in and kiss her stomach, sliding my hand down her leg with more pressure than before until I reach her bare pussy. Fuck, she's so ready, my fingers slide into her with ease. I press in and, when I drag my fingers out, I circle her clit a few times before pushing back in.

"How are you feeling, sweetheart?"

"It feels good. I need more, though."

I push deep and curl my fingers. "Like that?"

"Yeah," she whimpers, breathlessly.

I build her up for several minutes, checking in every so often, but it seems like she's somewhere else. I have never had an issue making a woman come before, but Charlotte isn't like any other woman. I pull my fingers out and suck them clean. A mistake. Fuck, she tastes incredible.

How am I going to go back to being just friends after I've tasted her?

I kiss down her leg, careful to apply enough pressure she won't ask me to stop. Once my face is between her legs, I lick up her center, making her shudder. It's the first real reaction I've gotten from her, and do it again—to no avail. I circle her clit with my tongue and press my fingers back inside her, making her gasp. *Okay, now we're getting somewhere.* I keep the same pressure and pace for a few minutes but… nothing. *Fuck.*

I sit back onto my heels, feeling a little defeated, but still determined. "What do you think about when you touch yourself, Char?"

"Oh, I'm not fucking telling you *that*. Absolutely not."

"You gotta give me something here. I'm flying blind."

Char chews on her lip. "Well, I'll tell you if you tell me what you think about when you fuck your hand."

Her blunt request takes me by surprise. "I can't tell you. What I'm into would compromise our friendship," I tell her honestly.

There is no way in hell I can admit I get off on the idea of controlling her orgasms, giving her one after another, even after she thinks she's done. Or, if she's mouthing off, edging her before she comes hard all over my cock and nearly passes out. I've dreamt about having her spread out for me like this for so long, I want to be the one that owns this piece of her.

"If I fake it, can we be done? This is getting a little embarrassing… for me. You're doing all the right things, I just can't. I'm sorry."

Fuck, I took things too far.

I move up the bed and lie next to her, offering my arm for her to cuddle into my side. "Come here." Charlotte rests her head on my chest and wraps an arm around my middle, hugging me tight. She drapes her leg over me. She's rarely *this* affectionate with me, and I revel in having her this close, kissing the top of her head. "You're not broken, there's nothing to be embarrassed about or apologize for. Are we… Are we okay?" My voice is caught in my throat. This is exactly what I was afraid of.

"Other than the fact that my best friend just had his face between my legs? Sure, we're okay." She lets out a small chuckle, but I worry this is a turning point for us, and not a good one.

Unless...

Charlotte mentioned she can't come if she doesn't feel something for the other person. It's a punch to my gut—she doesn't feel the same way about me that I do about her. I double down, and ask, "Can I try one thing?" She looks up at me curiously and nods against my chest. "Can I kiss you?"

Her breath hitches. "Oh, um, that's... that's not the best idea, right?"

"Why not?" I ask.

She sighs and hugs me tighter. "If feelings get involved... We shouldn't have done any of this because I already..." She clears her throat. "I, um, crossed the line."

"Don't lie to me, Char. What were you going to say?" *Please say you want me.* I don't know if my heart could take it if she pushed me away even further.

"It would ruin everything."

"If you don't want me, then you can kiss me and it won't mean anything. So, which is it?"

"We can't," she whispers softly.

"Because you want me as much as I want you." She stills in my arms. I risk everything and confess, "I've fought my attraction to you for years, sweetheart. If I only get one night where you're mine, can I have you naked and wrapped up with me, just like this? We can go back to being friends in the morning, but I want to pretend for a night that we're not just friends."

I still need to figure out the whole being married thing. With her in my arms right now, I dare to imagine what it would be like if we stayed married. As dangerous as that thought is, I've thought about it more than I'd like to admit. I want Charlotte. I want her as my wife, even if I shouldn't.

"I can do that. We can pretend for tonight. Tomorrow, will you still be my best friend?" Her voice cracks at the end.

"Of course, babygirl. You'll always be my best friend."

She dozes off and I let sleep claim me, hating that I'm in love with the one woman I can't have.

7

CHARLOTTE

As it turns out, faking sleep is much easier than faking an orgasm. *What the fuck am I doing?* My instinct is to run. I can slip out of here, message Eddie, and get on the first plane back to California. The one thing I've wanted for the last few years came to fruition, and I couldn't even climax from it.

So fucking embarrassing.

I try to pull away to use the bathroom, but Jason holds me closer. "Where do you think you're going, sweetheart?" he says sleepily.

"I just have to pee, I'll be back." I won't be back. I need to put distance between us. He said he wants me, which is honestly a dream come true. Except we can never be together, so why indulge in the fantasy when it will only end in heartbreak?

I use the bathroom. After, instead of climbing back into bed, I put on a pair of leggings and Jason's hoodie, grab a hotel key and my phone, and head down to the lobby. The bar is still open, and I hop up onto a stool, passing the time doom-scrolling on my phone as I wait for the bartender. It dies after a few minutes and I'm kicking myself for not charging it.

"What'll it be, love?"

I pocket my phone and reply, "Sorry, I'll have a vodka martini with a twist."

He nods and begins making my drink. "Where's your bloke?" he asks as he pours my drink from the shaker and sets it in front of me.

"Oh, he's not mine. We're not together," I reply, taking a sip. I remove the lemon rind from the edge of the glass and swirl it twice before placing it in my drink.

"Could've fooled me." He smirks. "If, uh… if you're up for it, and want to have dinner, I'm off in ten." He's actually quite attractive; tall with shaggy blond hair and piercing blue eyes. If I was in a better headspace, I'd consider it—even if it was only a friendly meal and nothing came of it.

"Thank you, but I'm going to finish my drink and go back to bed," I sigh with a lopsided smile.

He writes something on a bar napkin and sets it next to my drink. "If you change your mind. Drink's on me, either way." He walks away and I down my martini in three long gulps. I take the napkin and begin walking toward the elevators, throwing it away as I walk past a trash can.

The elevator doors open and as I'm about to walk into the elevator, I faceplant into a hard chest.

"There you are." Jason wraps his arms around me. "You weren't answering your phone." He releases me and I look up to find so much anger in his eyes. At least, it feels like anger.

"I just needed a few minutes alone." I step in the elevator. When I look back at his face, I don't know why, but I have this urge to kiss him.

Oh, right, I know why; we almost had sex and my emotions are all jumbled up.

"I was worried. You just left without so much as a text or note. I don't care that you went for a drink"—he slides a hand down his face—"I just wanted to be sure you were safe."

"Well, I am. I didn't mean to worry you, I just... I freaked out," I admit.

His arms wrap around my shoulders and I hug his middle in return. "I took things too far. I'm sorry, Char."

"Sex doesn't freak me out... it was the other thing that did."

Jason pulls back enough to look at me, but doesn't let go. "What other thing?"

I resign myself to the fact that he's going to keep asking until I tell him the truth. "That you've wanted me for years. We… we can't do this. It hurt to hear because, well, you're the one guy I'm not supposed to want. Not only could it destroy our friendship, but my sister—"

"Step-sister."

"*Whatever*," I groan. "She's still family. This would ruin my relationship with her. I could lose my best friend *and* her."

The elevator dings and the doors slide open. Jason takes my hand and leads us down the hall to the room. "Let's get some sleep. Tomorrow, none of this happened, okay? It doesn't matter how I feel. I didn't act on it for the last two years, what's another twenty?"

I don't want him to pretend. I don't want to forget him telling me. I don't want him to lie to me. I don't want him to hurt, or resent me for any of this. I want to be able to openly want him. The second the hotel door closes behind us, I ask, "Do we still get tonight? Where I'm allowed to want to be with you without consequences? I know it's stupid but we've already—"

Jason cuts off my words with his mouth on mine. His lips are soft in contrast to his beard scratching my face. I wrap my arms around his neck as he pulls me closer to him, our bodies now flush. I welcome his warm, tight hold on me.

He breaks away from me suddenly, leaving me breathless. "I'm sorry, I know you told me not to."

I roll my eyes. "Seriously? Did I not just kiss you back? Sure, it's incredibly reckless, but, fuck it." I cup the back of his neck and bring him in for another kiss.

"Just tonight," he says against my lips. I can't help the whimper that escapes me.

"Just tonight," I echo.

It's not fair. He could be mine if things were different— if I wasn't so much younger than him, if my step-sister wasn't his ex-wife, if he saw me as more than a friend… Okay, that last one is a bit of a plot twist, but I can't let one hot night change things between us. We can never be more than friends. I'll never be someone he dates, his girlfriend, or wife.

What am I doing? I can't fuck my best friend, even if I'm in love with him.

"Stop." I press my hands to his chest and he breaks away from me the moment the word slips from my lips. "I thought I could do this but…I can't. I'm sorry." He holds me close, but doesn't say a word. We stand there in each other's arms for a minute, until I feel the need to break the awkward silence. "Things aren't going to go back to normal tomorrow, are they?"

"I don't think so, sweetheart. I shouldn't have told you how I feel about you."

I squeeze him tighter. "It's not one-sided, but I can't risk losing you and Emma if we have sex or… anything else."

"You were never going to be a quick fuck, Char. You have to know that. If things were different…"

I look up at him. "They aren't, though. I've crossed the line. You've crossed the line. Where do we go from here?"

"I'll leave that answer to you," he replies, his eyes soft and earnest.

We've ruined everything. The moment his lips touched mine, we could never be "just friends," again. I can feel it in my bones… I've lost my best friend. None of this can be undone or erased.

"I'm sorry. I'll get another room," I insist. "I can't be here with you. Not when I want someone I can't have." I don't move out of his hold, awaiting his response.

"What do you really want?"

"You," I reply, as my heart tears in two. "I'm not supposed to want you. I know I *can't.* I'll grab another room. I'm sorry. I'll text you the room number, so you don't have to worry about me."

"Your phone's dead, Char. Stay here. I'll get a room, and if there isn't one available, I'll sleep on the couch. I know Edmund was fucking with us when he booked this room, anyway. Multiple beds…" He shakes his head. "How much does he know?"

I shut my eyes tight and pull away from him as I reply, weakly, "Everything."

Jason moves closer, kisses me on the top of the head, whispering into my hair, "I love you, babygirl. Goodnight." He moves away from me, takes my phone and plugs it in to charge before he walks out the door.

Did I just lose Jason?

8

JASON

The last week has been a blur. Charlotte has kept herself busy helping the girls with Sage and Tyler/Edmund's wedding. I still don't understand what's going on with their situation, but at this point, I couldn't care less. I have a feeling I've lost my wife, my best friend, and the love of my life in one heated moment where I took things too far.

The ladies kicked us out of the palace—yes, a fucking palace—so Ethan, Tyler… *Edmund*, whatever the fuck his name is, and I are headed to a pub to blow off steam before the wedding.

"Is baseball season in full swing?" Ethan asks me, his words mildly slurred after his fourth Old Fashioned. "See what I did there? Full swing?"

"Yeah, the team trains year-round, but the season started up this month," I reply, keeping my eyes on the

TV in front of me and trying my best to avoid all conversation.

Edmund jumps in, not allowing me the escape. "All right, mate, out with it. What the hell is happening with you and Charlotte?"

I take a long drink of my stout, trying to figure out how the fuck to answer that. It's none of their business, but I have no one to talk to about this and it's eating away at me. I take a deep breath and admit, "Well, a few months ago, after she got back from Paris, there was a focus group up at the cabins she was hoping to secure a long-term contract with. You know the ones? Dylan and Em have one up there—"

"I *also* have a cabin," Ethan interjects. "Mine's bigger."

"Don't be an arsehole," Edmund tells Ethan. He gestures for me to continue, which I shouldn't do. I'm normally an IPA guy and, after my sixth barrel-aged stout, I'm feeling more than a little buzzed.

"Well, there was a storm the week before. I offered to drive her in my truck—I didn't trust the roads. She was awarded the contract while we were up there and we went out to celebrate. The next morning, when we woke up, neither of us remembered what happened the night before."

"You fucked my friend, you cheeky bastard," Edmund laughs, sipping his whiskey

I shake my head. "No, we didn't sleep together. Something worse happened… *Fuck.* I don't know why I'm telling you this. You have to promise not to tell Charlotte. She doesn't know."

"She's my best friend," Edmund replies at the same time Ethan scoffs, "She's like a sister to me."

"Then I'm not fucking telling you, am I?" *Fuck these guys.*

Ethan and Edmund glance to each other and nod, then Ethan asks, "Do we need to pinky promise?"

"Fuck," I mutter, mostly to myself. They aren't going to let this go. I planned on telling Charlotte soon anyway. I pull out my phone and show them the scanned image of our marriage certificate. Their eyes widen in shock.

"Holy shit! No fucking way! You said she doesn't know. How does she not? What the fuck?" Ethan rakes his hand through his hair. "You gotta tell her. It's been, what, three months?"

"Almost four," I correct miserably. Pretty sure it's more than four. *Fuck.* I need to tell her.

Edmund growls, "Not making your case better, Jay."

Since when am I "Jay" to him?

"I know. I just… I was hoping to figure it all out first." I finish my beer and signal for another.

"For four months? Does anyone else know? If Emma finds out…" Thanks for the reminder, *Eddie.*

"You don't think that I thought of that? This whole thing is fucked up!" *And I'm in love with her.*

"I have to know, did you two hook up at Em's wedding?" Ethan asks and I shake my head. "Damn it! I was hoping something would happen. The low lights of the quiet sensory room…"

"She was having a rough time with the noise, so I just made sure she was okay. Even if she was doing okay, making a pass at my ex-wife's wedding is a bit of a dickish move, don't ya think?" She tried to kiss me that night, but I'll never admit that to him.

"But you like her! I fucking knew it. A little chaos never hurt anyone, Jason. Just go for it," Ethn insists. "I've been teasing her about you two since she moved next door to you."

"It's not like that. We're friends. I'm too fucking old for her anyway." Our age difference is just another constant reminder that Charlotte and I could never be together. I don't care if she's older or younger than me, but would she want to stay married to someone twelve years older than her?

"Too old? Sage is eight years older than me, do you think that stopped me? Get that out of your head, mate. Char's my best friend and I shouldn't be saying this, but Ethan only teased her because, well, she's had a thing for you for the past few years. If you want to be with her, be with her. Age doesn't fucking matter." Edmund has a point, but I don't dare get my hopes up.

"It's not that simple. Sage isn't your ex-wife's—"

"Step-sister. We know," Ethan groans. "I wasn't supposed to be with Melanie. She's my best friend's husband's sister. *Damn.* We sound like we are in a fucking soap opera playing musical chairs." He shakes his head. "You think the Ben Affleck clone cared that I was with his sister?"

"Um, he kind of did. But I know you have better names for him than that. It's not like you're innocent, though. For fuck's sake, you dated her for almost two months before telling his grumpy arse," Edmund reminds him.

I snicker at the descriptions of Dylan. "He's one of my best friends too. You're not wrong, he can be one grumpy mother fucker after a couple of gin and tonics. At least Emma keeps him in line. Why aren't they here, by the way?"

"I don't know them that well." Edmund shrugs. "This whole marriage is mostly a sham anyway. I wanted my best friend here because, even if I'm only married for six weeks, Char would never forgive me if she wasn't invited."

"Fair enough," I say, nodding. Charlotte can hold a grudge, and I'd never want to be on the receiving end of it.

Ethan's grins as he suggests, "Okay, I have an idea. I've known Sage for years and she would fucking love it. You want to grand gesture the fuck out of your quickie marriage?" He tells us his idea for Edmund, and I have to admit, it's fucking brilliant.

"Go for it. Makes a hell of a lot more sense than what's going on right now," I offer.

"You're right. Sage and I will be so much happier if I can pull it off."

We finish our drinks and… *Fuck*. I'm nearly drunk as we make our way back to a palace.

9

CHARLOTTE

"You did *what?* Shit." Melanie shakes her head. "Em can never find out."

"I *know.* No one can know. I shouldn't have told you but… I don't know what to do!"

"I would've just had sex with him. I love Ethan, but I can appreciate how fucking hot Jason is. I can't believe he told you he loves you," she sighs with a shrug as we prepare the platters for tonight's buffalo plaid party.

"Shh! Will you keep your voice down, someone might hear you." I glance over at Sage's friends, Andi and Georgiana, who are unloading boxes of wine and beer. "He doesn't love me, at least not like that. We're just friends."

"I know you're basically in love with him too, no matter how much you deny it. What's the worst that happens? You come too many times?"

Sage startles me as she asks, "Are you talking about that hot baseball player of yours? Just fuck him already."

"*Jeez*, where did you come from? You scared the shit out of me!" I grab my chest. "Does everyone fucking know?"

"We just all assumed you fucked in London because you guys have been so fucking weird this past week," Sage admits, grabbing a glass from the cabinet. She adds a few ice cubes and pours herself a whiskey. "Also, he looks at you like he's about to pin you down and do all sorts of dirty things to you."

"He doesn't. You two are full of shit," I grumble with my arms crossed over my chest.

"Come on. Make yourself a drink and let's go sit," Sage insists, gesturing to leave the kitchen.

We make a mocktail for Mel, since she's currently trying to get pregnant, and head into one of the parlors with our drinks in hand. We're all wearing our matching black and white buffalo plaid pajama pants, so Georgie and Andi leave to their rooms to change into theirs.

Sage is telling us about an event snafu she had a few weeks ago when Melanie interrupts, "Oof, I think we're in trouble, girls." Sage and I look behind us to find the three guys walking in. It's like something out of a movie. It's sinful how attractive the three of them are

Ethan wastes no time grabbing Melanie to pull her to him. "Hey, princess." They are so in love, it's gross.

I sigh. It's really not gross, I'm just jealous of my friends.

Mel pushes against his chest as he tries to devour her whole. "Whoa there. Why don't you guys get cleaned up?"

Eddie wraps his arms around Sage from behind and kisses her neck, whispering something to her. She turns in his arms as Eddie says, a little too loudly, "I'm too drunk for this conversation, Cinnamon." I'll never get over the ridiculous nickname he has for her. "Tomorrow night, I'm going to—"

I pinch the bridge of my nose and do my best to dissociate to drown out their conversation. It's so fucking embarrassing. My friends are all lovey dovey with one other and I'm over here, single and pining after my best friend like a fucking idiot.

Jason coughs loudly, probably to announce his presence, but I don't dare look at him. I direct my attention to Sage, who is trying her best to get out of Eddie's hold. He's all growly and can't keep his hands off her. It's both adorable and eye-roll worthy.

"Sorry," Sage winces as she's finally able to move away from him. I can feel Jason's eyes on me, but I'm still not brave enough to look.

Ethan breaks the silence. "You know what sucks? I only found out about Sage and Tyler... *Edmund*, two weeks ago! Some friends you all are." Melanie raises an eyebrow at him. "Right. Well, gentlemen, we should leave the ladies to their little get together," Ethan announces, kissing Melanie's cheek. Jason walks away. Ethan and Eddie follow.

Once they're gone, Sage asks, "Can we escort the elephant out of the room, Charlotte?"

My eyes narrow. "Screw you and your metaphors. Give me all the fucking elephants, bitch. Make it a party!"

We all laugh and Melanie asks, "I know it's weird, but when are you going to finally ride that stallion?"

I throw back my head and groan. "Why does everyone keep asking me that? We… we're just friends."

"Just friends? Such a fucking liar," Melanie insists, chuckling. "You're one of my best friends, did you, or did you not, enjoy that delicious man between your legs?"

I sigh. "Even if I did, it wouldn't matter. We aren't here for that, are we? No. We are here for"—I gesture to Sage—"this tall drink of water who my best friend is obsessed with." *I still can't believe he's getting married.*

Melanie gasps, clutching her chest. "I am not obsessed with Sage!"

The three of us laugh and Sage adds, "That remains to be seen. I don't think Edmund would want to share, though. Sorry, Mel."

"Damn it! Well, I guess Ethan is stuck with me."

With the couples all paired off, Andi and I have been talking throughout the movie. It's a welcome distraction from what's going on with Jason. As the movie wraps up, we notice everyone has left, except Georgie and Jillian, who are on their phones.

Andi calls out, "Jill, where did everyone go?"

Jill glances around, finally noticing everyone is gone. She taps Georgiana, who does the same, and shrugs. "Probably went to go fuck," she answers and resumes with her scrolling.

"Don't mind them. The four of us have been single a little too long," And chuckles. "I'm honestly surprised Sage is the first to settle down."

"Oh, believe me, I get it. I don't even remember the last time I had a boyfriend. Ever since I moved to California, I've been too busy to date."

Andi nods but then frowns. "What about that hot bearded guy, Justin?"

"Jason," I correct. "We're just friends."

"Bullshit. There's no way! I just assumed you guys had some sort of lovers spat. Fuck, if he wasn't obsessed with you, I'd hook up with him myself." Andi sips her wine and her eyes linger on me. *Maybe she's waiting for my green light?*

"He's not obsessed with me," I admit, though I'm not entirely sure if it's true. "We aren't together, so if you want to, go for it." *Even though it would hurt the moment I found out.*

"That man only has eyes for you, Char. I'm not going after an unavailable man, even for a quick fuck. Last thing I need is him calling out your name in bed." We both laugh, but a pang of jealousy hits me at the thought of him with another woman, especially one as beautiful as Andi. "Seriously though, go hit that." She glances behind me. "Speak of the devil."

I turn to find Jason walking toward us. He's close enough there's a chance he heard most of what we said. I'm hoping, with all my being, that's not the case.

"Hey, sweetheart. Sorry, the road to the inn is closed; we all have to stay here tonight. Edmund said there are three rooms left."

"Oh, great, I'm sure I can room with one of the girls tonight. Thanks for letting us know," I reply as casually as I can muster, even if what I really want is to stay with him tonight.

Georgie snorts. "I don't share a bed with anyone, unless they're providing me endless orgasms. You're all on your own tonight." She gets up and leaves without another word.

Fuck.

"Andi and I will room together," Jill announces with a smirk.

Double fuck.

"Well, have a good night, you two." Andi stands and, with her back to Jason, winks at me.

Once we're alone, I finally meet his gaze. "I can sleep on a couch. Don't worry about me."

Jason shakes his head with a soft chuckle. "No, babygirl, you're not sleeping on the couch." He sits down next to me. All of a sudden, the room feels incredibly warm and way too small. "Can we talk?"

"W-we are talking."

"About London," he sighs.

"Oh, right. Where I lost my best friend? Yeah, definitely *not* a fan of that city. Actually, I'd rather not talk about it." I shift to get comfortable, looking away from him.

Jason places his hand on mine, squeezing and not letting go. "You didn't lose me. I wanted to give you space after what happened. But it's been the shittiest week without you." He blows out a long breath and I hate that nothing will ever be the same between us.

"Yeah," I admit with a nod. "We kind of made a mess of things, didn't we?" He brings my knuckles to his lips, and the small gesture forces my gaze back on him. "You told me you love me, and I know you mean as friends, just as I love Eddie and Mel... but I don't love you that way." I squeeze my eyes shut for a moment, trying to keep my stinging eyes from betraying me. "I don't just love you as a friend, Jay. I'm sorry."

He leans in, pressing his forehead to mine. I fight the urge to kiss him. "Why are you apologizing? I don't just love you as a friend, either. You and me, it would be hard. I have to know, do you want to be with me?"

"I… Yes and no," I answer honestly. "We can't…"

Pulling back, his gaze is intense. Eye contact normally gives me a bit of anxiety, but not with him. "Will you still be my best friend, then?" he asks, and I want to scream 'no.' I want more. "I can't imagine my life without you in it. I'll take what I can get."

I draw in a deep breath in and exhale slowly. "Do best friends share a bed in a palace? I'm tired, and it's stupid for either of us to sleep on a couch."

"Come on." Jason stands and offers his hand. "Let's get to bed."

10

JASON

Selfishly, I hold Charlotte all night—wishing it could always be like this. As soon as we get back to California, everything will change, and I'm not sure whether it will be for better or for worse. Since we spent the night together in London, I haven't been able to think of anything but what happened. If it wasn't for Emma, our age difference, and Charlotte being one of the most important people in my life, I'd do everything in my power to make her mine.

It was one night. One night in the arms of the one person I shouldn't want and can't have. I should've moved on from it, but having her with me right now, what's *two*? Just for tonight, I can indulge my fantasy of keeping her. Tonight, away from home with her wrapped up in me, I can pretend she's mine. In a few short days, we'll go back to being friends and neighbors, no matter how much I hate it.

Charlotte stirs and lets out a long, contented sigh. I hold her tighter, but her sigh turns into a soft moan. *Fuck.* I would give anything for another taste of her—another shot at making her come.

I'm suddenly acutely aware of Charlotte's hand slipping down my side as it wanders lower to my hip, inches from my cock. I move it up, back to my chest. As much as I'd love her touching me, I'm not going to risk her doing this in her sleep when she isn't aware it's happening.

"Please," she whimpers softly. Her hand travels lower again, this time her fingers slip an inch into my boxer briefs.

"Sweetheart, you can't be doing that," I say loud enough that, if she's awake she'd hear me, but not if she's still asleep.

"Why not?" *Fuck.* She's awake. She slides her fingers lower, until she fists my cock.

"Because I want you too much to ask you to stop," I admit with a groan.

"Then, don't."

I should say no, should push her away. This isn't fair to either of us. Still, I've never been able to say no to her. She strokes up and down my shaft a few times, and I shiver, but grab her wrist. "You can touch me, only if I'm allowed to touch you."

She shakes her head against me. "I don't want you to be disappointed if you can't make me come."

"I told you last time: I don't come unless you do." I tilt her chin and lean in to press a chaste kiss to her lips. "I want to try something. Do you trust me?" She nods. "Turn around for me." I guide her body until her back is pressed against my chest. As I kiss her shoulder and neck, she reaches to the back of my head, tangling her fingers in my hair. I interlace our fingers and bring her hand from my hair to my lips, kissing her palm. "Show me how you want me to touch you."

Charlotte guides both of our hands down her soft body until they rest on top of her underwear. "Take them off for me," she demands with confidence I haven't seen in a while. I let go of her hand to tug them off her.

Placing my hand between her legs, I wait for her. "I want to see you come undone, Char. What do you think about when you touch yourself?" She stills. If I want her to open up to me, I need to admit my truth first. "Every time I come, I think of you." Her breath hitches and I continue, "I imagine what it would feel like to be deep inside you while you scream my name; your wet pussy clenched around me as you come over and over, until you can't take it anymore… only to give you one more." I replace my hand with hers, keeping mine on top. Kissing her neck, I whisper, "You think about me too, don't you? Show me how you touch yourself."

Her fingers circle her clit slowly but with a firm pressure. "Like this," she sighs breathlessly.

"Keep going, babygirl. Make yourself come for me." Charlotte continues playing with her clit, letting out the sexiest fucking moans I've ever heard in my life. I nearly come just from the sound of her.

"I'm close," she pants.

"Let go," I command. She listens beautifully, continuing until she comes all over both our hands. I bring her fingers to my mouth, desperate to taste her. She's better than I remember, even if it's only been a week. "How are you feeling, sweetheart?"

"I, um… good?"

I wrap my arm around her waist and bring her close to me. "Good. Let's get some rest."

"Rest? You think I can rest after that?" She turns in my arms. "We're on vacation. Vacation sex doesn't count, so…"

"Char, I can't have sex with you, especially after London. You know I'm in love with you, I can't just fuck you and walk away from it."

"You're not in love with me," Charlotte scoffs, shaking her head.

"I am," I insist, pressing my forehead to hers. "It wouldn't be just sex for me. I know tomorrow, or even when we're back home, things will have to return back to normal. We'll still have our nights watching movies, happy hour drinks after work, and taco night where I always overseason the beef. I can't do all that if I'm constantly reminded about how amazing it feels being inside you."

"How do you know it'll be amazing? I could be the most underwhelming lay of your life!" She's teasing but there's nothing funny about any of this. When I don't respond, she adds, "I know it's stupid, and I'm probably not even going to come, but being that this is the one and only time we might ever have sex... I want to."

"Why do you have to challenge me like that? You know the moment you said that you've never had an orgasm from sex..." *Fuck it.* I roll her onto her back, settling myself between her legs. Her wet pussy pressed against me soaks through my underwear. She looks all too pleased with herself, staring up at me and biting her lip. "Are you sure about this? Once we do this, there's no going back."

She laughs. "It's not like getting divorced in six weeks and pretending it never happened, like Eddie's doing."

Does she know?

"We're not getting divorced." The words slip from my mouth before I can stop them.

"Of course not." She grinds against me. It's taking everything in me to resist spreading her wide and taking what's mine. "It's the same thing, though. Once you take it out of the box, it's hard putting it back in. Isn't that how the saying goes?"

"Oh, um, sure." I don't think she knows we're married, but it only confirms why I haven't told her about us being married in the first place—I don't want to get divorced. I want to keep her.

"You might be older and wiser, Jay, but I know what I'm doing. I want you." She hooks her fingers into the waistband of my boxer briefs and tugs them down, freeing my painfully hard cock. I slide them down the rest of the way and toss them to the ground. Her smile is bright and playful, feeling more like us. "At risk of sounding like a desperate, cliché damsel over here... Will you make love to me?"

"That's not cliché at all, babygirl. I could never just fuck you." Sliding my cock in an inch, she gasps. "If you say stop, we stop. I don't care if I'm mid-thrust, okay?"

"Okay," she agrees, softly. I press in another inch, and she moans, "*Fuck*, you're huge."

"No, you're just tight." She laughs and I swallow the beautiful sound with my mouth on hers. I take my time, letting her adjust to me as I push in to the hilt. Scratching her nails scratch down my back, she whimpers. I don't pull out, wanting this moment of heaven to last. Between kisses, I ask, "Doing okay?"

"Mhm," she replies, nodding. Her lips never leave mine, kissing me as if it's all she's ever thought about. I pull out and slowly thrust back into her a few times. She's fucking perfect, made for me, and I can't imagine being with another woman the rest of my life.

Desperate to make her come again, I follow her body's lead to find the right pace that'll send her over the edge. Her breath quickens as her pussy strangles my cock. I kiss down her jaw to her neck, resisting the urge to leave a mark. The need to claim her as mine is almost unbear-able. I nip at her ear and demand, "Tell me what you need, so I can give it to you."

"Harder," she replies without hesitation. I do as she asks, but at this rate, I won't last much longer. "Right there, like that... I think... Yes... Don't stop... *Jason!*" I hold off as long as I possibly can. Charlotte screaming my name has me coming with her harder than I ever have as she pulses around around me. My vision blurs, and my whole body is lit up like fucking Forth of July.

I kiss her softly, both of us trembling. I pull out and lay next to her, wrapping her in my arms. It was far too quick for my liking, but more importantly, I'm very aware there's no coming back from this, and I'm offi-cially freaking out.

I had sex with my best friend.

I had sex with my ex-wife's step-sister.

I had sex with my wife.

I had sex with... the love of my life.

Fuck.

At least I had a vasectomy after Emma and I had Aiden, or I'd add the possibility of knocking up my wife to the list of things to freak out about. I take a deep breath. None of it matters, only Charlotte.

Except, my ego joins in the fun... *I made her come.*

"We can never do that again." Charlotte's voice is cold, and I feel like a bucket of ice water has been thrown over me. "Ever again."

What? Fuck that.

"Why not?"

She sits up, looking away from me. "Never again, Jay."

11

CHARLOTTE

"No. You didn't answer my question." Jason sits up next to me and places his hand on the small of my back. I resist the urge to shrug him off. "Why not?"

I turn to face him. "Because I'm not going to fake it with you again!" My hand flies to my mouth. *Why did I just say that?*

"You… faked it?" Shit, he actually looks hurt. "No, you didn't. I felt—"

"*Kegels*. You felt kegels. Every woman knows how to make their pussy flutter when they need to. I faked it." I blow out a shaky breath. "I'm sorry. I shouldn't have done it, but I knew you were close and I didn't want to burst your bubble."

Damn it, this was a mistake.

Jason ties his hair back into a messy top knot. "Well, fuck," he says with a chuckle. "Bubble definitely burst, but this wasn't about me. How have you not figured out that I get off on your pleasure? I only came because I thought you did, twice. I would have tried every position, bought every vibrator under the sun, and explored every possible kink until you came for me. I know you can because you came earlier on my hand; I'm just determined to do it with my cock."

"I... I don't even know what to say to that." I groan. "Why are you making this harder than it already is? I appreciate the sentiment, but my orgasms aren't your responsibility. I'm not your girlfriend."

"No, you're my wife," he roars. His eyes are wide and mouth agape. "I mean, you're *basically* my wife," he corrects.

"What did you just say? You know I suck at jokes and sarcasm, but I can spot lying a mile away. Why would you... Did you just..." *No, this is not happening.* "Did you just confuse me for *my sister?*"

I should've seen this coming, and I definitely should've known better. But no, I fell for my sister's ex-husband. This is just great. Perfect. I'm a fucking rebound since Emma is now married to Dylan, and now after we have sex, he calls me his wife by accident? Un-*fucking*-believable. I'm such an idiot. I should've known he was hung up on her. Who wouldn't be? She's basically perfect. If I was into women, I'd be one-hundred percent into her. Step-sibling romance be damned.

"She's your *step-sister,* and no. Absolutely not, Char."
Jason blows out a deep breath. "Fuck. I didn't want it to
come out like this… Do you remember the night we
went out to celebrate you getting the contract?" I
narrow my eyes, but nod for him to continue. "Do you
also remember joking that we should go get fake
married to freak out Ethan and Emma?"

"No… I mean, it sounds like me. I was pretty drunk that
night, and being roofied didn't help."

Jason grabs his phone from the bedside table, pulls up
his photos. He hesitates briefly before selecting one and
handing me the phone. "Apparently, we did it for real."

I zoom in and it's a… *What the fuck?* It's a marriage
certificate with our names on it. "This isn't funny, Jason.
What the hell is going on?"

"It's not a joke," he insists. "I looked into it."

I glance up from the phone to ask, "Hold on. This
was…" It's been four or five months and he kept this
from me? "Why are you telling me now? If this is real,
why didn't you say something the moment you found
out?" I throw the phone onto the bed and rush to put on
my clothes.

"I didn't know how to tell you. I tried to make it go
away, but then… I don't think I really wanted it to." He
stands and tries to take me in his arms but I step out of
his hold. "I'm sorry, babygirl, I didn't know how to tell
you."

"Oh no, don't you *babygirl* me. We're married? Fucking married? Is that why you wanted to have sex with me? Consummate the marriage? This is some fucked up shit, Jay." I begin pacing. This is worse, so much worse than the idea of him mistaking me for Emma. "Put your dick away, please. It's distracting." He snickers and slips on his boxer briefs and his buffalo plaid pants. "Actually, you need to cover up your model body. I can't think when I want to lick your pecs or your perfect fucking abs… *Fuck*."

"Char, I'm sorry. This isn't how I wanted to tell you." Jason lets out a hearty laugh and puts his shirt on.

"This isn't funny. What are we going to do? *Oh!* Melanie's a lawyer, maybe she can get us out of this?"

I begin walking out of the room to find her, but Jason snakes his arm around my waist from behind, pulling me to him. "It's the middle of the night, sweetheart," he whispers next to my ear, his beard tickling my neck. "We can find her in the morning. But, what if… what if we just let it be?"

Stepping out of his hold, I spin to face him. "You're kidding, right? First, you tell me that we're secretly married. Now, you're telling me that you want to *stay* married." I gasp. "What about your kids? *Shit!*" I begin pacing again. "Charlie and Noah wouldn't care, but Aiden? And what about Em?"

This is so incredibly fucked up.

"You mean to tell me that you've never thought about it? You and me?"

I stop pacing to glare at him. "In a hypothetical, that would *never* happen in a million years? Sure. This isn't like we organically dated and got married. We *accidentally* got married. The right thing to do is to get divorced or annulled or whatever, and pretend none of this ever happened."

"Do you love me, Char? Because I love you. I love you more than I've loved anyone. I—"

"More than Emma?" I snap. "You were married for over a decade and you have children together. You mean to tell me that you love *me*, more than you loved the mother of your children? No, never mind, I don't want to know. We—"

Jason cups my cheek and he kisses me. His lips are soft and warm and I melt into him in an instant. He teases with his tongue for me to open for him. I do. I can't help it. *Fuck, I love kissing him.* When I kiss him back harder, a growl erupts from his chest as his tongue swipes across mine.

No, we can't do this.

I push back from him, breaking our kiss. "Yes," he says, just above a whisper. "Yes, I love you more. Emma and I were young and got married because it's what you do after dating for a while. We were always better off friends. But you? You've never been my friend, Char.

You've always been more. Hell, I tried everything I could to fight it, but—"

"In the morning, we need to find Mel and see if she knows of any good discrete divorce attorneys. When we get back to California, we're getting divorced. We need to be sure no one finds out about this, especially your kids."

I love Jason, but we can't do this. I'm not about to destroy my friendship with Em, or my relationship with their kids, because of one fucked up night that I hardly remember. Tears prick behind my eyes at the thought.

Jason chews on his lip. "About that..."

"Fuck. Who did you tell?"

"Edmund and Ethan," he admits.

"Damn it, Jay! When?"

He pauses. "London."

Betrayal. That's what this is. Fucking betrayal. "Fuck Eddie. Fuck Ethan. Most of all, fuck *you*. I'm not even upset about the getting married part. You *lied* to me." It's only a matter of time before Emma finds out. I need to get ahead of it. "I need to tell my sister." He nods with his head low and I blow out a deep breath. "I need to take a walk." Grabbing my phone, I head toward the door. "Don't follow me, but I'll send you my location, so you know I'm safe."

"Charlotte—"

"We'll talk later. I… I just need to clear my head and talk to Em." I walk out and, thankfully, he doesn't follow me. I haven't had time to even process all of it, but I need her to know.

I turn on my location services so Jason won't be tempted to follow. Then, I call Emma. She picks up on the first ring. "Char! How's Delasnia?" she squeals.

I blurt out, "I'm married." There's a long silence on the other end so I ask, "You there? Did I lose you?"

"No. I'm here. You just caught me off guard. So, you met someone on vacation and got hitched?" She speaks cautiously, but I don't feel like she's judging me.

"Worse."

"You married Tyler… I mean, Edmund? Fuck, I bet Sage isn't too happy about that one. I thought he was obsessed with her?"

I sit on one of the couches in one of the several parlors that looks as if a great-grandmother decorated it. So much floral. "Worse, Em," I whisper. A tear escapes the corner of my eye. "So much worse."

"Out with it, then," she says brightly. "It can't be that bad."

"Jason." I'm met with silence and dread seeps in. "I'm so sorry, Em. It was an accident." A few more tears leave my eyes.

Emma bursts into laughter, but I can't tell if it's genuine. "Are you serious? This is too good. I can't say I'm surprised. I've seen the way he looks at you *and* the way you look at him. But how was it an accident? People don't accidentally get married."

"I'm sorry, so so sorry. This is a disaster! Apparently, we did it months ago the night we were drugged. He told me tonight. I never would have married your ex on purpose; please believe me." The guilt is eating me alive.

"Do you love him?"

It's such a simple but loaded question. No matter how I answer, it's wrong. "Yes," I admit, mostly to myself, even if she hates me for it.

"Then what's the problem?"

"*Everything's the problem!*" Crap, I think I said that out loud.

"You don't need to shout, Char. It's no big deal. Weirder things have happened. Did I ever tell you about that book where the woman ends up with two hockey players and an equipment manager? Now that's a predicament, but she lived happily ever after." She chuckles. "You're just married to one guy, not in love with three. Even if he is my ex-husband."

"Why are you being so cool about this?" I ask, my breathing getting heavier. "I'm freaking out. He lied to me, Em. I'm married to a fucking liar."

My fight or flight mode is kicking in. I want to run. Emma says something but it sounds like a song being played backwards. I begin rocking in my seat, humming to myself, trying to calm my body and mind.

Damn it! This is not the time for a meltdown!

Too late. It's coming in hot and I can't stop it. My ears are ringing and I can't keep my tears from painting my cheeks. *"Help."* The only word I can get out as I drop the phone, to cover my ears.

I hum a mash-up of songs to myself. Scripting from music usually calms me, helping me self-regulate, but my emotions are too big right now. My heart is pounding and I can feel it everywhere. *Thump-thump, thump-thump, thump-thump.* I try my best to concentrate on my breathing, even focusing on something small like the ornate detail of the rug, but it's all useless.

I'm sitting here for what feels like hours but could also only be minutes, before I hear a voice through the lyrics in my head.

"Babygirl, I'm here. Take a deep breath for me."

I don't listen. Two hands cover mine, which are still glued to my ears.

"You're safe, Charlotte. Shh. It's okay. I'm so sorry, sweetheart."

"Jason?"

12

JASON

"I'm here, babygirl. I'm not going anywhere."

I move from kneeling on the floor to sit next to Charlotte, lifting her to straddle my lap. There's a good chance she'll fight me in the middle of a sensory meltdown. I'm bigger than her and won't give up until her breathing slows.

Keeping her chest pressed to mine, I hold her tight. It's been almost a year since she had a meltdown, and this helped her last time. It only happens when her emotions are too much to handle... *Fuck.* If I'm what triggered the meltdown, I don't know how I'll ever forgive myself for hurting her like this.

Char asks again, "Jason?"

"Yes. It's me. You're safe. Deep breaths, okay?" I squeeze tighter, giving her the deep pressure she craves. She sobs into my shoulder, singing a song to herself. "It's okay, sweetheart. Shhh. I've got you." Her self-regulation isn't working. Since she isn't fighting me, I wrap her arms around my neck and stand with her clinging to me.

I carry her to our bedroom and sit down on the bed. After about fifteen minutes of my stroking her back and holding her tight, her breathing finally slows, but I don't let go of her. When Emma called to tell me to go find Charlotte, she told me she knew everything. She wasn't upset, insisting she's known how I feel about Char for years. I'm thankful she was so understanding, but I rushed her off the phone to find my wife. I'll call Emma back in the morning so we can have a proper discussion about all of it.

"Jason?"

"Yes, baby, I'm here."

"I'm—"

"Shh, it's okay," I tell her quietly.

"It's not, Jay." Her sobs have stopped but she doesn't move. I lift her face from my now drenched shirt to look at her. I don't dare require her to grant me eye contact; it has to be on her terms.

We sit there in silence for another half hour before she speaks again. "When we get back to California, I have to let you go."

"We'll talk about this later," I insist, doing my best to keep my tone even.

Charlotte shakes her head and meets my gaze. There's so much pain in her eyes. "I can't be with you. I'm sorry. As soon as we get to California, we have to get divorced or the marriage annulled. I don't know the difference, but I don't care. I can't stay married to you."

My heart shatters. This is my fault, all of it. I lost the perfect woman because I was selfish. "I should've told you the day I got the paperwork, but a part of me never wanted to let you go. I'm sorry I didn't tell you, it was just never the right time." The last two years, she's stolen a piece of my soul, one by one. Charlotte means everything to me.

I can't lose her.

"Why can't you stay married to me?" I continue, my voice beginning to crack. "It's not Emma, you know my boys love you, I love you. Why not just see what happens?"

Char breathes in deeply, and fists my shirt. She's fighting it. The logical answer is on the tip of her tongue. She's just as in love with me as I am with her, but finding out like this was too much for her. I don't blame her, this is on me.

"You lied to me," she states simply. I open my mouth to apologize again, but she continues, "But, honestly, it's mostly because we've never even dated."

Well, that's not what I was expecting...

"In a literal sense, you're right. But how many times have we gone out and someone thought we were together? How many times have I texted you '*be ready at six*' and took you out to dinner? How many times have I come over for a movie night, just to spend time with you because I wanted to be near you? We've been on hundreds of dates, Char." I shake my head, chuckling to myself as I remember Edmund telling me he asks Sage out every day for a date, and she still hasn't said yes. Those two are fucking ridiculous.

"I haven't even dated *anyone* in almost two years. I can't just go from being single to married just like that." She snaps her fingers. "Hell, I don't think *you've* been on a date since I met you."

"That's not true," I insist.

"Name one person, and don't you dare make them up."

I pause and frown. "I don't know, but I've been on a few dates. I just haven't been in a relationship with anyone." Truth be told, I've been on zero dates, but pretended I was going out from time to time to get her off my back about it. I'd go out for a drink and return an hour later to be grilled about a fictitious woman I was seeing. It was exhausting.

"Exactly. If you're serious, and you actually want to stay married to a hot mess woman who has the attention span of a squirrel on most days, and is prone to sensory meltdowns... Then I need to know that this is for real." This is her typical reaction after a bad sensory meltdown, needing control. I allow her to fixate on it. She sighs. "When we get back home, we're going to date other people. And I want to look into getting divorced."

"Absolutely not," I growl. "I'm married, even if I don't remember my vows. You can date, if it means at the end of it all you come back to me, but I'm not dating anyone but my wife."

Charlotte's obnoxious idea has been in full force for three days. I thought her focus would've moved on to something else by now, but here we are signing up for dating apps on her couch. Since I won't make one myself, she insisted she would create a profile on not one, not two, but *six* different sites for me. I'm in hell, but I deserve it. Even through the ridiculousness of it, I'm thankful she's talking to me at all.

I was sure I'd lose her over keeping this secret. Instead, she's obsessing over the fact that we've never dated— each other, or anyone else, for that matter. While she's not wrong, I'd rather do literally anything else, than go on a date with anyone other than Charlotte.

"Hey sweetheart, while you continue your attempt to find me Mrs. Right when she's already here on her couch, I'm going to run next door. I'll be back in a few."

Char briefly looks up from her phone, nods twice, and dives right back into whatever bullshit prompt she's answering for me. Once in my apartment, I call Dylan and he answers on the third ring, "Hey, married man, what's going on?"

Fuck. I should have guessed Emma would tell him. "Are you free for a drink?"

He chuckles, "Sure, give me an hour. How much time do we need? I promised Em I would make dinner tonight."

"I need to talk to someone about this and my best friend is currently preoccupied trying to find me a date I don't want."

Dylan chokes on his drink. "Okay, make that fifteen. Need me to call Ethan?"

"Please don't. He already knows the basics, but I don't need him giving me more shit about it."

"He gives *me* shit so often, I'd love to see him turn his attention to whatever the fuck you have going on. I'm inviting him. O'Malley's or Keith's?"

I groan. "Fine. O'Malley's"

"See you in fifteen."

We hang up and I stop by Charlotte's next door to make sure she's okay before I head out. She hardly pays attention to me, waving me off. I sigh and leave.

After I explain everything, Ethan won't stop laughing. To be fair, if this wasn't happening to me, I would be laughing too. But it *is* happening to me, and I'm fucking pissed about it.

"For fuck's sake, man. Just lean against a doorframe or slowly roll up your sleeves while keeping your eyes locked with hers. How else do you think I snagged this one's sister?" Ethan says, sipping his Old Fashioned and gesturing to Dylan, who groans at the mention of Melanie. "You're lumbersnack eye candy; she'll eat it up and forget all about the dating app thing."

"Why do you always insist I'm a lumberjack? I've never chopped a single piece of wood in my fucking life, but this is probably the tenth time you've said that."

"It's the man-bun," Dylan insists, signaling the bartender for another gin and tonic.

"And the flannel," Ethan adds. "Hold on, we're going about this all wrong. Put on some baseball warm-up pants, no cup. Would be hot as fuck."

I finish my IPA and order another, glaring at Ethan. "Not helping. This is Charlotte we're talking about; she wouldn't notice if I walked into the room naked."

"Whatcha packin' there?" Ethan gestures to my dick. "I'm sure she'd notice. I was in the room next door when you two hooked up in Delasnia. Maybe she just needs a gentle reminder of what you have to offer…"

Except I couldn't even make her come…

Dylan nearly spit out his gin and tonic. "What? You fucked Charlotte? I thought you were just married after a fucked up night in the mountains. Does Em know?"

"No one knows... no one *did* know." I side-eye Ethan.

"Eddie knows, too," Ethan says with a shrug. "Basically everyone who stayed the night before the wedding knows. You guys weren't exactly quiet. Next time she has a meltdown, you better come knock on my door. Charlotte is like a sister to me. I don't care if I'm balls deep in Mel's—"

"Ethan!" Dylan growls. "I do *not* need to hear about you hooking up with my sister. Fuck, man."

"Fine," Ethan groans, rolling his eyes. "But you get the point. Charlotte is family to all of us. If she needs help, we're here. I was pissed I had to find out from Mel hours later."

"She's my *wife*. She's mine to take care of, Ethan."

"Damn it! You too? First Dylan, then Eddie, now you? What is it with you guys and the growly *'she's mine'* book boyfriend manifestation? Don't get me wrong, it's hot, but it's getting old." Ethan shakes his head. "I warned you in Delasnia. You should have told her."

"If neither of you are going to help me, I'm going home to try to win over my wife and convince her to put a stop to this online dating thing."

I move to get off my stool but Dylan places his hand on

my shoulder. "Sorry, you're right, I shouldn't have invited him."

"Hey! Fuck you guys. Just for that, you can pay the tab," Ethan jokes.

Dylan chuckles. "Nice try, Barlowe. I know you know the owner and get comp drinks here."

"Hey, remember that one time I was here with Emma, and you thought she was on a date..." Ethan can't finish the story, he's laughing too hard. I also can't help chuckling. Ethan did a real number on Dylan when he started dating Emma, pretending to be her date for the night. Dylan fucking lost it. I can't say I blame him. If Ethan had pulled that shit on me, claiming he was dating Charlotte, I'd be seeing red too.

"Asshole," Dylan says with a smirk.

"Aw, come on you dusty ol' fart, it was funny!" Ethan insists. I've known Ethan for years, since he's best friends with Emma, but it's been a while since I've seen him rip into Dylan like this. It's a welcome distraction from my miserable situation.

"I thought it was Mayo?" I ask, adding fuel to the fire.

"Oh, fuck. Not you, too," Dylan groans. "I've got to get back to Em and the kids soon, so let's focus. How are we going to get you out of the dates?"

Ethan's grin couldn't be wider. "My time to shine, boys. My time to shine."

13

CHARLOTTE

Charlotte, 30
San Francisco, CA
Typical girly shit…

Ugh, what the hell am I going to put in this damn
profile? I can't seem to think of anything interesting to
include about myself, even if my life depended on it.
Jason's was so easy, why can't mine be sexy and engag-
ing? I pull his profile up again and read through it to see
if it'll spark any inspiration.

Jason, 42
San Francisco, CA
No, I'm not a lumberjack.
Yes, I played minor league baseball.
No, I won't let you open your own car door.
Yes, I will let you pick where we're going for dinner.
No, you can't pay for said dinner.
Yes, you're an independent woman, but you'll still let me take care

of you.
Lazy Sundays > Sunday Funday
Mountains > Beach
Books > Movies
Coffee > Tea
IPA > Everything else

If you're up for dating a single dad who has his life together, I might be your guy.

I scroll back to the top and see if he has any matches.

Inbox (74)

Fuck! I take a deep breath and close out of the app. My front door opens and I toss my phone onto the couch like a teenager caught with porn by their parents.

Jason walks in, tossing his keys on the table. "Hey sweetheart, want to grab dinner?"

"Oh, I-I can't," I stammer. "I have, uh, I have a date tonight. Don't worry, you have seventy-four matches on one of the apps, I'm sure you can keep yourself busy." There's an ache in my chest. *Why the hell am I doing this?*

"Send me the location and his information," he growls.

"Jay, I don't need a keeper. I'll be fine," I insist. "Besides, you're going to be with your own date. You'll be too busy with them to worry about me."

Jason pinches the bridge of his nose and groans. "Why are you doing this, Char?" When he glances up, he stuffs his hands in his pockets. "I don't want to date anyone other than you."

It's not that I don't want to date Jason, but I'm terrified we'll jump into this with two feet and he'll discard me in a month or a year when he figures out we're better off as just friends. After he lied to me, I don't know if I can trust him.

"We've been over this," I sigh. "You want to wife me up when I've barely dated and you haven't been with anyone since Emma. I don't want to be your rebound girl. What if, in five years, you get bored with me, or I get bored with you? I need to know if we do this, it's permanent. I refuse to be Emma 2.0." The admission is like a stab to my heart, but nothing compared to the pain in his face.

"Why do you think I've barely dated in two years, Char?" He waits but I don't answer. "You fucking know why. I wanted *you*. I couldn't have you, so I tortured myself being your friend when all I wanted was a chance to be with you. All the obstacles are gone, why are you adding one more?"

"Because I'm fucking scared, Jay! Is that what you want to hear? I'm scared to death that I'm going to lose you or you'll realize we were really *just* friends. It took you years to figure that out with Em—"

"You're not her," he insists. "She was never mine; she was *always* Dylan's. I knew it, but I tried to make it work. I realized, for the sake of our kids, that having a strong, healthy friendship was more important. After almost fifteen years, we didn't want our boys to have that as an example of what love is. The day she told me she was dating Dylan"—he shakes his head—"I've never been so happy for her." Jason sits on the couch next to me. "She may be my friend, but she doesn't hold a candle to you, sweetheart. I never loved her the way I love you. I buried how I feel about you for years, I won't do it anymore."

I know Emma loved Jason, but not the same way she's in love with Dylan. When Emma walks in the room, Dylan lights up with a wide dimpled grin. Hell, they both do. They belong together—anyone can see it. Whenever I saw Emma and Jason together, they always looked like two friends, not lovers. I just assumed it was the result of years of marriage and kids. I want what Emma and Dylan have—fireworks. I don't want to be accidentally married to my friend. I want to be chosen. Jason hasn't dated anyone seriously since Emma. It's like going from the fire to the frying pan being married to me.

"I don't want to be your wife," I admit softly. "I would be okay if we date as an actual couple, not as friends. But I also need you to see other people. Please."

"I get why you want to. I fucking hate it, but I get it. Go, date other people." Jason stands and makes his way to the front door. He turns and adds, "Tuesday night. I'll pick you up at seven."

He closes the door and I stare at it for a good minute

before frantically picking up my phone to text Melanie, Emma, Riley, and Lily.

> Buffalo plaid.

MEL

Fuck! Don't tell me he fucked it up already?

RILEY

Asshole!

LILY

I'm sure it's just a misunderstanding.

EMMA

We're on our way!

While I wait, I finish setting up my dating profile—it still doesn't hold a candle to Jason's, and I'm the one who wrote it. It'll have to do for now.

About an hour later, the girls arrive at my apartment with an assortment of alcohol and a plethora of snacks. We normally just drink wine, but the girls already know this requires the hard stuff. They set everything out on the coffee table while Melanie makes me a martini.

"What, no twist?" I tease as she hands it to me.

"This is twisted enough, no need to add to it," she replies with a wink.

"Holy crap! How many books do you own?" Lily browses my collection stacked next to my bookcase.

"I don't know," I reply with a shrug. "I really only listen to audiobooks. If I love it, I buy the paperback, especially if it's an indie author."

"You don't read them?"

I chuckle. "No, they're more of a trophy for my bookshelf."

"So… How's married life?" Riley asks, sipping her Moscow mule.

"I'm not really married," I groan. "I mean, *legally* I am, but Jason and I aren't even together."

I give them a rundown of everything that happened, complete with the faked orgasm—which I apologize profusely to Emma about. I have no idea what I'm going to do about all of this and hope they have solid advice to walk me through it. After everything, I still can't believe how Emma is okay with all of this. Except, what Jason said makes perfect sense—she was always Dylan's. I might be married to Jason, but I just don't feel like it's the same for us. I don't feel like I'm *his*… at least not now.

"Ready for some tough love?" Riley asks. I'm not, but she doesn't wait for my response. "Men are basic. Even Dylan, Andrew, and Ethan… even my boyfriend. They are all simple creatures."

All eyes are on Riley as Emma gasps, "Bitch, since when do you have a boyfriend?"

"Maybe I have two?" She shrugs and avoids the question. "Anyway, Char, if he says he loves you, he's not mincing words. Sure, he's probably going to fuck up. Put on your big girl panties, walk next door, and mount that lumbersnack."

"*Ugh*. Seriously? He's not a lumbersnack!" I laugh.

"He definitely is," Melanie insists. "If I wasn't married... Split me open, Daddy."

"Mel! *Shh*, he'll hear you. These walls are thin." There's a knock on my wall. "Fuck! See, I told you."

The girls burst out into laughter and Riley calls out, "We don't need the lumberjack getup. Break out the gray sweatpants, Jay! We wanna see it jiggle jiggle!"

"Fuck you guys!" I down my drink and get up to make another.

"I get it. You don't date much, but you're really not missing anything. The men out there are kind of trash. Do you think you're going to find someone better than Jason?" Emma asks, raising her brow.

"No." I chew my lip.

My phone buzzes on the table and Mel picks it up.

"Damn it. Face recognition. Unlock it, Char. You have a new message from the axe-wielding mountain man next door." Melanie hands me my phone. I unlock it and give it back to her.

I don't want to know what Jason has to say about any of this but I trust Mel won't send something back to him. Riley and Lily, on the other hand, are the reason Dylan and Emma are together—I don't trust their constant meddling, especially after that little comment Riley made about two boyfriends.

I plop down on the couch and the group is silent. "He doesn't own an axe, but what does he want?" I sigh, taking a long drink of my refreshed martini, with a twist this time.

"I… um… *fucking hell!*" Melanie's eyes are wide. I'm now regretting giving her access to my phone.

I snatch my phone back. It's not just a text message, it's a photo… of Jason… shirtless… in gray sweatpants with an outline of his perfect fucking cock.

I'm staring for far too long when Riley peers over my shoulder "Ask and you shall receive. You're welcome, *babygirl*," she chuckles.

I frown at her, confused why she would jokingly call me that. She points to the text below the photo.

> JAY
>
> Send the girls home, babygirl. We have unfinished business.

14

JASON

After leaving Charlotte's, my phone has been buzzing non-stop with email notifications. Thankfully, I was able to unsubscribe to the dating apps she set up but it took far too long to get rid of the nearly two hundred emails. When she hyperfixates on something, it takes hold of her; the obsession with this is by far my least favorite she's had in the past two years.

I can't handle the constant notifications, so I plug my phone in and take a shower, hoping the subscription cancellation will have taken effect by the time I get out.

Once dried off and in a pair of sweats, I grab a beer from my fridge and check my phone. There's several text messages from a group chat I have with Ethan, Edmund, and Dylan.

ETHAN

Did it work out?

DYLAN

Who are you talking to? Did what
work out?

EDMUND

What did I miss?

ETHAN

Jason becoming a book boyfriend and
seducing Charlotte.

DYLAN

Hold on. THAT was your plan?

I mean, it's not a bad plan, but I
expected more from you.

EDMUND

About fucking time, mate.

After Dylan left, Ethan said I should
seduce Char. I thought it was a joke.

ETHAN

There he is! Was wondering if you were
going to grace us with your presence.

It wasn't a joke. Have you seen what she
reads? Charlotte needs to be as
obsessed with you as you are with her.
She probably doesn't even believe
you're interested in her. Show her!

Time to turn into the ultimate book
boyfriend. You can do it! I believe in you!

DYLAN

Do I need to get Em's advice on this?
You know she works with romance
authors for a living.

ETHAN

I've got this! I'm pretty sure I've read more spicy romcoms than she has. Trust the process.

EDMUND

Go seduce your wife, just leave out the details. I don't want to think about one of my best friends naked.

ETHAN

A little chaos never hurt anyone, Jason.

The girls are laughing next door when one of them says loudly, "*Split me open, Daddy.*" I knock on the wall for them to keep it down. I know they all need to unhide and they're just having a good time, but I would rather not listen to them compare notes about their husbands.

All right, Ethan. You win. Don't worry Eddie, I'm not telling any of you how this goes.

I finish my beer and as I'm about to get another, some-one's voice calls out, "*We don't need the lumberjack getup. Break out the gray sweatpants, Jay! We wanna see it jiggle jiggle!*" I glance down at my gray sweatpants and laugh.

Ethan's right; Charlotte doubts how I feel about her. She's so insistent that I date other people to make sure she's the one for me. I already know she is, I don't need anyone else to prove it to myself. I've never courted her, never tried to seduce her, never even tried to show her how she's supposed to be with me.

That changes now.

I snap a cliché mirror pic, showing off the pants they were laughing about and send it with a text to Charlotte.

> Send the girls home, babygirl. We have unfinished business.

I wait a minute for a response. It says 'read,' but not only is there no new text from her, the girls next door are quiet. I hear one of them say, *"You heard the man, out!"* A few minutes later, her door opens and closes a few times before complete silence. I don't expect her to come to me, but I also want to be sure she's alone.

My phone buzzes with a text.

CHARLOTTE

What unfinished business?

> Invite me over and you'll find out.

You have a key and can stop by whenever you want. I don't need to invite you, you can just show up.

I consider my response for a moment, debating on how flirtatious or forward I want to be.

> This is different. If you invite me over, I want to walk in to find you on your bed. Naked. I intend to finish what I started.

Charlotte doesn't respond. Her door opens and closes and a moment later there's a knock at my door. Charlotte never knocks; she always uses her key.

Fuck, maybe I took it too far.

I open it to find her eyes cast down, fidgeting with the hem of her shirt. Slowly, she lifts her gaze to meet mine.

Taking cue from Ethan, I reach my hand up to rest it on the top of the door frame, leaning in slightly. "Forget your key, sweetheart?"

Charlotte takes a step closer, biting her lip. "You're doing the doorway thing, Jason."

"Doorway thing?" I ask coyly. "Oh, you mean this?" I wrap my free hand around her, pull her to me, then press her against the door jam, our faces inches apart.

"Yeah, that," she breathes.

"Admit you want me, Charlotte." I resist the urge to wrap my hand around the front of her neck and bring her lips to mine.

"You never call me Charlotte." She swallows hard.

"You never call me Jason." *Except when you fake an orgasm.* "Admit it. Admit you've fantasized about me spending hours worshiping every inch of your incredible body. Admit your heart stops when I kiss or touch you." I kiss her neck, making her whimper. "Admit a part of you has always belonged to me." I slip my hand from the small of her back, up her side, grazing her perfect breast. Finally, I claim what's mine, gently taking her beautiful neck in my hand. "Admit you're mine, babygirl, as much as I'm yours."

As she's about to close the distance, a throat clears behind me. "Put a shirt on, you hippie," our neighbor

Janis says, laughing as she passes us to her place next to Charlotte's. She's in her late sixties and has a great sense of humor… and the worst timing.

"Sorry, Mrs. Kennedy," Charlotte winces, pressing her forehead to my chest to hide her embarrassment.

"About time you two got together. Have a good night!" She continues walking down the hall.

I wrap Charlotte in my arms and kiss the top of her head, breathing in the familiar smell of coconut and vanilla that grounds me. "Stay with me tonight?" I whisper into her hair.

She rests her chin on my chest to look up at me. "We should get out of your doorway."

"Is that a yes?"

"I have an early morning," she replies, chewing her lip.

"I have an alarm on my phone."

"I don't want to disappoint you, again."

"I'm only going to say this once, sweetheart." I tuck her hair behind her ear, letting my fingers trace her jaw before pulling my hand away. "There is nothing in this world you could ever do that would disappoint me."

"We shouldn't—"

"No. As much as I have craved the taste of you, I don't care if we do anything tonight. I just miss having you in my arms and want to wake up next to you in the morning. Stay with me?" *Please say yes.*

She hesitates. "Will this be a one time thing?"

No. "If you want it to be."

"Doorway, Jay."

I chuckle. "Babygirl, you don't like saying yes to anything, do you? Stay the night with me?" *And let me keep you in the morning.*

"Okay… I'll stay. But I need to go lock up." She turns toward her place.

"I've got it." I'm not risking her going in there and not coming out. I grab my keys and beat her to it.

"I need to brush my teeth."

Nice try, sweetheart.

"It's early. I'll grab your stuff later if you need it. Come on, I'll order dinner. I doubt the girls brought you anything of substance." I guide her by the small of her back to my place after locking up. "What sounds good?"

We step inside my apartment and I lock the door behind us. When I turn, her eyes are fixated on my chest. "You should put on a shirt." She looks away with wide eyes as soon as she realizes I caught her.

I step toward her and shrug. "You've seen me naked." She lowers her gaze to my pants. I'm going commando and pretty sure she can tell. I follow her line of sight and, sure enough, there is nothing to hide. I'm half-hard but all it would take is her kissing me or even an innocent touch and I would be steel. "Do you really want me to put a shirt on?"

Charlotte gasps and looks away when she's caught staring again. I take another step closer. This time, her eyes meet mine and she doesn't fight it. She clears her throat. "I'm sorry, I shouldn't be staring," she whispers.

"I spent the last few years unable to keep my eyes off you. There's no reason to apologize." I glide my hand into her hair and kiss her softly. She whimpers against my lips as her hands find my waist. I don't push for more, afraid it'll end everything. When we slowly break apart, I admit, "I'm yours, only yours, babygirl. Let me prove it to you."

"I'm pretty sure your hard cock pressed against me proves it." She bites her lip and teases, "I suppose there's no reason to apologize for that, either."

"Fuck. Sorry, Char." I can't even adjust, there's nothing to keep this contained. "I'll go change." I turn to head to the bedroom, not wanting to make her feel uncomfortable.

I only make it three steps before she rushes out, "Stop." I turn back and she closes the distance. "Are you inviting me in?" I frown, unsure of how to respond. "Earlier, you said if I invited you in, you expected to find me naked in bed. Are *you* inviting me in? Can I have you naked in *your* bed?" She tries to contain her smug smile, but the rising blush on her cheeks gives her away.

"Tell you what, I'll get as naked as you are. I should grab a shirt to level the playing field." I turn again, but hear a light thump on the floor and glance back to find her shirt on the ground.

"No need, Jay. We match now."

I smile, biting my lip. "Not quite, sweetheart." She slides her black and white plaid pants down her legs and kicks them off to join her shirt. "Can I play with you tonight?"

She nods. *Fuck. Yes.* I've been dreaming about burying my face between her legs again since the night before Edmund's wedding.

"You have two minutes. I want you naked in my bed when I get back. I'm going to grab your clothes for tomorrow, your toothbrush… and something you keep in your bedside table." She stays rooted in place. I close the distance and press a chaste kiss to her cheek. "Two minutes, Charlotte."

15

CHARLOTTE

I scurry into Jason's bedroom and strip off my bra and panties. Do I stay on top of the covers all sexy? Do I get under them and cover up? Maybe he'll rip them away and growl like a wolf shifter in one of my favorite fantasy books…

As I sit in bed against the headboard, I pull the sheets up to cover myself as I hear his front door open, close, and lock. Footsteps approach the bedroom. The closer he gets, the more nervous I become and the faster my heart beats. When he reaches his bedroom doorway, he leans against the frame, crossing his arms.

"What?" I ask, feeling self-conscious.

"Let me guess, you spent the last two minutes over-thinking this." He pushes off the frame and steps toward the bed. I clutch the sheets to my chest, but he shakes his head. "I want to see all of you. Drop them." I follow his instructions and let them fall. "Better. *Fuck.* You're so beautiful. Never hide from me, babygirl." He climbs onto the bed and prowls toward me. I feel like one of those prey animals in a nature video, seconds away from being devoured. He tears the sheet away from my lower half. "I told you I want to see all of you," he reminds me with a smirk.

"You said you'd get as naked as I am," I manage, though my voice is shaky.

Jason chuckles. "You're right. I did say that, didn't I?" He slides off the bed and takes off his sweatpants, freeing his incredibly hard cock. "Almost forgot." He leans down to pick up his pants, pulls out my bullet vibrator from the pocket, and tosses them back on the ground. "Give me a number between one and ten."

"Um, four?"

He climbs back on the bed and pulls my legs until my back is flush with the mattress. It catches me by surprise and I can't help but giggle. "One, you're absolutely stunning." He kisses my neck, then moves lower to swirl his tongue around each of my nipples. "Two, you're fucking brilliant." He kisses my stomach twice. "Three, you're the most caring and compassionate person I know." His mouth is just above my pubic bone as he kisses me three times. "Four, you're strong and love with your whole heart." He licks up my center, massaging his tongue on my clit. "Bonus, five, I'm absolutely in love with you."

I involuntarily arch my back, seeking more friction. His words wash over me and, all at once, I realize this may be the missing piece. "Don't stop."

"Oh, I won't," he chuckles against me.

"No, I mean, don't stop talking." His fingers enter me and I gasp. "*Please.*"

"You should've picked ten," he chuckles. "Six, I've dreamt about you in my bed like this since the day you told me you were moving back. You taste better than I could have ever imagined." He drives his fingers deeper and kisses the inside of my thigh. "Count for me, babygirl."

"Seven," I rush out between moans.

"Attagirl. Seven, you make me want to be a better man, a man that deserves a woman as incredible as you." He sucks on my clit and it's almost too much.

When I realize he's not talking, I continue, even if it comes out as a broken whisper, "Eight."

"Eight," he echoes between licks. As he continues thrusting his fingers inside me, he curls up and hits right where I need him. "Your smile lights up the room and draws everyone to you"

"Nine. I'm close, don't stop."

"With my face right here, I'll know if you fake it, sweetheart. Don't worry about coming, just let me make you feel good."

"Okay," I whimper. Focusing on him talking instead of my body frees me.

"Nine, I love how your mind thinks differently. You're so creative and inspire everyone around you."

"*Oh, God! Ten!*"

Jason swirls his tongue faster around my clit and my orgasm is within reach. Replacing his tongue with the pad of his thumb, he gives me the extra pressure I crave so desperately. "Ten, if you'll let me, I intend to spend the rest of my life showing you how special you are to me." He peppers kisses up my body until he reaches my jaw. "There is only you, there will only *ever* be you. I love you, Charlotte."

"*Jason,*" I moan and come harder than I ever have in my life, my body quivering and legs shaking. The waves of my orgasm crash over and over again. He kisses me hard and it helps me regulate my breathing.

"Number between one and ten," he whispers against my lips.

I chuckle, still reeling. "Two."

"I'm going to take one more from you. Are you ready for it?"

I nod, not breaking our kiss. He rubs his length up and down my entrance before sliding his cock inside me, inch by thick fucking inch until he's fully seated inside me.

How did I take him before? I feel like I'm going to break in half.

Jason pulls back. "Hey, what's wrong?"

"Nothing, why?"

"You're in your head, aren't you?" He keeps his cock deep inside me, thankfully giving my body a chance to adjust. "What's on your mind?"

"Are you seriously asking me this, during sex?"

"Of course, I am."

I blow out a deep breath. "It wasn't even anything big and emotional... Well, it's *big*, but not emotional."

Jason huffs a laugh. "You can take it. You did before. Would it be easier to ride me? Wait, where's that vibrator?" He pats around the bed. "Ah, here we go." He rolls onto his back, still inside me. Turning on the vibrator on the first setting, he rests it against my clit. I shiver at the added sensation. "How does that feel?"

"Good, I just don't know if I can move. I'm still coming down from whatever the hell it is you did to me," I tease.

"I want you to grind on me," he demands, all playfulness gone. He grips one of my hips and pulls me deeper onto him, rocking me back and forth. "There you go, just like that." Handing me the vibrator, he adds, "Hold this on your clit while I take care of you." I do as he says, but it's too much.

"Stop." He takes the vibrator and tosses it aside. He

quickly lifts me off of him, and I instantly miss the fullness. "No, no... it was just the vibrator, it was a lot."

"Come here," he says softly, carefully wrapping his hand around the front of my throat and pulling me down to him. I grip his wrist, not to pull him away, but to keep him there; something about it that makes me feel safe. He kisses me softly. "Whatever you need, let me give it to you."

Reaching between us, I guide him back inside me and slowly sit back onto his cock. He doesn't break our kiss when he speaks against my lips, "You take me so well. You're fucking made for me, Charlotte. Don't stop until you make a mess all over my cock. Tell me if it's too much, okay?" I nod. "Fuck, you feel so good."

I continue to grind onto him, creating friction on my clit that will send me over the edge if only... As if he reads my mind, Jason keeps talking. I don't know if it's the distraction or his praises, but it's fucking working.

"You're so perfect." He continues telling me how gorgeous I am and how much he loves me. I'm so damn close, it's within reach. "Don't think, okay? Just listen. I just want you to feel good, my beautiful Charlotte. You're mine, babygirl. When you're ready, come all over my cock and show me who you belong to. Keep rocking back and forth, let go when you can't take it anymore... That's it, just like that. You're doing so well." My body tightens. I'm almost there. He kisses me hard, his tongue exploring my mouth. "I love you," he whispers against my lips.

I shatter, coming harder than the last time. He pulls me close and wraps his arms tighter around me, thrusting four or five more times before finding his own release. My body is vibrating. With his cock still hard inside me, and our breaths in sync, I admit quietly, "I love you, too."

16

JASON

I pull out of her slowly, already missing her warmth. Seeing her fall apart for me was the hottest fucking thing I've ever seen in my fucking life. Now that I know what it takes to make her come, I intend on pulling several more from her tonight… and every night, if she lets me.

"Come on, sweetheart." I pull her to my side, not willing to let go of her just yet. "I'll order dinner for us. Drunken noodles and potstickers from the Thai place down the street?"

"Sure," she hums.

I grab my phone from the bedside table and tap on the app for delivery. Once I order our dinner, I check my email for confirmation to see how long we'll have to wait, and spot an email from my buddy, Mike, who's the pitching coach for a major league team. I open it. It's a notification that his team scouts will be at the next game my college kids are playing at… for me.

After the slap tear ruined my career playing minor league baseball, I became the athletics director at the local college, where I've coached their baseball team ever since. My boys played amazing last year and this year is shaping up to be even better. There were rumors that a few minor and major league teams were interested in me as a third base coach, but I never put much stock in it. Could this be the one? A shot at coaching in the majors?

"What is it?" Charlotte's question pulls me from my thoughts.

"There's a few teams looking at me."

She sits up, excited. "Really? That's amazing! To coach or play?"

"Coach," I admit, chuckling. "My shoulder has never been the same; I'll never play again. It looks like they are interested in me as third base coach."

"Isn't that the position you played? I'm sure you'll do great. They'd be lucky to have you!" I'm pretty sure she's more excited than I am.

I take her chin between my thumb and forefinger and kiss her softly. "Let's hop in the shower. The food will be here in a little bit."

We take a quick shower, and while I don't stop kissing her, I also don't touch her beyond that. I don't want her to think this is only physical between us. After we're dried off, I grab one of my shirts for her to wear. She could slip back into her clothes from earlier, but there's something about the idea of her wearing it that makes me feel like she's mine.

We finish dinner and put on a cheesy romcom movie, since she didn't get to watch one earlier. This is the first time I've been able to hold her like this, where I can openly touch her without worrying about the consequences. I can hold her hand, not just to keep her safe and grounded, but because I want to. It seems ridiculous to be excited about it, but I am.

All of the nights we spent on her couch or mine, having dinner and watching a movie… this is the first time I'm not actively keeping myself from her. She's always been affectionate, but a few weeks ago, I never would've imagined we'd be watching a movie with her head in my lap, holding my hand, talking and laughing like we always do.

As amazing as it feels to hear her scream my name when she comes, it wasn't just words I said during sex, I love her. I need to be smart about this. Getting married was an accident, but if I have anything to say about it, there'll be no divorce in our future.

The next morning, I'm settling into my morning routine at my desk when a notification pops up on my phone with two new emails. I take a break from researching vendors for next year's jerseys and check them. The first is from Mike saying they will definitely be at the game tomorrow. I'm nervous about the prospect of coaching. The money would be incredible, but it would require a lot more travel and I wouldn't be able to see my boys as much during the season... or Charlotte.

I check the next message and it's from one of those damn dating apps Charlotte set me up with. I'm about to delete it but see it was actually forwarded from her, not from them directly. I pull it up and it's an invite for a speed dating event tonight.

What the fuck?

I thought last night would have swept this under the rug, but here it is—back with vengeance. I open my messages and text her.

> Not going, sweetheart. Nice try, though.

I set my phone aside and get back to work. A few minutes later, there's a reply.

CHARLOTTE
I'll go without you.

> You're not going either. We have plans.

We don't, but I'll make something up on the fly if I have to. I was supposed to take her out tomorrow night. I'll need to move things up.

No, we don't.

We do now though. Meet you there at 6!

I call her to put an end to this bullshit and she picks up on the second ring. "Hey," she says coolly.

"We are *not* going speed dating," I growl. "You think I want to watch guys hit on my wife, one after the other?"

She sighs, "I'm only your wife on paper. I told you, I need to do this."

"No, you don't. I'll admit, we never dated, and it's fucking weird to be married to your friend when neither of us remember it happening. But you told me you love me, was it a lie?" The words tumble from me before I can stop them. *Damn it.* I don't really want her to answer that if she's not in love with me.

"It wasn't a lie, Jay," she replies softly. "I do love you."

"If you love me, you won't do this. You want to date? Date *me*. I'll take you out every single night if it means you'll stop asking to see other people." I rub my hand roughly against my beard. "It hurts too much, Char."

"I'm sorry, I don't want to hurt you. That was never my intention." She pauses, blows out a deep breath, and continues, "You're right. I was hung up on the idea of being married to someone I never dated, when I haven't seriously dated *anyone* in years. I'm... I'm sorry."

"No, this is my fault. I should've made my feelings known before all of this happened. Would you be okay just dating me?" I've never been so nervous asking anything before in my life.

"I don't want to see anyone else, but I'm also worried about you. This is your second marriage and you didn't exactly sign up for it. What if—"

"I'm going to stop you right there. You didn't answer my question. Don't worry about me and what I want. Would *you* be okay only dating me?"

She doesn't respond right away. I wait patiently, giving her time to think about it. "Yes." Her words are barely above a whisper.

"It's settled, then. Delete the apps, sweetheart. All of them. You're with *me* now. With my traveling so much this season, I need to make sure we are all right… starting right now. I'll pick you up at six, we're going out tonight, *not as friends*."

My palms are sweaty and I may as well start reciting lyrics from Eminem's "Lose Yourself" at this point. It feels like I'm a senior in high school picking up my prom date, only I'm walking next door to pick up my *wife*. I never felt like this with Emma when we dated. Charlotte's special, the woman I was always meant to be with.

Shortly after Emma and I got married, Charlotte's mom married Emma's dad. I didn't go to their wedding because I was in the middle of spring training. Charlotte was going to school in New York at the time, and it wasn't until her twenty-first birthday, when she came to visit Emma, that we met officially. She was stunning, but I was a married man. Never in a million years would I have cheated on Emma, so I avoided Charlotte like the fucking plague.

Even when Dylan and Emma got engaged and Charlotte told me she was moving back home, I still considered her off limits. I have a great relationship with the now-happily-married couple and there was no way I was going to jeopardize that. It's easier to stuff my feelings away.

I can share anything and everything with Charlotte, but now, standing at her front door with my fist poised to knock, I'm freaking out. I'm now understanding why she was so worried about us being married when we've never dated. It's terrifying.

I blow out a deep breath and finally knock. There's rustling in the apartment, followed by a *"shit, he's early."* I can't help my smile; I'm only four minutes early. In Charlotte time, it's more like twenty. She unlocks the door and I'm stunned into silence. She's a vision in a sleeveless black dress that hugs her curves perfectly and lands just above her knees. Her hair is curled and pulled to the side, and her makeup is understated. She's just as beautiful wearing sweats and a tee, but when she's all dressed up like this, I'm speechless.

"Just need to grab my purse and shoes," she says as her eyes rake over my body. "Fuck, you look good, Jay."

Shit, how did I let her compliment me first? I'm such an asshole.

"Sweetheart, you don't just look good… you take my breath away."

Charlotte glances down at her dress then back to me, unfazed. "Oh, thanks." She shrugs and turns on her heel to grab her purse and nearly walks out barefoot.

"Forget something?"

She frowns and I gesture to her feet. "Right." Her cheeks flush as she puts on her heels. "So, where are we going?"

"It's a surprise."

"You know I hate surprises," she groans.

I lean in to kiss her cheek and say softly, "I know. Trust me."

After locking up, I take her hand and it feels… *right.* Unlike every other time I've held her hand, this is different. She's not squeezing back because she's overwhelmed, she's simply doing it because she wants to. A warmth blossoms in my chest at the realization that this woman is choosing me. I intend to keep it that way.

We pull up to a steakhouse where Ethan knows the owner. It usually has a month-long waitlist, but he managed to get us a table with less than twenty-four hour notice. I guide her by the small of her back to our table, not wanting to take my hands off her. Once seated, the waiter takes our drink order—a triple IPA and her favorite martini with a twist.

Charlotte opens the menu and quickly closes it with a snap. "We should go."

"Why? We just got here."

She whispers, "Did you see the prices? This is ridiculous. We could have groceries for a month for the price of dinner tonight."

I take the menu from her. "What sounds good? Name it. If you want tacos, we'll grab them. You want pizza? Done. But if you've been craving a medium-cooked filet with a side of potatoes and glazed carrots, then that's what we're getting." I narrow my eyes in a standoff.

"Filet," she says softly.

"You don't need a menu, then," I say with a wink. I set them aside as the waiter returns with our drinks.

"How was work?" I ask, taking a sip of my beer, unable to tear my eyes away from her.

"It was good. There's a huge taste test project I need to develop a screener for, but I'm not thrilled with the recruiting company. Last time we used them, we were promised over a thousand respondents and ended up with only half. I might switch companies, but I'm also worried it could be my screening process. My client wants a variety, but sometimes when you have a large project like this, beggars can't be choosers." Charlotte takes a sip of her martini that quickly becomes a gulp. "It's hot in here, right? It feels warm."

She's fucking adorable when she's flustered like this. "No, just you, babygirl." When she's nervous like this she does better if she can keep talking, even if it's hopping from subject to subject. "Tell me more about the mock jury trial you have coming up this weekend. Are your clients still giving you problems?"

Charlotte tells me about the issues she resolved today, including having to replace several respondents from the study. I listen intently, allowing her to shine. She's fucking magnificent at her job and I love that she's so excited about it.

Dinner arrives and we continue talking about work. We also make plans for this weekend to take the kids to the zoo. Aiden is obsessed with sloths still, so we make sure to go at least once a month. I stupidly didn't make any after-dinner plans, being so last minute. I'm hoping she'll be okay with an evening in.

As much as I want to wake up next to her tomorrow morning, I don't want to make a habit of it and having her shut down on me. I want to traditionally date her, so she's comfortable and secure in our relationship when I'm on the road. We might be married, but I don't want to rush things and scare her away. I've seen that almost backfire with my friends one too many times. Hell, it's backfired on me.

Walking to the car, I ask, "Want to stop for ice cream on the way home?"

"I'm way too full, but maybe we can grab a few pints and bring them home for later or tomorrow? Thank you for dinner, by the way."

"It was my pleasure." I kiss her knuckles and open the car door for her.

We pick up ice cream on the way home and when we arrive, I walk her to her door. I don't want to slip into our usual friend routine, but she insists I go to my place and change into comfortable clothes. I disgruntledly head next door to change.

When I return, I don't use my key, I knock. When she answers, she's not wearing sweats, she's wearing a silk top and shorts that leave nothing to the imagination.

"Charlotte," I growl.

She shrugs, a smirk tugging at her lips. "Yes?"

"I'm trying to be a gentleman and give you a proper date. Granted, most dates don't end in sweatpants and a movie, but you expect me to keep my hands to myself when you open the door wearing that?" I glance around to make sure no one sees her and guide her by the waist further into the apartment, closing the door behind me.

"Sure," she replies, biting her lip.

"I was promised a movie, but as soon as it's over, you're going to give me a number between one and ten."

17

CHARLOTTE
FOUR WEEKS LATER

Jason was right. I didn't need to date other people. I didn't need *him* to date other people. This past month has been an adventure, to say the least. We've been out a few nights, when he's in town and I'm not working on a late night project. He's truly the perfect man. After spending the past month together—not as friends—I am blissfully comfortable with my relationship with Jason and have a growing feeling that maybe we're supposed to stay together at the end of all of this. What started out as a mess is now… *easy*. No matter how happy I am, I'm always waiting for the other shoe to drop. It's too perfect.

I'm headed back up to the mountains for another round of focus groups and with Jason traveling with the team this week, Ethan offered to drive me so I could get some last minute work done on the drive up. Melanie wanted to come too but she has horrible morning sickness, so she's staying behind.

Ethan has a huge cabin that makes Dylan's look like a shack. I'm sure he bought it on purpose to piss off my brother-in-law. While they are friends, Ethan still takes every opportunity to mess with Dylan. They're grown ass men that act like middle school girls.

We pull up to his cabin and head inside. Once we're settled, Ethan suggests, "Why don't we go out tonight? Nothing crazy. Maybe grab a drink and a little table dancing?"

"Sure, I could use a bit of fun," I chuckle.

"How's everything going with the lumbersnack? Things boring already?"

I shake my head. "No, he's just gone a lot right now with baseball season in full swing. It's fine, but I don't feel comfortable going out by myself after we were drugged and accidentally got married, you know?"

"Come on, doll, let's go get wasted on my dime. I'm already married, can't do it twice." He snatches his keys from the table and wraps his arm around my shoulder to lead us back to the car.

"Wait, I should change first."

He laughs and raises his eyebrow. "Oh, my dear Charlotte, lest you forget who you're talking to? You seem to be in desperate need of a little pampering... and a little shopping."

Ethan takes me dress shopping to find something fun to wear for tonight. He also insists I go to a salon for a cut, color, and blowout. The stylist adds caramel highlights to my hair, giving it a lot of dimension. Every time I try to pay, Ethan beats me to it.

After a quick dinner and a wardrobe change at the cabin, we both look amazing. "Ethan," I squeal, "you're doing the shirt thing!"

He's cuffing the sleeves of his dark gray button-down and chuckles. "Don't get any ideas, Char. I'm a happily married man. But don't worry, I taught your lumber-snack all he needs to know."

"The door frame? That was you? Damn it, Ethan. Here I thought he was being all sexy and book boyfriendy but he was just taking cues from you?" *How much of it was real?*

"All I said is that he should lean against a doorframe once in a while." I must have it written all over my face when he adds, "Don't worry. That's *all* I told him. Well, I also told him he needs to get his head out of his ass... I think? Or was that Eddie? I can't keep track of all the idiot men and their questionable choices at this point. Moral of the story: Jason is his own man and the only thing you need to thank me for is a doorframe lean and maybe the occasional sleeve roll. The rest is all him."

I nod and blow out a breath. "Promise?"

"I'd never lie to you. I'm just glad you two are finally together. I called it years ago. Even before you moved back, I knew that you two would be good together." He finishes cuffing his sleeves and offers me his arm. "Shall we?"

The bar is packed for a weeknight. I'm glad Ethan is here—I'm feeling a little overwhelmed. We snag two seats at the bar and Ethan orders an Old Fashioned for himself and a martini with a twist for me. He slides my drink over and teases, "Here's your trouble with a twist, doll. Bottoms up!" I giggle and we both finish our drinks in a few quick gulps before playfully slamming our glasses down on the bar. He signals to the bartender for another round.

"So, you're going to be a dad now? Are you still going to have time to come out and party, ol' man?" I jest.

"Absolutely! You think I'm going to let your sassy ass stay at home while your husband is off enjoying his best baseball life? Fuck. That. I'm going to be a stay-at-home dad, I'm not dead," he laughs, lifting his refilled glass in salute before taking a drink. "What about you? Are you planning on getting knocked up any time soon?"

"Oh, no. I don't want kids. I have enough issues going on up here." I tap my temple. "No reason to pass those genes along. Plus, Jason had a snip-snip so at least we're on the same page, if things work out for us."

"Sorry." His face falls. "I didn't think of that. You would be a great mom, though. But, I guess you are... technically."

"What?" I frown.

"Well, step-mom," he says with a shrug. "How's that going, by the way?"

"Oh, um, we haven't told the kids. Things are way too messy right now. I'm still Aunt Charlotte. I don't know that I'd ever be a second mom to them, or that I'd want to."

As if Ethan can sense my discomfort, he suggests, "Want to dance?" I look around and while the tables and bar are full, there's no music.

He gets up with a wink, grabs my hand and drags me to the jukebox, putting on "You Belong With Me" by Taylor Swift. When Ethan started dating Melanie, he sang this song during karaoke, directed at me and my feelings for Jason. I can't help the laugh bubbling out of me.

"This is *your* song. Come on." He pulls me onto the dance floor, twirls and dips me. We belt out the lyrics. Eventually, the whole bar joins in. Ethan has an incredible voice. Me? Not so much, but I'm still having so much fun.

As one of the choruses begins, two strong arms wrap around me from behind, making me jump. My eyes are wide, but Ethan laughs, kissing my knuckles and heading back to the bar. Before I can turn around, a beard tickles my shoulder and neck. "Hey, babygirl." I breathe a sigh of relief as Jason kisses my neck as he sways with me, listening to everyone in the bar sing.

When it's over, he turns me to face him and takes my face in his hands, kissing me. I pull back. "What are you doing here? I thought you weren't supposed to be here until tomorrow?"

"Surprise," he replies with a wide grin. The song ends. Around us, cheers and applause erupt. He kisses me, and it's then that I realize the cheers were for us. I look around and find all eyes in our direction.

"Oh, fuck. You're not about to grand gesture it up right now, are you?" I glance over at Ethan, who's talking on his phone. Since he's not paying attention to us, I breathe a sigh of relief. If Jason had something planned, Ethan would be ready to stream it.

Jason bites his lip. "No, sweetheart. I got the job. I wanted to tell you in person because I have to leave tomorrow morning for Florida."

"What job? Florida? What's going on? Are you moving?" A mild panic sets in. Though mild turns to spicy quickly.

"I told you a few weeks ago a major league team was looking at me," he reminds me with a furrowed brow.

"Looking at you. *Looking*, Jay. You never said *anything* about being interviewed… and now you're leaving *tomorrow*? What the fuck?"

"I'm not moving. That's just where the team is playing right now," he replies quickly. "I'm supposed to meet up with them. Char… this is *it*. This is the major leagues."

He's the happiest I've ever seen him, and I couldn't be more proud. But all I can think is it's one more thing he hid from me.

"I know you've wanted this since your injury, but why didn't you tell me? First, you hide that we're married for months. Now, this?" I shake my head.

"Come to Florida with me?"

"I can't," I answer honestly. I take a step back, away from him. "I have studies all this week. When are you back?"

"Three weeks."

"What?" I shriek, my eyes widening. "Three weeks? Why three weeks? You've never been gone that long before." I try to sound calm but I'm freaking out.

"There are three series back-to-back. When the team is back here, I'll go to LA for a seminar and stay for a series, then two more travel series and home... Char, we'll video chat every night, I'll call you every morning, and we'll text every day. My schedule is going to be busy, but my wife is my number one priority."

"It's still so weird when you call me that." I shake my head. "I'm happy for you, truly. But, I'm pissed that you hid this from me."

Ethan comes up from behind me. "Char, you okay?"

"No, I'm not." I blow out a long breath. "Sorry guys, I'm not going to be a lot of fun tonight. We should be celebrating. Ethan's going to be a dad soon. And you've landed your dream job. I'm sorry. I should be so happy for you both."

"I haven't signed the contracts. I won't take it," Jason insists. Ethan laughs, almost hysterically. Jason narrows his eyes and asks coolly, "What's so funny?"

Ethan shakes his head, his laughter fading. "Nothing. Well, Mel and I went through this."

"At least she knew you bid on the Paris contract in the first place! Melanie wasn't blindsided." I look to Jason. "I'm going back to the cabin. You two stay and celebrate. We'll talk more about this later."

"Are we okay?" Jason's eyes are overflowing with worry.

"No." I shake my head. "We'll talk later." I hug Ethan and kiss Jason on the cheek.

I head toward the door but Ethan stops me just before I reach it. "I'm going to keep him away from the cabin for a few hours. Do you want me to see if Dylan's is available? Say the word, and I'll take care of it."

"It's fine. I just need to cool off." I look back to Jason with his hands in his pockets. Our eyes lock for a moment, but I turn back to tell Ethan, "I need to call Mel."

Ethan kisses me on the cheek and squeezes my hand. "Take my car. Text me if you need anything, but let me know you made it there safely." I don't need someone looking after me. He knows and must sense that I'm not thrilled about being coddled, when he adds, "I tell that to Mel and Emma, too. I need to know my girls are safe."

I nod and wrap my arms around him. "I'll be fine. My heart? Not so much."

He holds me tighter and whispers, "He loves you... but let him grovel. He should have told you."

With a small smile, I take his keys and walk out.

The drive is longer than it should be. I take my time with Ethan's car. After all, it costs more than I make in a year. As soon as I arrive at the cabin, I text both Ethan and Jason to let them know I made it. Once inside, I set my bag down, kick off my heels and rummage through my suitcase for comfortable clothes to change into.

I can't do the secrets on top of secrets and call Melanie.

"Hey, Missy Mel," I sigh, as soon as she picks up the phone. Already, I'm on the verge of tears.

"All right, which car are we going to take?"

I chuckle. "It's not that bad... or maybe it is." She doesn't say anything, so I continue. "Jason took a job coaching with a major league team. He didn't tell me, and he's leaving tomorrow for weeks."

"Oh, Char. I'm so sorry."

"Do you... do you know of a good divorce attorney? Someone who can make this go away?" The tears begin to fall.

"I do, but is that what you really want? I know you love him and that's a big thing to do," she offers cautiously.

"I do love him, but he hid that we were married for months. And now, just as I was coming to terms with it, he didn't tell me he was even interviewing with a team. I…" I'm having trouble catching my breath, but the next words tumble out as I admit the truth to Mel and to myself. "I don't trust him."

"I'll send you the information in the morning. Please, sleep on it first and tell Jason what you're going to do before you call?" She's so optimistic, it makes my heart ache, but I'm so hurt by being treated like a porcelain doll or… a child.

"Thanks, Mel. How's the morning sickness? Are you feeling any better?"

"Oh, fuck no! I feel like garbage. But this isn't about me, babe. You know what Ethan would say?"

"No," I answer honestly, though I suppose he'd send me on a wellness retreat to 'find myself.'

"Therapy. The answer is almost always therapy. You know I have anxiety and I talk to my therapist weekly. Ethan would tell you to do couples therapy, and I'd agree. Where is my husband, by the way? He didn't leave you alone, did he?"

I chuckle. "He gave me the keys to the car and told me he would look after Jason. He wanted to make sure I had time and space to think, and call you."

"You drove his car? I've only driven it once! Lucky bitch," she laughs.

Taking a deep breath, I consider my options. Jason is amazing but he continues to make choices for the two of us and I'm not okay with it. I can't be married to someone I don't trust. "I might still date Jason, but I need a divorce," I confirm, mostly to myself.

"Go take a long shower. By the time you're done, you'll have a little more clarity. We both know you're impulsive, so give yourself time to process this before you do anything. Call me anytime, I'll probably be up." She starts to hurl and I feel awful that no one is there to hold her hair back. "Gotta go, Char. Love you."

"Love you, too."

18

JASON

"You fucked up, man... *again*." Ethan takes a long drink of his Old Fashioned. "You know Charlotte doesn't like being treated like she's different. She can handle big news without having a meltdown. Why didn't you tell her about the job?"

"I didn't think I was going to get it. She's my biggest cheerleader and I didn't want to disappoint her if it didn't work out." I rub the back of my neck and continue, "I didn't think she'd react this way."

"We talked about this in Delasnia. I may have been a little buzzed, but I distinctly remember you not telling her about being married for four months. You were married to my best friend for years, and now you're dating someone who I consider to be like a sister. I laid into Dylan for fucking shit up with Emma. It's your turn before you fuck everything up with Charlotte." He sets down his glass with determination. As I'm about to defend myself, he waves his hand in dismissal. "No, you fucked around and now you're about to find out."

I try again, "It's not li—"

"*Ah, ah, ah.* Not so fast, lumberjack ball boy. You're going to sit and listen while I tell you how you can fix this." I nod in response and make a mental note to stop wearing flannels around the guys. "Good. Right now, she's talking to my wife, which means there's a good chance one or both of them have suggested divorce. Mel doesn't specialize in family law, but she knows some of the best lawyers in the state."

My heart stops. There's no way I can lose Charlotte because of something so small like this. "No, she wouldn't…"

"Wanna bet? I'd easily place a few grand on Char asking Mel for the best lawyer she has in her pocket. So, before I give you the answer to all of your problems, tell me what genius idea you have to win her back."

Ethan waits expectantly and it's then I realize I don't have one. I didn't think she would be upset by this, since she knows coaching is my dream job. "I don't know. I want to take the position, but it's not worth losing her."

"Don't be a fucking martyr. This isn't about you. You don't have to choose between Charlotte and the job. Hell, I just dealt with this with Mel when I got the Paris contract. Oh, and Eddie's in Delasnia while Sage finishes the contract for me in Paris. It's not distance that's the issue. Try again." He crosses his arms and leans on the bar.

"Obviously, I'll apologize, but I don't see what the problem is," I reply with a shrug.

"You don't see anything wrong with hiding things from the woman you care about? Seriously? She's your *wife*. Did you hide things from Emma?" I shake my head. "So, why do it to Charlotte?"

"I didn't want to freak her out," I answer honestly.

"Because…"

"I love her and I don't want to lose her."

He sighs in exasperation. "Wrong. You're making choices for her when you should be collaborating like a partner and *husband*. Just because she's autistic doesn't mean you have to handle her with care. She should have known about the marriage the day you got the paperwork in the mail. And you should've told her about the job the moment you had the interview on the books. Oh, and while we're at it, you should have let her kiss you at Emma's wedding."

"How do you——"

"Who do you think tried to push you two together that day?" He rolls his eyes and groans into his drink. "You're a fucking idiot, Jason."

Ethan wasn't kidding when he said he would lay into me. He's right about everything, though—I've been making choices for Charlotte this whole time. "So, how do I fix it? You said you have the answer. Out with it."

"How long have we known each other? Over a decade. When have I ever made things easy on you?"

Asshole.

My voice gets caught in my throat. "I can't lose her, Ethan."

"What did I recommend to you when things were rocky with Emma?" Ethan glares at me.

"Couples therapy?"

"Couples therapy," he confirms. "It didn't save your marriage, but it saved your relationship. Now, your boys have two parents who get along and Emma reconnected with a poor man's Bruce Wayne." I can't help but snicker. Ethan doesn't skip a beat. "Go to therapy. If she's not meant to stay your wife, at least your relationship has a chance of being repaired."

Ethan drank me under the table; I'm in no shape to talk to Charlotte like this. I have to be on a plane in the morning and I expect I'll have a hangover from hell.

"I forgot you're a beer guy! Whiskey hits differently. I'll make sure Charlotte's in her room when we get back to the cabin. You'll need to take an aspirin, drink a gallon of water, and sleep it off." Ethan pats me on the back and pulls out his phone to order a ride for us.

"Fuck. She's gonna be so mad! And she's already mad. It'll be mad on top of mad. I'm getting divorced, aren't I?"

He chuckles and replies, "That remains to be seen. App says our ride will be here in two minutes. Do we need a barf bag for you?"

"Fuck you, Barlowe."

"If I was single, I'd consider it. But, also, drunk men with top knots aren't my type." He types something into his phone. "Okay, Char is upstairs in one of my guest bedrooms. I told her you'll talk in the morning... Looks like our ride is just around the corner."

A black sedan pulls up moments later, and we get in to head to his cabin. Thankfully, the ride isn't too long, arriving fifteen minutes later. Now that I've slightly sobered, I have an overwhelming urge to march upstairs and take Charlotte in my arms and apologize for everything. Ethan was right about all of it; I've been sheltering her, and that's not fair to either of us.

"I know you said I should talk to her in the morning, but—"

"No. Absolutely not. You're drunk. No good can come from talking now. Sleep it off, big guy. Upstairs, second door on the right is yours. Leave her be for the night." He makes his way into the kitchen and opens the fridge.

Despite his suggestion, I go upstairs in search of my wife.

I knock on the first door before opening it. It's the master and empty. The second door he said was promised to me, which means the third might be hers. I knock three times before slowly turning the knob to enter. "Sweetheart, you in here?"

Opening the door a little further, the room is dark, but her phone illuminates her face. Char's laying in bed with earbuds in. She turns and takes one out. "Hey Ethan, is he in— Oh. Hi."

"Hey, babygirl. Can I come in?"

She takes a deep breath before sitting up and answering. "Depends. This isn't one of those *'invite me in and get naked'* things, is it?"

"No. But I want to stay the night with you, if that's all right?"

"I want a divorce, Jay," she blurts out.

My shoulders fall and her words cut through me, but I draw on my conversation with Ethan and suggest, "Only if you go to therapy with me first."

"Did Mel talk to you? Shit. Now I need to add one more person to the list of people I can't trust."

"It wasn't Mel; it was Ethan. Why? Did Mel suggest it to you too?"

"Yeah. Makes sense since both of them go."

"I'm not giving up on us. I made mistakes, and I need to make it up to you, but I'll be damned if this is how our story ends. You're my wife, I—"

"Fine, I'll go to therapy. Just please stop calling me that? We're only married on paper. I've been in love with you for years, but we've never been together. You never got down on one knee. We didn't have Eddie or Ethan plan our wedding. We didn't promise ourselves to each other in front of our friends and family... Don't you think I deserve that?"

I sit on the bed next to her. "Of course."

"And you need to stop lying to me and keeping secrets because you think I can't handle them. I don't deserve that either." There is so much hurt in her eyes. It's killing me that I'm the cause of it; I want to take it all away.

"Never again. I promise from now on, you and I will make decisions together. I want to tell you about my new job, but I've had quite a bit to drink tonight. Can we talk about it in the morning?" She nods and I take her hand in mine, waffling our fingers together. "Do you want me to stay in my own room tonight? I don't mind; the choice is yours."

Char chews her lip. "If you can keep your hands to yourself, you can stay. I'm in no mood to be touched that way tonight."

"Absolutely. But... Can I hold you?"

"Yeah," she breathes. "I think I could use my best friend right now."

"Scoot over, babygirl. I've got you." I kick off my shoes and peel back the covers before sliding into bed with her.

"Could you not wear jeans to bed? The texture is too much against my bare legs." Her tone is clipped, but it usually is when she's advocating for her sensory needs. I don't take it personally and just want her to be comfortable.

I remove my flannel and jeans and toss them on the ground. "Come here." She cuddles into my side and I hold her tight. "I love you. Goodnight, sweetheart."

"Night."

19

CHARLOTTE

"Do you want to come stay with us for the next few months?" Ethan asks, pouring his second cup of coffee. "We have the space."

"I'll be okay. You don't need to worry about me."

Ethan quirks an eyebrow. "That's not what this is about. You lived on your own in New York, so your neighbor-husband being gone off and on for a few months should be a walk in the park. Just know the offer stands, if you change your mind. If you need family, we're here." He sits down next to me at the kitchen table.

"You know, I was coming around to the idea of being a wife, but now… I need a good divorce attorney and an even better therapist." I blow on my coffee and take a sip. He made it just how I like—a splash of hazelnut creamer and a sprinkle of cinnamon. Ethan's attention to detail never ceases to amaze me.

"Mel can help with both of those. I moved to virtual therapy a few months ago when I was in Paris, but you should probably get the whole experience. You know, the chaise lounge and the *'how does that make you feel?'* from a therapist in-person?" He offers a small smile. "You're gonna be all right, doll. Hold off on the divorce until after therapy."

"That's what Mel said," I interrupt.

"She's brilliant, you should listen to her. I didn't just marry her because she's pretty," he teases.

There are footsteps coming downstairs making my heart stop. Ethan looks to the sound and back to me, placing his hand over mine. I turn mine over and squeeze his tight. As Jason walks in, he ties up his hair. When he spots me, our eyes lock and all the air leaves my lungs.

For years, I wanted him to want me and to look at me like this, as if I'm everything to him. Ethan and Mel are right; I shouldn't be impulsive. If he's willing to do the work, I should give him a chance.

"Hey, sweetheart. Did you sleep okay?"

I nod, unsure of what to say. I tossed and turned all night, my mind wouldn't shut off. Ethan jumps in to my rescue. "There's a fresh pot of coffee and I had your truck delivered this morning. What time is your flight?"

Jason remains rooted in place, his eyes never leaving mine. It normally makes me uncomfortable, but this morning, I can't look away. "Five hours, but it's a long drive to the airport." He breaks eye contact first and glances to Ethan, "Thank you. I'll get out of your hair after I talk with my wi— Charlotte."

Ethan nods and stands from the table. "I'll leave you to it." He claps Jason on the back, grabs his ereader, and walks out onto the back porch to finish his coffee. I look down at mine, keeping my hands busy tracing the lip of the mug. I normally listen better while I'm doing something others deem distracting. But this is pure avoidance and I want to dissociate.

Once Jason pours his coffee, he sits next to me in Ethan's seat and breaks the uncomfortable silence first. "I should've told you."

"Told me what?" I snap, finally looking at him. "How you failed to tell me we were married for *months*? Or that you've been interviewing for an incredible job opportunity, but didn't bother to tell me until the night before you needed to leave?" My gaze falls back to my cup. "As soon as you're back, we'll do couples therapy, but until then, we should see a therapist separately. After all of this, there are things I don't want to share with you."

"We share everything with each other," he says gruffly. I scoff and he corrects, "Okay, you got me there... What haven't you shared with me?"

"Why didn't you tell me we're married?"

He takes a moment to respond. When he does, I still don't meet his gaze. "I told you, I thought I could figure it out and make it go away. I wanted to fix it at first...

Until I realized I didn't want to." His words only make me angrier. I begin tapping my nails on my mug, sounding like Morse code. My years of therapies trying to make me more neurotypical is going to battle with my urge to dissociate and stim. "I never found the right time to tell you."

My cheeks are hot and my heart is beating faster, thumping wildly against my ribcage. "Right time? You waited until we had sex before you admitted I was your *fucking* wife. You had months. So, fine, you selfishly wanted to be married to me. Sounds romantic in theory, but it's just one more instance of you making decisions for me." I finally look up, my eyes stinging from tears I refuse to shed. "I'm not broken, Jay."

Maybe I am? I was told by specialists for years that I wasn't normal. Maybe they were right and I am broken. But even so, it doesn't excuse this.

I continue, "You don't need to treat me like I'm one step away from a meltdown. It's not good for either of us."

"I've always had this instinctive need to protect you from, well, *everything*. I like being the one you depend on, but you're right. I didn't tell you about the marriage because I *wanted* to be married to you. I knew as soon as I told you, there was a chance I could lose you. I selfishly lived in the fantasy that you were mine. And I didn't tell you about the job because I didn't want to disappoint you if I didn't get it." He rubs his beard and adds, "You're it for me, Char. I made a few big mistakes, but I promise I'll make it up to you as soon as I'm back."

"You still haven't apologized for the job."

"What? Yes I ha—"

"No, Jay, you haven't. Not once have you said you were sorry." One of my neurospicy superpowers is my uncanny ability to remember everything. It's a blessing and a curse.

Jason thinks for a moment and I wait for realization to hit him. "Fuck, you're right." He places his hand on mine. I resist the urge to pull away. "I'm sorry… and I'm not just saying that because you pointed it out. I made a mess of things. I'm going to fix it."

I let out a shaky scoff. "No, *you* aren't going to fix anything. That's what got us into this mess. *We* will fix this. If it can be fixed."

He squeezes my hand and brings my palm to his lips; his beard tickles my fingertips. "I love you. I love you so fucking much, sweetheart, it hurts. Please don't give up on me, on us. *We* will fix this, I promise." I kiss his cheek but don't respond. This is all too raw. "I wish you could drive me to the airport. It's going to be a rough three weeks without you."

"Don't get all sappy on me now. You'll be fine," I insist, waving him off. "Send me the schedule, and if I have a free day, maybe I can fly in for a game or two. I really am so damn proud of you. I just wish you had told me… No more secrets?"

He kisses me softly and mutters against my lips. "No more secrets, babygirl."

———

My focus groups went great, but my mind is elsewhere. I do love Jason, so fucking much. It hurts to be upset about all of this, no matter how justified I am. More than anything, I really want to forget it ever happened, even if only for a night.

As soon as I'm back at the cabin, I'm welcomed by the scent of fragrant garlic and sautéed onions wafting from the kitchen. "Honey, I'm home," I call out to Ethan. Fuck, I'm so excited. He's an excellent cook and my mouth is watering at whatever the hell he's making. Setting down my bag, I kick off my shoes and wander into the kitchen. "That smells… *Jay?* What are you doing here?" He left for the airport hours ago; he should've landed in Miami by now.

"I pushed it back a day. I told them I had something to take care of before I left," he replies with a shrug.

"Okay… Where is Ethan?"

"I asked him if I could drive you home in the morning. I hope you don't mind? He wanted to get back to Mel and jumped at the offer. I wanted it to be a surprise, but now I'm second guessing everything."

"It's fine. Really." I wrap my arms around his waist,

tucked into his side as he continues stirring over the stove. "What's for dinner?"

"Spaghetti and garlic bread. You know I can't cook, but I was hoping to have you all to myself tonight. The less distractions, the better."

I'm not sure what he means by distractions but I admit, "It smells amazing. Can I help with anything?"

Jason turns down the heat on the stove and sets the spoon to the side. All at once, I'm being lifted onto the counter. He steps between my legs and pulls me to him until my body is flush with his. "No, babygirl. Sit that pretty ass down and let me make you mediocre pasta."

I bark out a laugh. "You're really selling it there."

"Would you rather go out tonight? I know I kind of ruined last night, so if you want to get dressed up and have dinner out, we can do that."

I shake my head. "No, this is great. Thank you for making dinner. I'm exhausted after back-to-back groups and didn't expect you here. It's tiring keeping everything bottled up every day and I don't think I'd survive through a dinner in public."

"You don't have to mask for them, sweetheart. They love working with you, as you are." He kisses my neck. "*I love you,* just the way you are. No mask."

I'm so incredibly distracted by his simple touches that I nearly forget what we're talking about. It's so easy being caught up in him after fighting my attraction for years, but I still need to keep my emotions in check around him until we figure everything out.

Jason trails kisses up my neck to my jaw, until he reaches my mouth. I ask against his lips, "Sorry, what were you saying?"

"I don't remember," he chuckles as he pulls back. "I'm going to finish making dinner, but then I'm going to do something I've been dreaming about since I drove up here."

Frowning, I ask, "What's that?"

"If you're up for it, I want to spread you wide, right here on this counter, and feast on you. Seems like the perfect appetizer to me."

My cheeks heat and I feel warm and tingly everywhere. "*Oh...*" I'm speechless. He's going to be gone for weeks. Weeks of him not touching me. I might still be pissed about everything, but I also have needs. "Okay."

He turns off the stove, then returns to me. "Give me a number between one and ten, babygirl."

20

JASON

"Ten," Charlotte replies confidently.

"You think you can handle coming ten times? Challenge accepted, sweetheart."

Her eyes widen as her breath hitches. "Oh, no! I thought you were going to do that"—she lowers her voice—"sexy talking thing you do."

I slide my hand into her hair and bring her lips to mine. It might be weeks before I can kiss her again, and I don't want to waste a second not tasting every inch of her. I need to make up for everything, and while my apology shouldn't be physical, I need to show her how much she means to me.

She moans into my mouth as I devour hers, teasing and exploring as if it's the last time. I'll be taking ten from her by morning.

"Oh, I'll be doing both. Did you hydrate today? You're going to need it for what I have planned for you."

Charlotte chews on her lip. "I filled my steel water bottle twice…"

Definitely not close to enough.

"Will you be mine tonight? To do whatever I want with?" I kiss her softly and add, "Do you trust me to take care of you?"

She nods but whispers against my lips, "If it's too much—"

"We stop immediately. Hard stop. I don't ever want to hurt you. I spent years fantasizing about testing your limits, to take what I want from you. Our schedules have been so busy lately, I haven't had the time to pleasure you the way you deserve." *If I have it my way, I won't be coming until she's had her ten.*

She stills. "What do you mean 'take what you want?'"

I trace her bottom lip with the pad of my thumb. "It turns me on to have full control over how and when you come. I want to take from you, over and over, until you have nothing left to give me. Only then will I come deep inside you."

"Should we eat first?"

I let out a hearty laugh. "Oh, I intend to eat…"

"Food, Jay. We should eat *food* if you plan on having some sort of sex torture marathon."

"No torture, I promise." I turn back to the cabinets and grab a glass, filling it with water from the fridge and handing it to her. "Drink up, sweetheart."

"Oh, you were serious about the water thing?"

"Drink," I repeat, a little more forcefully.

She takes a few long gulps and sets it down. "Happy?"

"Absolutely. Now, lay down for me. I'm starving." I set her back onto the counter and slip her pants and underwear off. We have so many important things to talk about, but right now, I want to take care of her too much to consider anything rational.

"You don't have to— *Oh fuck.*" I lick a few firm circles around her clit and she moans my name. She gets off on me being a little rough with her—a gentle touch is too much for her sensory needs. I grab her thighs and spread her wide. I fucking love her curves; I always have something to grip onto. Her body is *perfect*.

Charlotte won't come on my face, at least not without a little help. I replace my tongue with my hand, massaging her clit with my thumb and pressing two fingers deep inside her. She gasps at the pressure.

"You're so fucking beautiful. So wet and ready for me." I kiss her soft stomach and she covers her face. "No, baby-girl." I remove one of her hands and kiss her palm before setting it to her side. "You don't have to look at me, I know it can be too much for you sometimes, but I want to see you when you come undone."

She tightens around my fingers and I'm immediately regretting wearing sweatpants. It would be so fucking easy to pull them down and push inside her. My boxer briefs are too tight and I have to adjust myself. Watching her writhe at my touch is almost too much.

"Jay, I'm close," she whimpers as I drive my fingers deeper, curling inside her.

"Just relax for me, baby. Let me own this piece of you." I lower my face between her legs and circle her clit with my tongue. "There you go, babygirl," I murmur against her.

"Right there… I… I'm… *Jason*," she cries out as she comes for me. Her pussy clenches around my fingers and I nearly come in my pants, wishing it was my cock inside her instead.

My beard soaked, I remove my fingers, sucking them clean. "I fucking love it when you come for me."

Breathlessly, Charlotte asks, "How are you supposed to do that nine more times?"

"Let me worry about that, sweetheart." I help her sit up. Her cheeks are flushed and her eyes a little glazed. "How are you feeling?"

She responds without words, snaking her hand around my neck and pulling me in to kiss her. I chuckle against her lips. They part, beaconing me to taste her. As we break apart, she fists her hands in my shirt and states matter-of-factly with all of the confidence in the world,

"I hope you don't think that's going to get you out of everything that happened yesterday."

I gently claim her throat with my hand and kiss her brutally. When we come up for air, I finally answer, "Never. You're my everything, Char. Expect me on my knees for you until you're mine, not just on paper."

Kissing her one last time, I turn away from her to finish dinner. She's going to need her energy for what I have in store for her.

***

"Seven," she whispers into the darkness.

I've had her straddling my lap, beneath me, spread out like my own personal feast, in the hot tub, in the shower… and now my personal favorite, on the chaises on the deck, in our bathrobes, with her between my legs and my hand between hers. Not once have I been inside her.

"Come here." I wrap my arms around her and she rests her head on my chest. "Let me know when you're ready for your final three."

Charlotte sighs against me and I kiss the top of her head. I breathe in her coconut shampoo I'm going to miss while I'm gone. I needed the extra day to make things right between us.

Okay, so maybe I'm trying to make it up to her in orgasms.

I already have the name of a few therapists that take virtual clients and will be calling in the morning to set up an appointment. I'm not thrilled about unpacking my baggage with a stranger, but I'll do it for her.

"Why don't we get some rest?" I suggest.

"You… you didn't…" Her voice trails off.

I hold her tighter. "The night is young." It's not. It's four hours after when I would normally be in bed. "I don't need to come, I just want you to feel good." She hums in response. "Time to get some rest. Don't worry, I'm taking three more from you when you wake up. I want you well-fucked before I leave."

She sits up abruptly. "You don't think I would cheat, right? I would never!"

"No. The thought never crossed my mind. I just like the idea of you craving me while I'm gone." I scoot her forward so I can get up. Once standing, I lift her up and wrap her legs around me. She clings to me like a koala and I bring her inside. "I love you, babygirl."

Charlotte lets out a yawn; she's tired and spent, still managing a soft, "Love you." My heart swells at the admission. Once she's tucked into me in bed, for the first time in a very fucking long time, all feels right in the world.

"Jay?" Char pats my chest to wake me. "Jay, you gotta get up. We need to leave soon."

I pull her closer to me. "Nope."

She kisses my chest. "If we don't give up, it means I won't get my ten," she teases.

Rolling her onto her back, I press my already hard length against her. "Don't joke about that, baby. I'm a man of my word." I free my cock from my underwear and slip her panties to the side, driving into her in one swift motion. She's so wet and tight, I won't be able to pull three more from her without coming. Kissing her softly, I press closer, applying some of my weight on top of her. She likes the deep pressure, but I'm careful not to crush her.

"I'll make you a deal, Jay. Come with me and number nine and ten will happen when I come to see you next weekend?"

I stop my thrusts. "This weekend?"

She nods, biting her lip. "I checked your schedule. I can come to Florida on the last day of your series there."

I thrust harder. "Really? You'll come visit me?"

"I… *ahhh*… wanted to surprise… *oh*… you."

"Just for that, I'm taking my three right now, babygirl."

I pull out of her, kissing down her body. I bring each of her perfectly pink nipples into my mouth, nipping as I release them. Moving down her stomach, I land on her soaked pussy. It used to be a challenge to get her to come, now I expect it. I've learned her body and can play her like a fiddle. She loves when my beard gives her extra friction, so as I suck on her clit, I make sure to scratch it against her a little.

Charlotte's also in her head and I make sure to keep talking her through everything. "Baby, you're so fucking perfect. I love that you're dripping for me." She tangles her fingers in my hair and pulls me closer. "That's right, sweetheart, make a mess on my face so I can taste you all the way to Miami."

"I need more," she moans.

I hum against her clit to give her a little extra vibration, then press two fingers in her pussy. Testing my luck, I graze my pinky over her tight hole to see if she's into it.

Charlotte gasps. "Oh!"

Fuck, yes. She's into it...

I press in—just a knuckle—to test how much she can take. I push further as I lick and suck on her clit. She shatters beautifully for me.

Two more.

If I time it right and work quickly, I can make her come almost immediately after. I crawl up her body and rub up cock up and down her entrance before thrusting inside her.

"Jason, it's... it's too much..."

"Say stop and we stop, babygirl."

She shakes her head. "No, I am just so... *full.*"

"It's because you're the perfect fit, baby." I kiss her fiercely and continue to drive into her at the pace that will have her coming hard in minutes. Like clockwork, she screams out *"nine"* as she comes. I don't let her come down from her high, building her up again. Pulling out, I flip her over and bring her back to my chest. "Hands on the headboard, sweetheart." She reaches up and looks over her shoulder at me with a smirk. "You want it gentle or rough?"

"Gentle. I don't think I could handle rough right now."

I kiss her shoulder and place one of my hands over hers, interlacing our fingers. My other keeps her hip in place as I thrust in and out of her. "You really are the perfect woman, Charlotte. You're mine." I kiss her neck and debate marking her. I don't want any man coming within twenty feet of my wife. Sucking hard, I leave a beautiful dark red imprint on the side of her throat.

My wife.

"I'm close, I just need a—" I drop my hand between her legs to play with her clit. She moans, *"Yes..."*

"I know, baby. You're going to give me number ten, are you ready?" She whimpers in response and I bite down on her shoulder gently. "Let go for me, babygirl. Come all over my cock."

Charlotte backs into me, taking what's hers as she comes for the tenth time since we started this little game. My own release follows the moment I feel her pulse around me. With my cock still throbbing inside her, I sit back on my heels and wrap my arms around her. She sags into me, completely spent.

I graze my teeth over the mark I left and whisper. "I love you, Charlotte."

"Not sure how romantic that is, considering you're still inside me. You love my *pussy*, Jay." She chuckles and I love the feel of it against my chest.

"You know that's not true." I pull out and lay down, gesturing for her to do the same. She tucks into my side, barely able to move. "Are you really coming to see me this weekend?"

"Yeah, I booked a flight when you were sleeping. I wasn't sure if you were rooming with the other coaches or if you had your own, so I didn't book my hotel yet. I was just thinking if we are going to make this work, it should be fifty-fifty. If you put the work in, so should I."

"I'll take care of it... *Fuck*, I'm so happy you'll be there. I'll arrange for everything else, just send me your flight info." I wrap my arms tighter around her. I would give this woman anything.

"Okay." She sighs into me, and in this moment, I think I'm the happiest I've been in a long fucking time.

21

CHARLOTTE

I'm a selfish woman and I make no apologies. When a hot, bearded man tells you he's going to make you come ten times, you say "yes, sir" and let him.

Okay, so I don't think I could ever call him that, but it's the thought that counts. He did delicious things to my body and I didn't regret a second of it...

Until reality settles in.

He's going to be gone for a few weeks. We need to talk about what's going on between us and I need to talk to someone who isn't *him*.

I'm a "just kidding" wife. We didn't sign up for this, and I certainly don't want to remain married to someone who never even proposed. I don't care what the marriage certificate says, I'm not his wife. Girlfriend? Maybe. But not a wife.

While I'm still upset about the whole not telling me about his new job thing, I try to push my emotions aside. I've become a master at it over the years. I can't count how many times I've practiced my smile in front of a mirror. I don't want my resting bitch face to be the thing he remembers from the last few hours of our time together before he gets on a plane.

I was serious when I told him we need to work on everything together and separately. Jason can't be the only one making an effort. So, later this week, I'll be on a plane to fly across the country to see him.

The ride home is too quiet. I can't stand awkward silences and have the overwhelming need to always fill them. He can sense my uneasiness and asks, "Everything okay, sweetheart?"

"Sure, why wouldn't it be?" I lie.

"You're full of shit, Char. What's wrong?"

Damn it.

"I don't want to talk about it right now. We only have" —I glance at my watch—"forty-five minutes together. I don't want to waste it talking about anything that might cause a fight before you leave."

Jason pulls off the freeway at the next exit. "If we need to fight, then we fight."

"Can we just wait until we get home?"

"Nope," he replies, popping the 'p.' He parks in front of a coffee shop, turns off the engine, and faces me. "I know you don't like confrontation, but we're going to let everything out in the open—right here, right now. I'm not getting on that plane until I know we're okay."

"We're okay—"

"No. You're going to worry about whatever is upsetting you, for weeks, and I'll have no control over it. What's on your mind?"

I groan, crossing my arms over my chest. "Not everything is an ADHD or autism thing. I'm not going to be obsessing on this. I reserve my hyperfixation for bigger issues and fun hobbies."

"*Everything* is an autism and ADHD thing, Char. It's part of who you are. It's not bad; don't dismiss one of my favorite things about you." Jason narrows his eyes at me and I glare back.

"You're not going to like what I have to say…" *Especially after last night.*

"It doesn't matter. Out with it. You don't want me keeping secrets; this is no different."

He's right. I take a deep breath. "I know we said we'll go to therapy, but I also *really* don't want to be married to you."

Jason pauses and swallows thickly. "Ever?"

"Yes? No? I don't know, I just… We did this all wrong and it's really bothering me. I want to be with you, I do, but the boys don't even know about us dating, and we're fucking married. You're one of my best friends, so I don't want to fight and ruin that… Come to think of it, have we *ever* had a fight? I feel like we should fight about something and get it out of the way——"

He cuts me off with a searing kiss I feel all the way to my toes. It actually keeps me from spiraling, but we also need to talk about this. When we break apart, he presses his forehead to mine and admits, "We don't fight because I always say yes to you, sweetheart. That's not healthy, either. Give us a shot. We'll go to therapy together. If you still want to get divorced, I'll admit, it'll break me, but I am not going to force you to stay married to me."

"For how long, though? How long do we have to go to therapy before I'm not married anymore?"

"What's really bothering you? Remember what Tyler… *Edmund* said about marrying your best friend? When I look ten or twenty years down the road, I see you and me."

He's not getting it. "Jay, this isn't just about the future. This is right now. When I pictured getting married, I imagined dating someone for years before walking down the aisle."

"I'll tell you what." He tucks my hair behind my ear. "Everything has been so fucked up, between the drugged wedding and my new job. We've been on a few dates, but I haven't had a chance to properly be with you. I know you want a deadline, but it's not that simple. You know baseball season is long and I'll be on the road a lot. It'll give you an idea of what our life would be like if we stay married. Give me until the end of the year. On January 1st, if you still want to get a divorce, I'll draft the paperwork myself."

"Really?" I breathe a sigh of relief.

"You have my word. I take marriage seriously, so I won't be seeing anyone but you when I'm on the road. How could I? I'm in love with you, Char. But beyond my monogamy, I'll treat our relationship as if the piece of paper doesn't exist. I also need to talk to Em about telling the kids. I'm fine not telling them about us being married, but they should know I'm with you. It's going to be a weird as fuck conversation, but they deserve to know." I place my hands on his cheeks and pull him in to kiss me. He chuckles against my lips, "I love you, babygirl."

When we break apart, he starts the truck and holds my hand in my lap. He asks the smart speaker in his car to call Emma. She picks up on the third ring. "Hey, Jason! How's Miami?"

"I'm not actually there yet, I'm driving down the mountain with Char. I stayed an extra day. You're on speaker, by the way."

Emma lets out a light laugh. "Of course, you did. So, what do I owe the pleasure of this call? Is Dylan not answering his texts again?"

"No," I chuckle. "But is he around? I want to talk to you both about something." He glances briefly at me. "*We* want to talk to you about it."

"Oh fuck. Did you knock her up? Char, did he knock you up? Come on, you two! We leave you alone for a month and you're already making babies."

"No, Em," I reply, giggling. "Definitely not. Can you grab Dylan?"

"Sure thing." She yells away from the phone, "Hey, grumpy pants, get over here… No, it's not Ethan, you know he has better names for you than that… Want me to call him and request insults? Unsalted pretzel is still my favorite… Because you're super grouchy since you figured out Harriet is interested in dating… *Ugh*, we don't have time for this. Jason and Char are on the phone. If you get over here and I'll…" She whispers something to him and I snicker to myself, knowing Dylan is about to get some tonight. Thankfully, Jason doesn't pick up on it. "Sorry, guys. We're here. So, what's going on."

Jason responds without hesitation, "I want to tell the boys about my being with Charlotte." He squeezes my hand. "We don't need to tell them about the marriage, but I want to tell them in person that I'm with her. I would hate for them to find out before I have a chance to talk to them."

"Char, how do you feel about this?" Dylan asks.

The question takes me off guard. "Oh, um, well… You know I love your boys, as well as Harriet and Lizzy, and technically I'm the boys' step-mom right now—*which is so fucking bizarre*—but I want to be Aunt Charlotte still. Is that okay? Jason's right, it's better to come from you guys and Jason."

Emma hums. "Well, it should come from *all* of us."

"What if"—I chew my lip—"what if you come with me to Miami this weekend? It'll be one of Jason's first games as a coach in the majors. I'm sure the boys would love it."

"Yes!" Emma squeals.

Dylan adds, "Sure, we'll absolutely be there. Noah has soccer on Saturday and Harriet has a *date* Friday night, but we can come for the Saturday night game, or the Sunday game if we time it right." He growls at the word date. I can't help but laugh at my brother-in-law being a typical protective father. I don't blame him, his daughters are stunning and so fucking talented and intelligent, they deserve to be treated as queens.

"I have a project Saturday, so I'm flying on Sunday morning, I can meet you guys there," I offer

I glance over at Jason and he whispers, "I'll pick you up."

"It's settled. We'll see you both on Sunday!" Emma's excitement is infectious and I can't wait to see her and the kids.

Harriet and Lizzy are Dylan's teenage daughters from his previous marriage. I don't see much of them, but I do see Em's twins Charlie and Noah, and her youngest Aiden a few times a month. These past few weeks, I've barely seen any of them since my work schedule has been so chaotic. I was already excited to see Jason in action this weekend, but now I'm giddy thinking about spending time with all of them. They're my family, even if I don't share blood with any of them.

We hang up and drive the remaining forty-five or so minutes home. Once we arrive, Jason walks next door to his apartment to grab his bag, before coming by my place.

"Hey, babygirl. I gotta head out."

Hunched over my fridge, I pull out a sparkling water, then make my way to him. "Have a safe trip!" I plaster on a bright smile.

Jason wraps me in a tight hug and kisses the top of my head. "I'll see you at the airport, Sunday, okay?" I nod against his chest. "I love you, sweetheart."

I tilt my head, resting my chin on his chest, and whisper, "See, that's way more romantic than when you're inside me." He chuckles and kisses me. I mutter against his lips, "See you Sunday."

22

JASON

Things are fragile with Charlotte. I have no intention of getting a divorce. Quite the opposite. She isn't where I am at emotionally, but I've had months to process everything and know what I want, while she's only had a few weeks.

My first virtual therapy session is scheduled for two hours after I land in Miami. I want to be sure Charlotte knows I'm taking this seriously and making her a priority. Besides, the rest of the week is incredibly busy building rapport with the team and working with the new third baseman the team traded for. There will be very little time to sleep, let alone fit in a therapy appointment.

Robbie's only nineteen, but he's better than any college kid I've worked with. He played in my college program for six weeks before he was picked up by a minor league team for two months. Then, he was sent to the majors and traded to my new team—which was part of the reason I got this job. I'll have quite a bit of work to do with him, but after a few years, he's going to be fucking amazing. Third base has been their weak link, regardless of whether it's the top or bottom of the inning. I'm excited for the challenge.

Once I'm checked in at my hotel, I fire up my laptop and begin the video call with Dr. Bryant.

"Hi, Jason. Great to meet you."

"You, too."

He checks over a file. "It says here that this isn't your first rodeo. So, let's dive right in. To start, why are you back in therapy?"

Shit, this guy's straight to the point.

"My wife and I have a unique situation. We, uh, accidentally got married." *Please don't ask how that makes me feel.*

"Care to explain?"

I blow out a deep breath and recount how Charlotte and I ended up married and also how I took my new job. This man may be my saving grace to keeping Char, and I divulge everything, every single detail.

"The 'getting married' or 'getting a new job' aren't what concern me, Jason. Your wife should be your equal in a marriage, regardless of how you came to be her husband. I can understand why hiding both from her can be difficult to share, but could you elaborate on how you've treated Charlotte since she moved to California?"

Taken aback, I ask, "What do you mean? We're friends, but I've been in love with her for years. I've treated her as a friend all this time because I didn't think she felt the same way about me. When I figured out she did, it became more of an issue of how my ex-wife would respond."

"Do friends keep secrets from each other?"

Should have seen that one coming.

"No." I shake my head. "But I was worried about how she would react."

He nods, writing something on his notepad. "And how do you think she would react?"

"I don't know. Maybe demand a divorce? Or decide she doesn't want me in her life at all anymore—even as friends?"

"What if she had demanded a divorce?"

I swallow thickly and reply, "She already did, but I suggested we go to therapy and date through the end of the year before she made a decision."

"Except, she already decided. You said she wanted a divorce."

Shit, he's right.

"I can't lose her and I'd do anything to keep her."

"Our time is almost up, but there are a few things I want you to consider: First, take some time and write down the last three times she made a decision on her own, without your help or suggestions. Second, consider your role as a husband and how you can shift from her friend to someone she's dating. There is a bit of an age difference between you two, which could've led to a bit of a protective streak or a problem with a power dynamic on your part. This is a typical response. You mentioned Charlotte has diagnoses of autism and ADHD. Fostering independence should always be the number one priority. Next week, I'd like to discuss these further. Before we hang up, do you have any questions for me?"

I shake my head. "No. Thank you."

"It's been a pleasure getting to know you today. I see we have a recurring meeting scheduled moving forward, but if you need a last minute appointment between our meetings, please contact my office and we'll make sure to fit you in. Therapy isn't supposed to fix your problems, but help guide you to finding your own solutions. You're on the right path, and with a bit of work, I'm optimistic you'll see a positive shift in your relationship."

We hang up and I marinate with everything we went over. Essentially, I've been treating Charlotte like a kid all these years. Sure, it was to protect her, but if he's right; I need to let her ask for help instead of jumping in to save the day. I fucked up these past few years, much more than I ever realized, but that changes today.

23

CHARLOTTE

I blow out a deep breath. The lights might be low, but the flicker of the bulb on the ceiling to my right is distracting me. *Flick flick, pause, flick, pause, flicccccck, pause...* There's no rhythm to it. I can't sing along. I can't hum. There's no amazing drum beat I can tap along with...

I'm uncomfortable and the urge to stim is unbearable. I take a deep breath in through my nose and out through my mouth.

There are no lights, there are no sounds. Just the potted plant to the right of the assorted magazines I have zero interest in flipping through... The plant. Focus on the plant.

"Ms. Wentworth?" A voice pulls me from my botched grounding exercise.

"Oh, hi. That's me."

"She'll see you now."

Nodding with my well-rehearsed smile, I enter a sterile room that quickens my heart rate and shortens my breath.

"This feels wrong," I admit, mostly to myself.

"Charlotte, what feels wrong?" It's as if she has no fucking clue about how some neurodivergent people have been poked and prodded most of their lives, and struggle with environments like this.

I glare at her. "All of it." My words are laced with venom, but fuck her for coming at me with this condescending energy.

No… this isn't her fault. Deep breath in, exhale three, two, one.

"I'm sorry. This isn't my first time in therapy," I admit. "I've had bad experiences with it."

"Apologies directed at me aren't allowed in this office. How can I help? Are you experiencing sensory or emotional overload?"

I ponder her question for a moment. "Both," I answer honestly. "But I also don't do well in medical settings."

She asks her smart speaker to dim the lights, leaving a small ball to my right illuminated in a dark blue.

Shit, is she going to do the whole color and emotion thing? Here we go…

"How are we feeling now Charlotte?"

I sigh at the pointlessness of it. "The ball is blue, so I'm supposed to feel sad, right?"

"No. You can feel however you like. I'm going to change the color of the ball and I want you to tell me how the color makes you feel."

Called it.

Closing my eyes tight, I grumble, "I know this game. I don't need to look, Doc. What color is the light?"

"Yellow," she replies.

"Happy."

"Charlotte, if you are comfortable, open your eyes."

"It's not yellow, is it? Is it red? *I'm angry.* Or is it orange? *I'm feeling creative...*"

She chuckles. "Should I put on green and assume you're envious? I want to give you a tool to express yourself if your feelings are too big."

I open my eyes. "Been there, done that. Let's just start the tests that determine I'm broken."

"You aren't broken, but I sense you have trauma from previous medical or therapy experiences. Let's try something different." She stands and gestures for me to do the same in front of a full length mirror. "What do you see?"

"A woman who doesn't know what the fuck... *frick* she's doing."

"Try again," she says softly. "This time tell me exactly as you wanted to say."

"A woman who doesn't know what the fr—"

"Lace it with whatever you're feeling, good or bad, Charlotte. Profanities aren't a bad thing. Fuck, shit, asshole... all of it is allowed."

I blow out a breath and stare at myself in the mirror. I lift my chin slightly. "A woman who doesn't know what the *fuck* she's doing."

"There we go," she chuckles with a smirk. "Now, why don't you know what the fuck you're doing?"

"Because I'm in love with my best friend, we got married, and now I'm afraid he hasn't seen the ugly side of me. When he does, he... he might not love me," I admit.

"That's a lot of pressure to put on yourself; hiding who you are from someone you love. Are you masking right now?"

Staring at myself in the mirror, I nod. "Yeah. I don't like people seeing me when I'm stimmy or sad. I like being the happy, fun friend."

"Are you happy, though?"

I chew on my lip. "No."

"What color?"

"Red, blue... So, I guess purple?" I reply with a shrug

"Allow yourself to be angry and sad, Charlotte. There's nothing wrong with purple. You can feel as big or as small as you want. It's never bad or wrong. Identifying it is the first step. After that, you get to decide what to do with how you feel. You've been masking for years, letting yourself feel your big emotions is the hardest part."

She's the first therapist I've met who's encouraged me to feel angry or sad, not just how to overcome it or asking me to explain *'how it makes me feel.'* When I want to feel anything but happy, I hide it, squashing it down for no one to see. But, the truth is… I'm not happy. I'm pissed and hurt.

I take a deep breath and let my pleasant but neutral expression I've perfected over the years fall.

I don't hide scratching my nails against my palm.

I remove my mask.

It's too raw and too real, but I need to do this. Not for Jason. Not for a therapist. *For me.* I need to be honest with myself.

I speak my truths to my reflection, "Jason lied to me. He hid our marriage for *months*. Now, he's in Florida, living his dream. But he didn't tell me about that, either. He doesn't trust me, how can he love me?"

"Why does that make you sad or angry?" Her words pull me from my confession. I recoil back into my safe place, replacing my pursed lips with a small smile that doesn't meet my eyes.

"Sorry, I was just talking out loud. It doesn't matter what I feel. It is what it is."

"First, no apologies. Second, it *always* matters how you feel," she asks again, "Why does what Jason did make you sad or angry?"

I look back to the mirror and admit, "He doesn't think I could handle it. I know I'm younger than him, but sometimes I feel like he..." I trail off, not wanting to admit the truth.

"How old is he?"

I sigh. "We're twelve years apart. That's weird, right? Oh, and he's my step-sister's ex-husband. Shit, this all sounds like a bad sitcom."

She steps away and gestures for me to sit. "There are a few things we should probably unpack there. The age difference is the least of it, I'm more interested in how he treats you."

I reluctantly tell her, "Sometimes he treats me like I'm a child he needs to protect. I've been on my own since I was eighteen. I don't need a keeper, but I've always had someone keep an eye on me. In New York, it was my friend, Eddie. Here, it's Jason. I'll admit, I do need someone to check in on me from time to time, but I've been on my own for my adult life. He's been my person, the one who makes sure I'm safe, but I never asked him to. His son is autistic, so maybe that's why he's so protective? As I say it all out loud, I feel like a burden to him."

"I know we scheduled couples therapy for when he is in town. Since he isn't here to talk about this, why don't we talk about some ways to empower you. You aren't broken, Charlotte. You have comorbid diagnoses, but that is all they are, diagnoses. Slapping a label on it just means you are better equipped to understand how you think; that's all."

"I don't feel like anyone understands. I was diagnosed with ADHD when I was a kid and put on meds that messed with my head. It's not my parents' fault. They saw me struggling and medication seemed like the best solution at the time, but I didn't like how they made me feel."

She picks up her notebook and begins writing as she says, "What were you on?"

"Various stimulants. My body gets used to them and I have to switch every few years."

"What about antidepressants?"

I shake my head. "No."

"Something I would like to explore is that you could have undiagnosed depression or high-functioning anxiety. A lot of ADHD and autistic people—especially those who identify as women—are great at covering up their real emotions in front of family and friends. I imagine it was similar in a clinical setting, and they could have missed it."

Maybe she gets me, after all. "Yeah," I chuckle. "I know how to pass them with flying colors."

"I would like to evaluate you for depression at our next session and determine next steps. But for now, let's talk about options to help you be a bit more independent. Do you have any self-harm or self-injurious behaviors?"

"No."

She continues taking notes. "What about sensory or emotional meltdowns?"

"Rare, but I am usually good about self-regulating."

"When was your last one?"

I think back to that night with a grimace. "When Jason told me we were married."

She hums. "Do you have any pets?" I shake my head. "What are your thoughts on an emotional support or service animal?"

"I haven't thought about it," I admit.

"I have lists of resources I can send home with you. It could be a great solution for not relying on your husband. Before we end our session, I would like to get an updated medical history that wasn't in your intake."

We talk for the remainder of the hour, and she sends me home with a referral for a psychiatrist who can prescribe a low-dose antidepressant, if I want to go that route, and information on service animals. The more I consider it,

the more I think she's right; both would be a great
option for me.

As soon as I'm home, I text Jason.

> I just had my first therapy session in
> forever. Are you free tonight to talk?

JAY

Of course. Just name the time.

I bite my nail. I should just call him and get this conversation over with.

> Now?

The game is almost over, but I can call
as soon as I am done.

> Shit, I'm so sorry. I forgot about the time
> difference! When do they have you on
> the field?

Sunday will be my first game.

> That's exciting! I'm glad your boys will
> get to see you in action for your first.

So am I. I'm also glad you'll be there.
I've gotta run, but I'll call you as soon as
I'm back to the hotel.

Love you, babygirl.

I type out "Love you, too" but delete it before sending.

24

JASON

We went into extra innings, but I made sure to text Charlotte on my way to the hotel. The last thing I need is for her to think I'm blowing her off, especially since she went to therapy today and was nervous about it.

Once I'm in my room, I take a quick shower and call her. "Hey," she answers, sounding relatively calm. It's a good sign.

"Hey, babygirl. How was your day?"

"I want to get a service animal," she blurts out.

"Aren't those for people with disabilities?"

"Yes, and they also help people with other conditions, like epilepsy and autism. I think it would be good for me, so I don't have to rely on you so much."

It feels like a stab to my gut. I like that she needs me, but I think back to my conversation with my own therapist yesterday. This might be a good opportunity for me to give her the independence she deserves.

"I'll always be here for you, Char, but getting a dog or other animal to keep you safe is actually very smart. I know your meltdowns are rare, but if I'm on the road and Ethan or Edmund aren't around…" I swallow thickly at the thought, hating that I won't get to see her as often. "It's a good idea, sweetheart."

"Will you help me get one? There's a lot of options and it's expensive. I don't want to be taken advantage of, you know?"

I chuckle softly. "Of course. I just got a signing bonus from the team. Will you let me pay for it?"

"Oh, no. I couldn't—"

"Char, it's really expensive and I have the money for it. Please, let me do this for you? I don't want the cost to be the reason you can't get one."

"I understand, but I really want to do this on my own. I can't have you always coming to the rescue."

That is exactly what I'm doing. *Shit.* I take a breath and start over. "I'll make you a deal: I'll help pay for the difference. I'd hate for you to not get what you want because of money. Whatever you can't afford, I'll take care of."

She sighs deeply, and gives in. "Fine, but he better be cute."

"It'll be the cutest pup in the whole damn world. So, how did the rest of it go?"

"I have a lot of things I'm going to work on, like not masking while I'm with you. Also, I'm going to see a psychiatrist about medication options. Oh, and I'm going to be evaluated for depression, so... I'm more broken than I thought."

My heart hurts more and more with every word that comes from her mouth. "Hold on, let's start at the top. You mask with me? I know you talk about doing it when you're with new people but... *me?*"

"It's bad enough you've seen Meltdown Charlotte, I don't want you to see Sad Charlotte, too. Or worse, Stimmy Charlotte."

"I want all of it. The good and the bad. Don't you trust me? Shit, Aiden—"

"Is your son," she sighs. "I'm... replaceable. If I show you all of me, you might not like what you see, Jay."

"Replaceable? You're kidding, right? I know you're still trying to wrap your head around all of it, but I'm in love with you. Fuck, I didn't want you moving next door because I was so attracted to you. I knew I would fall hard if I got to know you better, and I was right. If you're sad, I want to see it. If you're pissed off, show me. You think I don't see you stim? You're good at hiding your emotions, I'll give you that. I know when you start scripting that you're either really excited or nervous. You scratch the inside of your palm, too, but I don't see it as often anymore. Don't hide from me, Char. Please."

She sighs. "I thought I was pretty good at hiding it."

"No, babygirl. You suck at hiding it." She sniffles and I hate that she doesn't trust me. "I'll love you when you're sad or pissed off or overstimulated. Always. This is why it's good that we're both talking to people. I tend to always say yes to you and I want to protect you from, well, everything. If we're going to spend the rest of our lives with each other, we need to get it all out in the open and talk through it."

"We're not supposed to talk about the whole being married thing."

I stifle a groan. "Answer me this, in ten years, do you see us together? What about twenty?"

"I haven't thought about it." Her voice is small and I'm probably going about this the wrong way.

"I love and adore everything about you. I don't see any part of my future without you in it. After this weekend, I'm not back in California for another week, but we're playing LA before I'm back home. Can I fly you out there, so we can spend time together? Go to an amusement park, eat a bunch of fried food, ride everything that will make me want to hurl…"

"Yes."

"Yes?"

"Yes, Jay." She sniffles again, but with a soft laugh. "I'll come to LA. I'm nervous as fuck about everything, but I think spending time together, like we did in London, would be perfect. It's honestly the last time that I felt like we were *us*. I want that back."

I can't help my wide smile. If I play my cards right, I may get to keep the one woman who makes me feel whole. It's only been one day since I saw her, but I fucking miss her. I hit the video chat option on my phone. She answers it and I'm glad to see she's smiling; it's one that reaches her eyes. I love that she's not putting on a brave face for me.

"I wanted to see you before I head downstairs to meet the boys for a drink."

Charlotte's sitting on the couch, folded laundry stacked next to her. "We should only do video calls from now on. Just don't mind me if I'm walking around the apartment doing chores when you call. You know I like to keep my hands busy... I mean..." Her cheeks flush and she hides her face with an unfolded tee from her basket.

"I'm sure I could help you keep your hands busy. But I prefer them above your head, holding mine, as I'm buried deep inside you."

She removes the shirt from her face that's now bright crimson. "Jason..."

"Yes, babygirl?"

"You can't be saying things like that," she whispers.

"Give me a number between one and ten."

Her eyes are wide. "What did you just say?"

"You heard me. Give me a number between one and ten."

"One," she says quickly, embarrassed and looking away from her phone.

"Tell me one thing you've always wanted someone to do to you?"

"Sex in public," she rushes out, then immediately covers her mouth.

"I want you to come for me tonight, just once, thinking about me taking you from behind in public. No cheating if a second is within reach. You get *one*. Use your favorite vibrator or touch yourself. And as soon as you're spent, I want you to text me with proof."

She frowns. "What kind of proof?"

"I want to see your glistening pussy for myself after it's soaked your sheets. I expect photographic evidence, sweetheart. It'll be for my eyes only, but you better believe I'll be fisting my cock to it, wishing it was you riding me instead."

Charlotte gasps and a good thirty seconds pass before she replies, "Okay, but only if you show me how hard I make you after I send it."

Fuck, this backfired. My jeans are entirely too tight.

"You're on, babygirl. I've gotta run. I'll talk to you later."

Charlotte pauses. "I love you, Jay."

She never says it first... *ever*. My heart just about leaped out of my chest. "I love you, too."

———

At the bar, I meet up with a few other coaches. Two of them have their wives with them. It's another reminder that I need to slow things down and give Charlotte time. Maybe next year, she'll be here with me as my wife by choice, not because of an accidental wedding we don't remember. There are barely six months left before the January 1st deadline. It's both too much time and not nearly enough.

"Hey, Jason! Pull up a seat." Todd gestures to the empty table next to them to grab a chair. "Man, that Robbie kid is somethin' else. Can't believe he's only nineteen."

Pride warms my chest. I only worked with him for a few short months before he was recruited, but I'm so damn proud of how far he's come in such a short time.

I excuse myself to grab an IPA from the bar. When I return, Todd's wife, Kendra, asks between bites of her burger, "Didn't you say your family was coming to your first game?"

"Yeah, they're all coming out. I have to pick up my wife

from the airport, so I might be late to the meeting Sunday morning."

Mike nearly chokes on his beer. "What did you just say?"

"I know," I sigh. "I hate being late, but it's important to me that I'm there when she lands. Dylan and Emma couldn't get on the same flight with her, and Charlotte hates long flights."

"No, fuck the meeting... *wife?* Since when are you married? I didn't even know you were dating." Mike shakes his head in disbelief.

I shrug, not wanting to recount the whole situation to them. "Only for a few months. We, uh, eloped."

"First season as a coach's wife." Kendra blows out a deep breath. "I remember my first year when Todd was with Houston. We nearly divorced... *twice*," she laughs, but my heart leaps into my throat.

Todd wraps his arm around Kendra and kisses her temple. "It was absolute shit. Being newlyweds and only seeing your wife a few days at a time... Fuck, it was hard."

"It's why Alicia and I split. It was too much," Kevin says into his glass.

Mike's wife, Emily, asks, "Is Charlotte going to be traveling at all?"

"No, not really." I shake my head. "She landed a large contract for work. But, if the schedules line up, I'll be flying her out as often as I can when we're on the road."

We finish dinner and drinks. All of this is a reminder that Charlotte didn't sign up for this, I dragged her into this life. I just hope we're strong enough to survive it, especially with how delicate things are between us right now. I make a mental note that we probably shouldn't sleep together until I've earned her trust again. While things are great physically between us, I need to work on winning *all* of her over if I want to keep her.

25

JASON

It's my first game coaching in the major league, and it's fucking unreal. Years ago, I played for them, and now I am ushering baserunners to the same bag I used to take up myself. I only played two games before my injury sent me back down to the minors, but it was the best two of my life.

Robbie is a beast, and I intend to teach him everything I know. The kid is going to do big things—if only he'd stop checking out Dylan's daughter sitting in the row behind the dugout.

Between innings, I stop him before he takes a seat. "Keep your head in the game and stop eye-fucking the girl in the stands."

"I was not—"

"Harriet's my buddy's daughter, and still has over a year before she's legal. Off. Limits."

"Shit, Coach. She doesn't look sixteen. I didn't know, honest. She's fucking beautiful, it was kind of hard not to look, but… Fuck, she's sixteen?" He shakes his head. "Please don't tell your friend. The last thing I need is some rumor hitting a media cycle that I'm into a minor."

I grip his shoulder. "I'm not saying anything, but touch her and if her dad doesn't kill ya, I will. Understood?"

"Absolutely." He rejoins the team, looking defeated.

I take my spot by the foul line and glance back at my girl. Charlotte's wearing my number from when I played, and it has to be the hottest fucking thing she's ever worn. She's flanked between Emma and Harriet who, according to Emma and Charlotte, has a little crush on Robbie—she showed up in his jersey, not trying to hide it. After my talk with him, I'm not worried anything would happen between them, but I also don't want to see her heart broken. There's nothing wrong with a harmless crush.

My boys are sitting with Lizzy and Dylan. Noah is watching the game intently, while the other two are fixated on their devices. I shake my head, chuckling to myself. They came all this way to LA to play games on their tablets. Dylan raises his drink to me, my guess is it's his usual gin and tonic based on the lime garnish. I tip my hat in reply.

A few uneventful innings pass with only a few singles and a double. Next up is Robbie. We have a man on second, so if we play this right, we could bring in another run.

Strike one.

Ball.

Strike two.

Crack.

The ball pops up and has a decent amount of air on it. There's a chance it'll make it to the wall. For half a second, I hold my breath as I watch it fly. Just barely, but it made it over—home run. It's Robbie's first, and I get to be one of the first to congratulate him. I swear I can hear Harriet cheering through the crowd from here. Robbie fist bumps me as he rounds third base and sprints for home plate.

With one inning left, the game is practically in the bag. Since I won't need to deal with the press today, as soon as the game is over, I'm taking everyone on a quick tour. I'll show the kids my office and introduce them to a few players—*not* Robbie, who will thankfully be busy with the press from his performance tonight. It's best to not formally introduce him to Harriet if I can avoid it.

After an eventful day, Dylan and Emma take the kids back to the hotel. We plan to meet up later tonight for dinner, but I want some time alone with Charlotte.

"Can I see the field?" She's bouncing on the balls of her feet, entirely too excited to be here.

With everyone gone, I reply, "Of course. Come on," taking her hand and leading her out on the field to third base.

"Shit, the bases are so far apart in person. They seem closer on TV or even from the stands."

I jog back to the dugout and grab a ball and a bat before returning to her. "Do you want to pitch, or hit?"

"Hit, obviously!"

I hand her the bat and she practically skips to home plate. I stand halfway between home and the mound. My arm isn't what it used to be, and I don't want to accidentally hit her with a rogue ball. "You ready?"

She nods and I toss it underhand to her—to be safe. Her form is a little too good and she hits it out to left field. As she begins running to first, I call out, "This isn't your first time!"

Laughing as she rounds the base, she yells back, "Nope, high school softball team!"

"Cheater!" I stop her at third and wrap her in my arms. "Next time, I'm not going easy on you."

"I'd prefer it if you went a little *harder* on me," she replies, wiggling her eyebrows. Lifting onto her toes, she wraps her arms behind my neck and kisses me. I'd claim her right here and now, but there are cameras everywhere.

"Ready to get out of here?"

"I have an idea." She takes my hand and leads me to the dugout. Once we're down the steps, she playfully pushes me against one of the walls. Her hands wander from my chest, down my stomach to my belt. "You should have kept the baseball pants on."

"As much as I want to be deep inside you right now—" She grips my cock through my pants. "*Fuck*."

"What were you saying?" Char kisses me and nips my lip as she pulls back. "You want to know what I thought about that night, when I told you I wanted to have sex in public?"

"Fuck. Here?"

She nods excitedly and I slide my hands under her jersey, exploring her bare waist. I should tell her no, but I've never been able to. "Can you be quiet, babygirl?" She bites her lip, nodding again, and her eyes are alight with mischief. "We have to be quick." I check where the camera is and the right corner is a blind spot. I guide her to it. "One and ten, sweetheart."

"Ten," she teases.

I kiss her roughly, muttering against her lips, "No time, but I'll give you two now and eight after dinner."

"I was fucking kidding!"

"I'm not." I nip at her earlobe as I unbutton her pants, trailing kisses down her neck. "I've been dreaming about the taste of you since I left." As I slip my hand into her underwear, I'm pleased to discover she's already wet for me. My fingers graze her clit as I push into her, making her gasp. I curl twice, then remove my hand, groaning as I suck my coated fingers clean. "I'm addicted to you."

"Do you want to know what I thought about while I was touching myself or not?"

"Fuck, can I show you with my tongue on your clit? If not, you can tell me later."

Charlotte slides down the wall until she's on her knees. Before I can react, she's unbuttoning my pants and tugging them down. "I want you in my mouth, Jay."

"I'm not coming in that pretty mouth of yours. Especially since you didn't come first."

Charlotte frees my hard cock and slowly licks the underside before taking all of me. "Fuck." I hit the back of her throat, making her gag lightly. She's so beautiful on her knees for me, I fight the urge to wrap her ponytail around my hand and fuck her mouth. She moves up and down my shaft with perfect suction—any faster and I might come, which definitely isn't going to happen until she does. I her hair around my fist and tug her off me. "You got me close enough, sweetheart. It's my turn." She stands and I command, "Take off your pants. I'll shield you but I want your sexy thighs against my cheeks."

With a wicked grin, she slips them down her legs and kicks them off. I fall to my knees and pull one of her legs over my shoulder. "Fuck, I missed you." I selfishly taste and tease her. As much as I loved watching her pouty lips glide up and down my cock, I'd rather spend the rest of my life on my knees for this woman, making her come over and over. I glide two fingers inside her as my tongue firmly circles her clit. Her hips buck forward and I grab her ass to get closer.

Time isn't on our side. Tasting her was more for me than it was for her; I'd need more time to build her up. I press a kiss to her thigh and stand.

"Fuck, I need you," she pants. I lift one of her legs over my hip and use the wall for leverage. Lining my aching cock up with her, I teasing her entrance before pushing inside. "Jason." My name comes out as a strangled whimper.

I kiss her neck, grazing my teeth over where I marked her last time; it's still a little pink. "You're so incredible, Char, taking my cock like this. You're fucking perfect." I thrust harder, giving her the pressure she craves. She stifles a moan, biting down on my shoulder. "That's right, sweetheart. You're gonna come twice before I empty myself inside you." I lower my voice and whisper softly, "My favorite thing in the whole fucking world is watching you fall apart for me. You're a fucking goddess, letting me take what belongs to me."

"I'm close, Jay. Keep talking."

"Do you how fucking hot it was seeing you in my old number in the stands?" I pick up my pace, even if it puts me at risk of coming too soon. "Sexiest fucking thing I've ever seen in my life. I want you laid out on the bed later wearing it."

"Right there... don't stop..."

I swallow her screams as her pussy pulses around me. She feels too fucking good. I continue driving into her, building her up to give her one more. As I carefully take her neck in my hand, I keep her mouth on mine to quiet her moans. She whimpers against my lips and it's the sweetest fucking sound.

"You're mine, babygirl. You're going to give me one more right now, but I'm absolutely taking another eight tonight."

"Can you fuck me from behind? It hits my—"

I don't let her finish, pulling out and turning her around. "Hands on the wall, sweetheart. I'm not sure how you imagined it the other night when you touched yourself, but this isn't going to be gentle. Say stop and I stop, but otherwise I'm going to fuck you hard until I get one more from you." She nods and glances over her shoulder at me with a smirk. I grip her hips and thrust into her hard and fast.

"Oh fuck... Yes, just like that... I'm... *Jason!*" I cup her mouth to quiet her. As hot as it is to hear her call out my name, I don't want to get caught.

"My turn, baby." I thrust harder and it only takes a minute before I find my own release. Wrapping my arm around her middle, I pull her flush with me, holding her close as I catch my breath. "How are you doing?"

"So fucking good."

I kiss her shoulder and neck. "It's official, you're coming to all my games." I pull out and turn her toward me, kissing her softly. "You're irresistible and I need to work on the whole 'always saying yes to you' thing... But not today."

"I should put my pants on. You know, before we get caught."

I tug up my own pants and bend to help her slip into hers. Never in a million years would I have guessed my sweet, innocent Charlotte would suggest sex in the stadium.

And I'm never going to look at a dugout the same again.

26

CHARLOTTE

The whole game, I couldn't take my eyes off Jason. He looked so fucking hot in those tight baseball pants, but nothing beat when Robbie hit that home run—I've never seen Jason so happy. I didn't intend to do anything physical when we were alone on the field, but the dopamine hit was definitely worth it. I'll be riding the high all night.

Emma and her crew picked a family-friendly restaurant for dinner, right on the beach. We're seated at a large table on the patio and I'm enjoying the salty air whipping around us as the calming waves crash into the sand. Aiden gives me a knowing look—this is sensory heaven for both of us.

I opt to sit across from Jason. If we are about to have a serious discussion with the kids, I don't want to make it any more awkward than it already is. Emma takes a seat to my left and squeezes my hand once before releasing it. She has been entirely too cool about this whole thing; I'm grateful for her support.

Harriet sits to my right and, while she might only be sixteen, she's a lot like her dad and a voice of reason— even if Dylan has made questionable choices of his own in the name of love. I don't need to be sandwiched between a couple of romantics; it's a perfect balance.

"So, kids, we have something we want to talk to you about," Emma starts.

"Oh shit, please tell me you're not getting divorced!" Lizzy's eyes are wide and moments from welling with tears.

"Absolutely not," Dylan assures her, covering her hand with his. "Hell will freeze over first. Emma's stuck with me the rest of her life. This is actually about Jason."

"He's gay. I knew it," Harriet says, crossing her arms and sitting back in her chair.

I bark out a laugh and Emma joins me with a chuckle before clarifying, "No, he's actually dating someone—a woman. But even if he was into men, we'd support him and his new partner all the same." She looks to Jason to continue.

Jason clears his throat and as he is about to explain, Aiden blurts out, "You like Aunt Charlotte." I picked the wrong time to take a sip of my martini and choke a little. Emma pats me on the back gently as I compose myself. "What? Dad's liked her since she moved next door."

Fuck, I forgot how perceptive Aiden is.

"You're not wrong," Jason admits with a wide grin. "I've been in love with Charlotte for a few years, but apparently I'm really bad at hiding it. We wanted to talk to you, to make sure everyone is okay that I'm mar— *dating* Charlotte."

Damn it, Jay. If he isn't careful, Aiden will pick up on his slip ups.

Noah shrugs. "I mean, it's a little weird." He looks to me. "You're mom's sister."

"Step-sister," Emma corrects. "We didn't grow up together, so it's more like we're good friends."

"Does that mean we get a second mom, like Harriet and Lizzy have?" Charlie asks.

"No," I answer quickly. "I mean, I love you all. You're family to me, but I'm only dating Jason. If we get mar—"

"*When* we're married," Jason talks over me.

I glare at him. "*If* we get married."

"Charlotte…" Jason warns, his voice commanding.

"*What?*" I mouth to him. I direct my attention back to Charlie. "I'd prefer to still be your aunt, if that's all right. I've enjoyed being your cool aunt up to this point,

I don't want that to change because of my relationship with your dad."

"Is this like when Dad was obsessed with Mom and basically steamrolled her until she married him?" Harriet asks with a knowing smirk. She gasps and pulls out a notebook. "This would actually make for a great story; do you mind if I use it? You'd be a werewolf or a vampire, so no one would know it's you. Forbidden love is always a hit in YA fantasy."

"Go for it." I lean in and whisper, "But please make Jason and your dad a couple of obnoxious fae lords." She bites her lip as she scribbles away in her notebook. I raise my voice to address the table. "I know this isn't normal. Trust me, I get it; I'm still trying to wrap my brain around it all. No matter what happens, I'll always be your aunt."

The answer seems to satisfy everyone and Dylan thankfully moves on from the subject as our dinner arrives. "The guys are looking good this year. I noticed they play San Diego in a month." Em perks up at the mention of her favorite team. "Maybe we can take a trip and come visit on the road."

I glance at Jason and the frown hasn't left his face since I corrected him about getting married. In an attempt to smooth things over, I offer, "You know, I heard there's an amazing taqueria there with tacos that outmatch anything we've ever had."

Jason visibly relaxes and a small smile tugs at his lips. "Yes, yes there is." He takes a sip of his beer and continues, "I'd love if you could visit on the road. I know I'll have the boys when I'm at home, but away games get lonely."

Wait, what? He never mentioned anything about his custody changing. I'm all for it, but it feels like one more thing he hid from me and my heart twists.

"I'll check the schedule and let you know which game we'll be at," Dylan offers as he takes out his phone to look it up.

The rest of dinner is uneventful. The boys update me on what's going on in their lives, since I haven't seen them in almost a month, and the girls share what books they've been reading. Emma and Dylan talk about where they want to stay in San Diego, asking my opinion. Jason's eyes linger on me, but I avoid his gaze.

On the car ride to the hotel, he finally breaks our awkward silence and asks, "What's wrong, sweetheart?"

Don't you sweetheart me...

I stifle a growl. "We'll talk at the hotel."

The rest of the drive is quiet, and the moment the hotel room door clicks shut, I huff, "Number between one and ten."

Jason shakes his head, chuckling. "No. I'm not having sex with you when we're not talking."

"Fine. Eight. I'm owed eight orgasms, according to you, but I would rather you tell me eight things you've never told me before." I cross my arms. I rub my bicep and scratch my nails slightly, seeking sensory input.

"Where is this coming from?"

"You didn't tell me you adjusted your schedule with Emma and Dylan. I'm not upset about it. It's fucking amazing, actually." As happy as I am for them, I can't stop my words from coming out ice cold.

Jason closes the distance and wraps me in his arms. "But I didn't tell you," he finishes. "I'm so sorry. The last few days have been a whirlwind and I didn't have a chance to tell you. It wasn't intentional, I promise."

My arms involuntarily embrace him back. I sigh against his chest. "Eight things, Jay."

He doesn't hesitate. "One, I want you on the road with me as much as possible. It's selfish, but I miss you. I *always* miss you when I'm gone."

"I…. miss you, too," I whisper. He pulls me closer.

"Two, the boys are going to be with me for most of the time when I'm home. They asked for it. It wasn't something Emma or I brought up. I really am sorry I didn't tell you; I wasn't trying to hide it. I know you said tonight that you only want to be Aunt Charlotte to them, but… you're not just their Aunt Charlotte. If we're going to do this, really do this, I want you to be part of those big discussions I have with Emma and Dylan."

I consider it. "I think it's great that you'll have them more. I just don't feel right making any sort of parenting decisions. I've known them almost all their lives, but those should be conversations you have with Dylan and Emma, not me. I just want to be clued in and not find out at dinner, in front of everyone."

He pulls back and glances down at me. I would normally shy away from eye contact, but I'm lost in his dark blue irises. "You don't like secrets, neither do I. I can't promise I won't accidentally forget to tell you something, but I can promise that I will never do it on purpose, ever again." I nod and he continues, "Four——"

"No skipping ahead, *Sir*. You're on three."

A rumble comes from his chest. I have a sneaking suspicion he's way too into me calling him that. He corrects, "*Three*, I told Ethan and Eddie about the marriage when we were in Delasnia, while you were setting up for the buffalo plaid night. They promised..." He laughs, shaking his head, and I feel it everywhere. "They *pinky* promised, actually, that they wouldn't say anything. I told them I would tell you soon. I wanted to hold on to the fantasy in my head a little bit longer. I learned my lesson, I won't ever do that again."

"I admit, I'm still a little pissed at the two of them— pinky promise or not. People always hide things from me because they're afraid it might set off a meltdown or something. You know I can have big emotions but you have to tell me things, no matter what my reaction is."

"I know, babygirl." Jason tilts my chin with his thumb and forefinger and kisses me softly. "You're stronger than I give you credit for. I'm working on not bubble wrapping you. You aren't fragile, but I've treated you like you are. We're partners now, and as much as I love taking care of you, I also need to not jump in and try to save you when you don't need saving."

"I feel like we're going to stand here all night at this rate. Can you rapid fire?"

He smiles, making little wrinkles appear next to his eyes. "Four, I used to get jealous of your relationship with Eddie. For a while there, I thought you might end up together and it killed me. That's why I was a dick to him sometimes. Five, when I come over to your place, I only watch your cheesy romance movies because I want to spend time with you. I would watch static if it meant I could spend the evening with my arm around you. Six, I know you wanted to kiss me at Emma's wedding. The signs were there, but I assumed it was a lapse in judgment after sensory overload. I should've been selfish and let you. So many times I wanted you and every time I told myself there was no way in hell you'd want me back."

I wrap my arms around his neck and kiss him. He has no clue I wanted him just as much. Both of us wasted years pining after someone we thought we couldn't have.

I intend to make damn sure he knows just how much I wanted this.

When we break apart, he asks, "Should I keep going?" I nod. "I know you don't want me talking about how we're technically married, but mark my words, when you're ready, I intend to get down on one knee and do it the right way. You deserve a wedding with our friends and family there. When I told you there will only ever be you for the rest of my life, I meant it."

"Have you been reading books on my ereader or listening to my audiobooks? Ethan let it slip that he told you about the leaning and whatnot. How much do you know?" I eye him suspiciously but can't hold in my laughter.

"I guess that would be number eight. Yes, I've read romance books. I used to read them a little here and there when Emma would need a male perspective on a manuscript, but I knew after talking to Ethan that I'd need to pull out all the stops if I wanted to keep you. I wrote down a few of the titles from your bookshelf and read them." In a swift motion, he bends to lift me, and tosses me over his shoulder.

"Jason, put me down! I weigh too much for this! I'll break your back."

He throws me onto the bed as if I weigh nothing. "You better not be talking negatively about that beautiful body of yours. I'll let it slide this once, but never again." Caging me in, he closes the distance and trails kisses down my neck. "I'm in love with every inch of you. But since you decided to swap out your own pleasure for confessions, I'll worship you another day."

"You're such a tease." I swat at his chest. His beard tickles as he makes his way back up my neck to my lips. His kisses aren't full of fire, they're soft and gentle. It's... *Shit, he's trying to make love to my mouth, isn't he?*

"Not a tease, but I admit, I get off on the idea of controlling how and when you come."

Something about that statement feels familiar, but I can't place it. "Since I'm being rejected, can I force you to watch a movie you hate?"

"Only if you let me hold you all night."

27

JASON

After fighting how I feel about Charlotte for years, one would think it's easier when I don't have to hide how much I want her. It's worse. So much worse. Traveling the last few years never felt like this when I had to leave her. I dropped her off at the airport a few days ago and, no matter how much we talk, it feels like a piece of me is missing.

I'm sure my new therapist will have a field day with this one…

Opening up my video chat link, he greets me and the first question is harder than I thought it would be. "So, how are we feeling today? On a scale of one to ten, ten being the best day of your life, one being the worst."

"Can I answer based on different parts of my life?" I wince. "It's too complicated."

He nods. "Of course."

"Well, work would be an eight. Personal life…" I blow out a deep breath. "Four."

"What happened in the last week to prompt this?"

I recount the dinner with my boys, glazed over Charlotte and I on the field, but I'm honest about how I feel right now as I tell him, "I've always given her whatever she wants, without a second thought."

He writes something in his notebook. "Can you tell me a little more about how you met?"

"I was always drawn to her, even while I was married. Charlotte was away at college, then landed a job in New York, so I never had to see her. But when I did… Fuck, I promise I never cheated on Emma; I never would have hurt her that way. Em's an incredible woman, but something about Charlotte always pulled me to her. When she moved back, I was divorced, but it felt wrong to think about her that way. It got worse when she moved next door and her infectious joy was hard to avoid. Over the years, we became"—I can't help my smile—"best friends. We did everything together. I fucked everything up, not on purpose. I told you last time about how we ended up married." I pause and sigh. "There's something I have always felt when I'm with her, I can't explain it. I would rather be just her friend, than not have her in my life."

"So, why is your personal life a four?"

It hits me. "It's one-sided." He nods for me to expand on it. "She told me she loves me and the sex is, *well,* amazing. It's just… It fucking sucks that she doesn't want to stay married while I can't imagine ever being with anyone else."

"Let's put Charlotte aside for a moment, as if she never existed. What is your relationship process when you start dating someone new?"

I rub my cheek, realizing my beard is thicker than usual as I try to come up with an honest answer; I can't imagine my life without Charlotte and dating hasn't been on my mind since I was in my twenties. "I guess I would take someone out, eventually things would progress into more. If it worked out, we would get married." Shrugging, I add, "I don't know. It's been so long since I've been with anyone else or had to think about anything like that. Emma was my last serious relationship."

"Have you followed that same process with Charlotte?"

"No," I admit, mostly to myself. I meet his eyes through the computer screen. "That's why I'm *trying* to take a step back. I really thought I'd be able to keep it in my pants with her but all it takes is her giving me her bright smile or feeling her in my arms and I'm fucking done. I can't even smell anything coconut without thinking of her. This can't be normal…"

"Normal doesn't exist," he insists matter-of-factly. "If you took everything physical out of the equation, what's left?"

"I've been under her spell for so long, where do I start? She's so fucking smart, loves her job, loves her family— *my family*—with her whole heart. I love that she thinks about things I never would have thought of. Her autism and ADHD aren't a disability, they make her who she is and I wouldn't change a single thing about it. Sure, the sensory overload sucks, but her mind is so damn beautiful that I would hold her through any meltdown if it meant I still get to hear her tell me how excited she is about a new theme park ride she researched or sing songs off-key from Taylor Swift's newest album. I feel more connected to her than anyone I've ever known. Even my kids. I know that's a fucked up thing to say, but Charlotte and I are... I don't know."

"This isn't your first time in therapy. What do you think the answer is?"

I have to say no to the woman I love.

"I don't like the answer, Doc."

He laughs. "Take this week to reflect on it. When we talk next, let's talk more about how we establish boundaries and work through how you can support her diagnoses and your family. My priority is to give you the tools to navigate your unique situation. Same time next week?" I nod. "Relationships are two-sided. You should give as much as you get, especially with the age difference. But always keep in mind that she is neurodivergent and may not be on the same page. We need to work at being in the same chapter."

The last week without Charlotte has been absolute torture. I had one more session with my therapist; we discussed how I need to take a step back and let Charlotte process everything on her own terms. In my mind, I'm married. She's my forever. My wife. Do I need to work on myself? Absolutely. But when she comes to LA, I'm going to take the opportunity to enjoy time with her. I need to get serious about dating her and showing her she can trust me… trust *us*.

On Sundays, I'm used to Charlotte parading around her kitchen in sweatpants and an oversized tee, singing along to a Taylor Swift album while she makes waffles. It's become a ritual and, on days when I have the boys, they always look forward to her insistence that breakfast is essential on Sundays. They always join in and prefer time with her over me, most of the time. They'll miss Sunday time with Charlotte more than I do.

I'm surprised to see Char texting a picture of Aiden singing into a wooden spoon, another of Noah singing and dancing on a chair, and one of Charlie at the kitchen counter with his nose in a book.

CHARLOTTE

Miss you xoxo

Instead of texting back, I video call her. Aiden answers. "Hey Dad! What time is your game? We don't want to miss it but Aunt Char is taking us to the zoo."

"I already told you, it's this afternoon," Charlotte shouts from the other side of the room while Noah is singing "Shake It Off" by Taylor Swift at the top of his lungs.

"She's right," I remind him. "It doesn't start until four. Hey, can I talk to Char really quick?"

He hands the phone to her. She's joining Noah in his sing-along but stops once she sees me. "Hey, Jay. Ready for this afternoon?" She props the phone up against the backsplash as she makes their waffles.

"Yeah, the guys are looking good. Garcia needs to work on his pace from second to third, but it's going to be great."

"Well, you better win… Oh, hold on. Gotta pull these." She removes a few waffles from the iron and hands them to Charlie, who asks her something. Her head hangs back in laughter and she wraps him in a tight hug. "Yeah, go for it," she tells him, then her smile is back on me. "Okay, sorry, I'm here."

"He's not giving you trouble, is he?"

Charlotte glances behind her to ensure he is out of earshot. "No, Charlie just wants to listen to an audio-book." She pauses to give me a knowing look, "Not *that* kind of book. They requested a repeat of a middle-grade fantasy book earlier."

I suddenly realize Emma and Dylan aren't there. I trust her with my boys, but this isn't my weekend. "The boys are with you today?"

"Oh, sorry." She winces. "Noah asked Emma if he could come by for waffles. You don't mind, do you? I'm going to take them to the zoo for an hour so Aiden can get his sloth fix and then come back here, since the twins have book reports due tomorrow. Emma and Dylan asked. I'm sorry I didn't tell you!"

Fuck. If I wasn't already madly in love with this woman, she goes and does something like this…

Charlotte checks behind her for the boys and hollers, "Pajama party ends in ten, boys!" When she returns to the phone, she lowers her voice, "I've gotta go, sorry. We'll be watching, so you better win."

"Oh, we will, babygirl. Love you."

She blushes and glances around to make sure only I can hear her. Biting her lip, she whispers, "I love you, too."

28

JASON

Charlotte's coming to Los Angeles tomorrow morning and we've made plans to meet with a breeder who specializes in service dogs while she's here. I've spent the last couple years protecting her, and always will, but this will be a great step to help her gain the independence she deserves. It'll also give me peace of mind knowing she's always safe.

After the week I've had at the conference, I decide to meet a few of my new coaching buddies down at the hotel bar for a quick beer to let off steam. Jace and Gavin are a few minutes late, so I snag a stool at the bar and order an IPA.

A few sips in, I pull up my text thread with Charlotte.

> I can't wait to see you.

CHARLOTTE
> Me too. What are you up to tonight?

> I'm going to grab a beer with a few of the guys I met, then head to bed. I have to pick up someone special early tomorrow morning.

Going out tonight? Don't get roofied! 😉

> I won't. Don't worry, sweetheart. I don't think anyone would come within a hundred yards of us. Jace is a beast.

What are you up to tonight?

I'm also grabbing a drink.

Shit. I straighten, alarm bells ringing in my head.

With the girls?

Currently I'm solo. I'm a big girl, Jay! I can handle a drink by myself.

Are you at Keith's or O'Malley's?

No.

No? What the fuck? I blow out a deep breath and rub my hand down my face. I need to play it cool, and I'm feeling anything but. Char's out alone drinking by herself and it's not somewhere Ethan or Edmund know the owner. My heart rate quickens. I trust Charlotte. I don't trust the assholes who will absolutely hit on my gorgeous wife with me not there.

Before I can reply, another text comes in with a picture of her. My breath fucking catches and it takes a few seconds before I exhale. She's wearing her hair up, with bright red lips, and is sipping a martini. *Fuck, she's so beautiful.* It looks like a sports bar in the background, but I can't really tell. I definitely don't recognize it. Instead of texting back, I call, and she picks up on the first ring.

"Hey, Jay." Her tone is teasing and as much as I adore her sweet voice, I'm on edge.

"You're a little overdressed for a sports bar, don't you think?"

She chuckles, "Yeah, but it's because I have a hot date tonight."

A growl involuntarily leaves my throat. "What did you just say?"

"Yeah, he's super hot."

"What the fuck, Char? I thought… I thought we weren't seeing anyone else." It comes out a little strangled. I can't help it.

"Check your six."

"My what?"

"Turn around, you grumpy lumbersnack."

I swivel in my seat to find the most perfect woman I've ever known sitting alone in one of the booths, sipping her martini as if she didn't just give me a mild heart attack. I hang up and stuff my phone in my back pocket before I make my way over to her, not stopping until I take her face in my hands and kiss the ever loving hell out of her.

"Whoa, this isn't kiss-proof lipstick!"

"You think I fucking care?" I mutter against her lips.

Charlotte pulls back and swipes her thumb across my bottom lip. "I'm kidding. Of course it is. You think I would come here unprepared?"

"What are you doing here?" I slide further into the booth unable to tear my eyes from her.

"I'm here for the conference." She can't hold a straight face and a laugh escapes her.

I brush a soft kiss to her cheek, well aware that my beard will tickle her a little, and trail my lips down to her neck. She giggles and it's music to my ears.

"Fuck, I missed you," I mutter against her soft skin. Charlotte lets out a small whimper; all of the ideas I had about keeping my hands to myself have nearly thrown out the window.

Char clears her throat. "I'll be getting my own room while I'm here."

Cue the record scratch.

I pull back to look at her. "You don't want to stay with me?"

"It's not a matter of want, Jay. In therapy this week, I realized we need to slow things down. Sexually. When I was asked why I enjoy being with you, most of the reasons I came up with were either us being friends or... *you know.*" She chews on her lip.

"That's not why I want you to stay with me." My brows pinch but I quickly school my expression and take a deep breath. She's here a day early for *me.* I should be excited, not upset. "We aren't friends with benefits, Char. If that's how you're feeling about things... Fuck, this is on me. I'm clearly not treating you like my wi— *girlfriend.* What do you say I blow off the guys and we go out tonight?"

"You mean the two guys at the bar smirking at you?"

I glance over my shoulder and find Jace and Gavin quickly turning in their seats. "Yeah, one sec." I get up and head over, clue them in on my wife surprising me, then make my way back to Charlotte. "All right, I'll admit, I didn't plan anything. You surprised me, so what are you in the mood for? Night out or night in?"

I offer my hand to help her out of the booth. As she takes it, she replies, "Don't worry. We already have plans in an hour."

What are you up to, babygirl?

I should be offended. Charlotte signed us up for a cooking class because, and I quote, "*I suck at cooking.*" She's not wrong. Grilling is the extent of my culinary skills and I could learn a thing or two, so I welcome the random but creative date Charlotte planned.

The instructor begins. "Welcome, class. Tonight we are making filet with roasted potatoes and glazed carrots."

Hold on... isn't that what Charlotte ordered on our first real date?

"Char," I whisper, "did you have anything to do with the menu?" A small smirk tugs at her lips as she refuses to meet my gaze. I kiss her neck. "I love you."

"*Shh*, listen. He's about to give us instructions," she laughs, and I direct my attention back to the instructor.

"We'll begin by seasoning the beef and letting it rest. Seasoning will vary person to person. Start with flavors you're familiar with and add them to the small bowl in front of you, then experiment by adding in one or two that match what you're looking for."

Charlotte adds salt, pepper, and rosemary to hers. I add the same, but with a little onion powder and garlic. Once the steaks are seasoned, the instructor asks us to chop the carrots and potatoes. She's meticulous with her cuts, while I don't care what size or shape mine are.

There's an overwhelming warmth in my chest; this is exactly what I've always wanted. I'm so comfortable with Char and can imagine preparing dinner in the off-season, with my boys around the kitchen table finishing homework, and her walking in the door after her last focus group of the day. I want more late night impromptu dates like this, keeping each other on our toes. Maybe it was all part of some master plan? I'm a firm believer that it was always supposed to be the two of us in the end. There's no way in hell I can tell her any of it without her running for the hills. She's not ready, and I need to respect her boundaries.

"You want to know what I was thinking?" Her voice pulls me from my daydream.

"Always."

"When you're back home, can we do a few more of these?"

"Am I that bad of a cook?" I laugh.

She chuckles softly with a shrug. "I mean, you're not a *good* cook." I nudge her with my elbow. "What? I'm serious. This is actually very relaxing. If you're up for it, we should schedule one closer to us."

Even if I hated cooking, I'd do it for her. "We can take a look at the schedule and see what nights I have off, so we don't have to wait for the end of the season."

Charlotte nods slowly as she seasons her vegetables. "I know you're busy, it can't wait."

Fuck that. I'll quit my job before I let her think she's not my priority.

"I'm not waiting for November to take you to a cooking class, Char. We're going to make this work."

Her eyes snap up to me. "Oh, no, I didn't mean it how it came out. Seriously, I'm not worried about timing. This year is super busy for me, too. College is different from the majors, but this is the third season I've seen you through. I'm used to your ridiculous schedule. I'll travel more next year, maybe schedule projects for cities you're playing in so I can use it as a write-off."

She's thinking ahead to next year?

"You'd do that?" Hope blooms in my chest.

Charlotte shrugs as she admits, "If things work out with you and me, we'll both have to make sacrifices. Traveling is one I don't mind making."

The instructor approaches our work table. "How are things going here?"

"So far, so good," she replies with a bright smile.

He nods, but totally checks her out as he walks away. My eyes narrow and I resist the urge to growl, *"She's mine."*

After our prep, we place the vegetables in the broiler and cook our steaks in cast iron skillets. Everything looks and smells amazing, but I can't even enjoy it because this asshole keeps coming over and complimenting my girl. I don't consider myself a jealous man, but it seeps in more and more every time she talks with him.

Great, more things I'll need to talk through with my therapist.

I plate up our food and we walk over to one of the tables to eat. Before I sit, I tell Charlotte I'll be back in a few minutes. While I may have only had one beer earlier, I feel as if my bladder might explode. I avoided going earlier due to the flirty chef. He's absolutely going to take advantage the moment I leave the room. I need to make it quick.

After using the restroom, he's sitting at our table in my seat, and they're laughing about who the fuck knows what. *Called it.* I clear my throat.

Charlotte glances up and bites her lip. "Hey, Jay. You're gonna love the potatoes. They are *amazing.*"

"Of course they are, you made them," he says with a wink.

Are you fucking kidding me?

"Well, thanks for keeping me company, but you're in my husband's seat."

That's right, babygirl, you're mine.

His eyes are wide. "Oh, I didn't realize. My apologies." He stands and scurries off.

I take my seat and dare to ask, "Husband?"

"Don't read into it." Charlotte waves me off. "If you were Melanie, you'd be my wife right now. Oldest trick in the book. How else do you think women fend off men in public?" She takes a bite of her steak and I completely deflate. "*Mmm,* you need to try this, it's so good!"

Charlotte offers me a bite of her steak. I cover her hand with mine to bring it to my mouth. I don't want to let go of it when she pulls away. She's not wrong; hers is perfectly seasoned and cooked. I try mine and it's not half as good. I could definitely use a few more cooking classes.

"So, what were you talking about?" *Okay, so maybe I'm a jealous prick after all.*

"Oh, he promised me *eleven* orgasms later if I went home with him," she replies, pulling her lips into her mouth to stifle a laugh. I nearly choke on my steak and she hands me my water. "Jay, I was kidding! Please don't die!" She's cracking up while I take a few long gulps. "I'm sorry. I thought it was funny."

Once I compose myself, I lean in beside her ear and whisper, "You're mine, babygirl. Joke about that again and I will lay you down on this table, in front of everyone, and feast on that delicious cunt of yours until you come *twelve* times... Or until you black out. Whichever happens first." She swallows hard and I pull back.

"I... um... Are you ready to go?"

I glance down at my plate and back at her. "Only if we can grab something to eat later. I fucked up my steak and it's not entirely edible... Oh, and you're staying with me tonight."

"Yes to getting an alternative dinner. No to staying with you." She's so sure of herself and I both love and hate it. As much as I'd love to sink myself into her, more than that, I want her with me.

"If I promise to not touch you, will you stay with me?" I offer.

"That's the problem. You can't make a promise I don't want you to keep."

"What do you want, Char?"

"You," she breathes.

"Stay the night with me." I tilt her chin to meet my gaze. I know she'll likely look away if she's uncomfortable, but she doesn't. "I want to fall asleep next to you and wake up with you in my arms. Can I have that? But never joke about another man touching you."

She scoffs playfully. "Or what?"

"Or I can guarantee I'll do more than just sleep next to you. That's not a challenge, sweetheart."

"Okay, I promise I'll be a good girl and not talk about other men flirting with me, *Sir*."

"*Charlotte…*" I warn. "You keep it up with that smart mouth of yours, and you won't be riding roller coasters tomorrow, you'll be riding my cock, instead. Over and over until you can't walk for a week."

"Good thing I already booked my own room tonight. No chance of a sleepover."

"You didn't."

"Oh, I absolutely did. Don't worry, Jay. It's next door to yours."

29

CHARLOTTE

I tap my key card against the hotel door lock and open it after the satisfying click. Stepping inside, I open the door wider and gesture for Jason to come in. He doesn't budge, leaning against the frame, arms crossed over his chest.

"You really did get the room next to mine." He shakes his head, chuckling to himself. "What are you playing at, Char?"

Admittedly, I thought it was the safer option. I need to spend time with Jason when he's not between my legs, but I also selfishly wanted to see him first thing in the morning. I kick off my shoes and suggest, "Go to your room really quick."

Jason frowns, pausing for a moment, then pushes off the doorframe to stalk off to his room. As soon as I hear the door close, I open the adjoining one and knock on his. He opens it and uses the doorstop to prop it open.

I toss his white and black buffalo plaid pants at him that I packed. "Get changed and order room service."

"Really?" he laughs as he catches them.

"I'm going hop in the shower." Pivoting away from him, I glance over my shoulder. "Can you unzip me?" The dress I wore makes me look fucking amazing, but I'm done looking cute for the night.

He slowly unzips it, grazing my spine. The simple touch lights me up; this whole "not having sex" thing is going to be harder than I thought. When he reaches my lower back, he presses a gentle but firm kiss where my neck and shoulder meet. I can't help whimpering, desperately wanting more.

"All set," he whispers against my skin. His warm breath sends shivers down my limbs.

Turning to face him, my hands find his chest, and I lift onto my toes to kiss him, leaving an inch for him to close the distance. Jason slides his hand into my hair and tugs gently, bringing his face to the side of mine, his beard scratching my cheek as he growls, "Go shower, sweetheart."

I pull back, disappointed. "I'd ask you to join me, but…"

"But, what? You think I can't control myself? I can shower with a beautiful woman and not have sex with her."

"Are you taking a lot of showers with beautiful women?" I tease, but in truth, the idea of him with another woman hurts too much.

Jason finally kisses me and I fucking melt against his soft lips. "Only you, babygirl."

"You never say no to me," I mutter between kisses. "If I asked you to touch me, you would. I'm trying really hard to work on boundaries, but damn it... this is hard."

Jason pulls back and takes my hand, leading me into the bathroom. "You're right." He slips my dress off my shoulders and it slides down my body until it hits the floor. In an instant, he's kneeling before me, kissing my bare stomach. "I never say no to you." I use his shoulders for balance as I step the rest of the way out of the dress and kick it to the side. "But let this be a test. I'm going to shower with you, but everything below the waist is off-limits." He stands, removes his shirt and unbuckles his belt. "Do we have a deal?"

I swallow thickly, unable to tear my eyes away from his firm chest. "Yes."

His pants drop to the ground with a thud, and he removes his boxer briefs. Fuck, he's already hard. *Because of course he is.* This test is officially worse than taking the GMAT.

"Eyes up here, Charlotte." There's something about how he says my full name that does something to me. He turns on the shower, checking the temperature until it's extra hot—just how I like it. I step inside and my whole body is buzzing.

Jason joins me, and this has to be the worst idea he's ever come up with. He props himself with one hand against the wall behind me and I feel a little caged in. It causes my fight or flight response to kick in, and my heart rate and breathing are erratic. This isn't like when he prowls toward me on the bed; he's towering over me.

"Stop," I whisper.

He steps back immediately. "I'm so sorry. What's wrong?"

"It's not you." I close the distance, stepping toward him. Turning us so my back isn't against the shower wall, I have more space to take a deep breath. "I was feeling a little like prey for a moment there."

"It doesn't help that you're so small," he admits with a chuckle.

"Small? Um, newsflash! I'm not that short, and size fourteen isn't small, Jay. You're just a mountain made of muscle."

Jason frowns. "You're small if I say you're small, sweetheart."

"Whatever." I roll my eyes and cross my arms over my middle, feeling incredibly self-conscious.

He gently removes my arms, kissing the inside of one of my palms. "Don't you dare try to hide your beautiful body away from me again, understood?" I nod, speechless. "I love you, every single inch of you." He swipes his thumb across my bottom lip then kisses me. It's sweet and affirming, but also causes an undeniable heat to pool in my belly.

"We should get cleaned up," I suggest. "I'm sure you're starving since you didn't have dinner."

Jason chuckles and pulls me closer. "I'm starving, all right."

I swat at his chest. "Come on. I'm being serious."

"And I'm not?" There's so much fire in his eyes—his pupils are dilated and I feel like prey all over again. Except this time, I don't want to run. He leans in and presses a soft kiss to my neck, then nips at my earlobe. "I know you're not on the menu right now. It doesn't change the fact that I'd love nothing more than to spend the next few hours tasting and teasing you until you can't take it anymore… And only when I let you, would you come for me."

"You can't say stuff like that." My breath hitches. "I'm really trying here…"

Without another word, he grabs one of the washcloths and lathers it with soap. As he drags it up and down each of my arms with firm pressure, I relax against his touch. I can't help my heart beating faster as he begins washing my chest.

"Jay, I can wash myself," I laugh.

"Oh, I know. But this is the closest I'm going to get to touching you tonight, so I intend to take full advantage."

He moves up to my shoulder, then down my arm. When he reaches my hand, I snatch the washcloth from him and toss it to the ground. "If you want to touch me, then touch me."

"Be careful what you ask for, Charlotte. I promised above the waist, but that doesn't mean I won't have you aching for me to make you come." His thumb grazes one of my already pebbled nipples, causing me to gasp. "Is that what you want?"

"You and I both know you can't say no to me. So… I leave it to you. I won't ask for anything."

A growl rumbles in his chest. Wandering his hand lower until he rests it above where I desperately want him, he insists, "I'm going to touch you everywhere but…" He lowers his hand slightly, swiping his knuckle over my clit. "Here." I suck in a breath. "Think you can handle it?"

"Probably not," I answer honestly.

"Good."

"Good? What you're proposing is literally the opposite of good. You want me on my knees, begging to come. That doesn't sound like a fun time to me, sounds a lot like…" My voice trails off as I think back to a few books Ethan recommended a while ago, where the guy controls her orgasms and gets off on it.

Oh, fuck. Is that what this is? Is Jason some kind of… no. But, maybe?

"Char?" My eyes snap to his. "Are you okay?"

"Yes, sorry."

"Hey, why are you apologizing? We don't have to do this. Come here." He wraps me in a tight hug, kissing the top of my head as he whispers into my hair, "I'm sorry. I took things too far."

I glance up at him and insist, "No, it's not that. I was just thinking about something and kind of zoned out. I'm okay, I promise."

"What do you mean? What were you thinking about?"

"I'd rather not say. I need to talk to Ethan about it when I see him next."

Jason's jaw tics. "And I'd rather you not talk about another man while I'm naked with you. Though, I suppose I'm glad it's not that chef guy from earlier."

"Sure, he was friendly, but why would you bring him up?"

"He was checking you out from the moment we walked in," he laughs.

I shake my head. "No, he wasn't. But even if he did, I have a growly boyfriend to ward off any sexy strangers." I look down to my hands, rubbing my fingers together. "I'm getting pruney." He nods and I grab a fresh wash-cloth to quickly wash the rest of my body; my hair can wait. "And I need to get far away from your magical cock... *Shit.* I said that out loud, didn't I?"

He tilts my chin, pressing a chaste kiss to my lips. I sigh on contact. "Yeah, babygirl. You did."

Feeling as if I'm becoming more wrinkled by the second, I work quickly. Once dried off, I wrap myself in a fluffy robe and put distance between us before I do the one thing I promised myself I wouldn't.

It's short lived when Jason comes up behind me, wrapping his arms around my middle and kisses my neck. "Call Ethan," he insists. "I'll give you privacy. I don't want you worried about whatever it was that had you dissociating while I touched you."

"Shit, I'm so sorry. I really wasn't—"

"Shh, I'm not upset. I just don't want you thinking about it all day tomorrow and ruining your churros and roller coasters."

I nod and he presses a kiss to my temple before heading into his room. My mind's jumping from one thing to another, like a trailer for a movie.

"No honorifics."

"It turns me on to have full control over how and when you come."

"How have you not figured out that I get off on your pleasure?"

I pull out my phone to call Ethan, grateful he picks up on the third ring. "Hey, doll. Everything okay?"

I blow out a long breath. "Yes… no… Wait, why wouldn't it be okay?"

"We are texters, you never call."

"Shit, you're right. Sorry to worry you. So, remember that book you recommended to me? The one where the guy gets off on controlling orgasms?"

"Ah… So, Jason *is* a bit of a pleasure Dom," Ethan snickers.

"No! I mean… I don't know? That's why I'm calling you." I begin pacing. "I didn't sign up for a BDSM boyfriend, Ethan."

"Husband," he corrects.

"*Ugh*, thanks for reminding me. What the fuck? Is that what he's into? I'm not a sub, could never be a sub, will never be a sub. What should I do?"

Ethan chuckles. "Well, I had my suspicions that he might be kind of into it. I thought it might be more discrete to send you smutty book recs than to outright tell you. But, I doubt he's looking for that kind of relationship, it's probably more of a kink than a lifestyle choice. There's one way to find out though…"

30

CHARLOTTE

Last night, after my call with Ethan, I stayed with Jason in his room—clothes on. We had dinner in bed; he ordered a burger that was room temperature for himself and an ice cream sundae for me. Unfortunately, mine was more of a milkshake by the time it arrived, but I still appreciate that he got my favorite. No matter how curious I am about what he may or may not be into, I can't bring myself to ask. Still, I want to be close to him. Wrapped in each other's arms before falling asleep, he insisted nothing would happen and was a man of his word.

Waking up to the sun peeking through the curtains, we get dressed and grab a quick continental breakfast downstairs before heading to the park. It's early, but I love being at amusement parks when the rope drops with all of the diehard fans. It's about an hour from the hotel and Jason lets me blast my pop playlist the whole ride with no argument. Then again, he never argues with me, or picks the music… He always lets me have whatever I want. I love and hate it, but after speaking with my therapist I'm not enjoying his amenability as much as I normally do.

Jason interlaces his fingers with mine, keeping our joined hands remain in my lap for the drive. Two songs in, I turn the volume down. I scroll my playlist options, and ask, "What music do you want to listen to?"

"That was fine, you can keep it on."

I roll my eyes. "That's not what I asked. What do *you* want to listen to?"

Jason kisses my knuckles. "I don't care either way, sweetheart."

Why is he being so difficult?

"If I wasn't in the car, what would be on the radio?" I let go of his hand and reach for the radio settings. It'll be static since we're so far from home but it'll give me an idea if I recognize a station.

"Whoa, what do you think you're doing?" His hand covers the buttons. "Never touch a man's radio, Char."

"Well, you're not giving me answers," I chuckle. "Desperate times call for desperate measures."

He lets out a sigh and asks his hands-free system, "Play nineties rock." Rage Against the Machine's "Guerrilla Radio" begins and I can't hide my smile.

How has he hidden this from me for over two years?

As I sing along, it occurs to me that I don't remember the last time we did anything he suggested. He always asks what I want and I get my way. I turn it up, enjoying the drums and bass vibrating the seat and it's almost as if I can feel the beat in my chest. When the song ends, I can't help asking, "When were you going to tell me?"

"Tell you what?" His eyes on the road, I still spot a crinkle in the corner of one as he hides his smile.

Just as I'm about to answer him, "Sabotage" by The Beastie Boys comes on and excitement bubbles up inside me. I used to listen to The Beastie Boys in my early twenties when I lived in New York with Eddie. It brings back so many amazing memories of our late night coffee chats and sharing earbuds on our walk to a midday Broadway show.

Dancing in my seat, I lean in and press a kiss to Jason's cheek and whisper, "I thought we weren't keeping secrets." He begins to pull off the freeway. "Jay, what are you doing? We're barely five miles from our exit." My shoulders slump and I grumble, "*Fine...* Go find a coffee shop we can park at."

Jason chuckles but says nothing until we're parked. He takes his phone, presses a few buttons, and puts it back in the cup holder. "I never say no."

"Yes, we've established that."

He shakes his head. "That's why it's *technically* a secret. Every time we're in the car, I let you pick the music because I know it makes you happy and it doesn't make me unhappy, so why would I tell you no?"

It stings at first, but for so long I selfishly enjoyed him letting me always get what I want. "Do you want to go today? Be honest. Are we going to an amusement park solely because I want to?"

"Yes and no… I don't mind them, but I know how excited you get and we rarely get to go."

"I wanted to do rope drop to fireworks." I chew on my lip. "But that's not fair to you."

He surprises me by gently gripping the front of my neck and bringing me in to kiss him. It's sexy and possessive; it makes me want to do all sorts of sexy things in a coffee shop parking lot.

No, stop it. We're not having sex.

When we break apart, he says softly, "We are doing rope drop to fireworks today. All I want is for you to be in the stands tomorrow afternoon, wearing my old number like last time, and cheering on my boys while they bring home another win… No dugout sex required."

My hands cover my face. "I still can't believe we did that."

Jason pulls them away. "It was hot as fuck, Char. I'll admit, I've thought about it quite a few times while fisting my cock, wishing it was you riding me instead."

"Good thing you have your own room. I'm not sure the other coaches would appreciate you moaning my name every night."

"It's not *every* night." He huffs a small laugh and I quirk an eyebrow. As he kisses me again, he speaks against my lips, "Okay, *nearly* every night."

I sit back to confirm, "Me being at the game is really all you want? If we could go do *anything*, that's your big amazing ask?"

Jason blows out a long breath. "Charlotte, I'm not going to have this conversation with you."

My brows pinch. "Why not? You're the one who pulled over."

"I want *you*," he rushes out, adjusting his hair. I still at his words. "*Fuck*. Sorry, it's just... I don't care if we go to a concert, a cooking class, an amusement park, or sit on the couch doing absolutely nothing. I enjoy spending time with you, whatever that looks like. And I sure as fuck don't want it to end when the clock strikes midnight on New Year's Eve. I know we're not supposed to talk about this because it might scare you off but I'm not getting any younger, Char. I know what I want. I want you. I don't want to get divorced; I want to spend the rest of my life with you. So... if my girl wants to ride roller coasters and eat so much fried food that we both feel sick, then that's what we're doing, because all I want is to spend the day with you."

How is anyone supposed to respond to that? I have no words. But damn, now I'm craving theme park food.

"Um." I swallow hard. "So, what I'm hearing is that I need to prepare for you and me. I'm..." I chuckle to myself and sigh. "I love you, Jason. I know this. You know this. All of what you said is incredibly sweet, but... I'm a *little* stuck on the food thing. It's 'Shark Week,' so that fried food you mentioned? It sounds *amazing* right now." I pause. "I do love you, and I'm sorry. Did I ruin your beautiful declaration? I feel like I did."

Jason shakes his head with a hearty laugh. "I told you. If my girl wants churros, coasters, and pretzels shaped like cartoon characters, that's what she gets. But are you feeling okay? Please don't suffer through anything if you aren't feeling up to going. We can always go another time."

"Could you be any more perfect? You really are a damn book boyfriend." He chuckles and I take a deep breath. "I'm high on ibuprofen for my cramps, so I should be fine." I chew on my lip. "I don't want to get divorced, Jay. I just want to get married the right way, not forced into it, you know? This was an accident. I want to be your wife on purpose, if it comes to that."

"I know, babygirl. None of this was fair to you. You deserve so much better than a wedding you can't remember. I promise we're going to do this properly. Let's grab a coffee, then get back on the road; parking can be a nightmare there. We're still early so you won't miss the infamous rope drop... and you better believe we're staying for fireworks."

"We don't have——"

"No. We will stay as long as you want. If you want to go back to the hotel to relax halfway through the day, and go back to the park later tonight, then that's fine too."

"Okay." I nod, and my heart swells. How did I get so lucky to call this sweet man mine? "I've got the coffee. Do you want your usual?"

"I ordered it on my app as we pulled in. You're not the only one who can multitask, sweetheart." He leans in to kiss me. "We have maybe two minutes before our drinks are ready."

"Then you better not stop kissing me for two full minutes."

31

JASON

I purchased our tickets ahead of time so we wouldn't have to worry about an additional line when we arrive. While waiting at the main gate for our tickets to be scanned, Charlotte befriended a woman in line behind us. She seems nice, but there's something a little odd about her. I just can't put my finger on it. Her name being Apple doesn't help matters; it has to be a stage name or something.

"Okay, full disclosure, I was totally going to see if you wanted to buy tickets off me, but you're just way too much fun to talk to." Apple lowers her voice to just above a whisper. "Trying my hand at ticket scalping. I kinda suck at it."

I interrupt and turn Charlotte away from her. "All right, it was nice to meet you."

"Don't mind him, Apple." Charlotte slips out of my grip

with a beaming smile. "Come find us in the park later and we'll ride something together."

As soon as we are out of earshot, I whisper, "Char, be careful with that one."

She frowns. "She literally told me she sucks at scamming people. Who discloses that unless they have a good heart underneath it all? I'm pretty sure she's also neurospicy, or just a really cool person who is somehow stuck selling passes for a job. Don't be so judgmental."

"She did sort of give herself away, didn't she?" I chuckle. "You're right." I need to stop trying to swoop in and save Charlotte at every opportunity; she can handle herself.

We pass by the first concession cart and she jumps in line, beaming. "Do you mind if I grab a churro really quick?"

"There's no schedule, sweetheart." When we get to the front of the line, she tries to pay, but I steal her credit card away from her before she can hand it over. "Absolutely not." I hand the cashier my own card and put Char's in my wallet. "You're not paying for anything today. You can have your card back later tonight."

She narrows her eyes. "What if we get separated?"

"Then you call me."

The man hands her a churro and she continues her ridiculous line of questioning. "What if I lose my phone?"

"That thing is glued to your hand; there's no way you'll lose it. Just be lucky I didn't toss your phone or wallet into a marina like Dylan did to Emma a few years ago."

Charlotte lets out a hearty laugh. "I totally forgot about that. I still can't believe he did it." She shakes her head, still chuckling to herself. As she takes a bite of her churro, she moans, "I forgot how good these are. Want a bite?" She offers it to me and I indulge her. "Good, right? Can't beat the ones you get at amusement parks. Okay, so what do we want to ride first?"

I pull out my phone and check the app to see what the wait times look like. "The lines will be getting long soon. What's the longest you want to wait?"

"I can probably handle up to thirty minutes. The new antidepressant I'm on has helped a lot with my anxiety spiking when I have to wait for things, but I don't want to risk feeling claustrophobic surrounded by strangers for an hour."

When I come to places like this with Aiden, we usually get a disability pass so Aiden can wait the same amount of time as the queue, without having to stand in the line itself. It's helpful for when he wants to ride the big coasters with long waits, getting to have a magical experience like everyone else. Being proactive with his sensory meltdowns in a busy amusement park is a must.

I take her hand and tilt my head to gesture toward the customer service area. "Come on. I've got an idea."

We speak with one of the representatives, who asks Charlotte questions about why she struggles with waiting in line. They don't ask for her diagnosis but she's able to describe why it's hard for her to be in lines that are longer than half an hour. They give her a pass that we link to the app on my phone, so now we can ride anything she wants and not have to worry about a potential anxiety or sensory meltdowns.

"I don't want to use it for all the rides, just the ones that have longer waits. I like to have the full experience. Is that okay?"

I lean in to press a chaste kiss to her lips. "Whatever you need. I just want to be sure you have a good time."

After a few rides, a pretzel, popcorn, and walking what feels like a hundred miles, we're waiting for the return time of our next ride. There's a quiet area tucked between kid rides and the space-themed area that overlooks a pond, and we're enjoying a break from the crowds. I've actually had a great time today. Coming here without kids is a completely different experience. No one is arguing about what we're having for lunch, or complaining about the wait of a ride. I need to plan more trips like this, just the two of us.

A woman and her two children approach us. "I'm sorry to bother you, but are you Jason Kelly?"

"Yes, ma'am."

One of the boys' eyes lights up. "See, I told you, Mom! He's the new third base coach. He used to play for them, you know? Mr. Kelly, could I have your autograph?"

"Oh, um…"

"He'd love to," Charlotte answers for me.

The mother fishes in her purse for a pen and hands it to me. I admit sheepishly, "Sorry, I never get asked for autographs. Who should I make it out to?"

"Jordan, please." I nod and sign my name in his character autograph book. "Wow, thanks Mr. Kelly. We'll see you at the game tomorrow!" They turn to leave and the mom mouths "thank you" to me.

"Look at you, Mr. Famous Third Base Coach."

I sigh. "It's fucking weird, isn't it?"

"I mean, a little," she replies with a sweet smile and a shrug.

My phone alerts me that it's our turn to ride the next one. "Ready to head over?"

Charlotte shakes her head. "It's nice and quiet here. Can we stay a little longer?"

"Of course." I wrap my arm around her shoulder and she snuggles closer into me. In no world would I ever be able to live without this woman.

A few hours later, the cloud cover has burned off and now it's a scorching one-hundred degrees. For LA, that's normal, but neither one of us are used to it.

"Would it be okay if we go to the hotel and jump in the pool?" Charlotte asks, fanning her face. "I'm melting."

I let out a sigh of relief. "If you weren't going to ask, I was going to suggest it. I think I sweated out every ounce of water I consumed today."

We leave and head to the hotel, and thankfully it's within a short walking distance. I booked a room here, just in case she needed a break in the middle of the day. Turns out, I needed it just as much. I change into swim trunks and she puts on a black one-piece. It's low-cut in a V, showing off her incredible tits.

"Eyes up here, Sir," she teases

I didn't realize I was staring and meet her gaze as she ties her hair up. "What did you just say?"

"I said eyes up here." Her eyes twinkle with mischief.

What are you up to, babygirl?

I cock an eyebrow and correct, "I was referring to what you called me."

Charlotte bites her lip to hide her smile and shrugs. "I don't know what you're talking about."

"Right…" I eye her with suspicion as I tie up my hair. I then pull her to me and she sucks in a breath as her chest collides with mine. "You look delicious, by the way."

"My boobs look pretty fucking hot in this, right?" She briefly glances down at her chest. "I mean... *damn.*"

"Your ass looks amazing, too." I playfully smack it and she yelps. "Come on, let's go cool off."

I take her hand and we make our way down to the pool. Of course, every fucking douchebag here is checking out my wife. She's oblivious to the attention she's getting, but I can't help the pointless tinge of jealousy I feel— she's mine, they don't stand a chance.

We secure a couple of chaise lounge chairs next to each other. After a quick dip in the pool, we lay out for a bit, soaking up the warm sun. I read a book on my ereader while she listens to an audiobook and thumbs through a magazine. I keep my hand on her thigh, publicly claiming her in front of the two dozen men who have been ogling her since we arrived.

Charlotte takes out an earbud. "All right, Jay. I get that you want to be an alpha caveman right now because my tits look great, but if I end up with a tan of your hand-print on me, I'm going to be upset."

I chuckle and lean over to kiss her temple. "Don't give me ideas, babygirl." She rolls her eyes and sets down her magazine, covering my hand with hers as she closes her eyes and takes in the rays. "Want to grab an early dinner before heading back into the park?"

Charlotte shrugs, not looking at me when she replies, "Why don't you decide, Sir?"

"Charlotte," I warn.

Her eyes snap to mine. "Yes?"

"What are you doing?"

"Honestly? I'm trying to see how growly I can get you today. Is it working? I wore this super hot swimsuit, but thought I would throw a few 'sirs' in there for good measure."

Unable to help myself, I gently grip her neck and bring her lips to mine. She opens for me and I explore her mouth, not caring who sees. I want her naked right fucking now, but since that won't be happening, tasting her is the next best thing.

When I pull back, her lips are swollen and eyes are wild, just how I like them. "Yeah, it's fucking working," I admit and sit back. She touches her plump lips, still looking over at me, but I don't make eye contact and return to reading my book.

Two can play that game, sweetheart.

32

CHARLOTTE

I hop in the shower after we finish at the pool; the last thing I need is my fresh caramel highlights turning green from the chlorine. As the water pelts my back, I lose myself in thought.

Fuck, I hope Ethan's right and it's just a kink.

"Jay, can you come in here?"

A few moments later, he's outside the shower door. "Everything okay?"

I poke my head out. Jason's only wearing gray sweat-pants and is definitely not wearing underwear. He catches me staring and I quickly look away. "No, yes, um… yeah?"

"What do you need?" His voice comes out like a purr.

"Sorry, I forgot. Nevermind." I close the shower door, but through the frosted glass, his silhouette doesn't move.

Fuck. I turn to wash my face that is undoubtedly crimson.

The door opens and I still, holding my breath. He steps in, but even though the anticipation is killing me, I don't turn around.

We are not having sex in the shower.

We are not having sex in the shower.

We are <u>not</u> having sex in the shower.

I startle when he touches my shoulder. Gliding his hand down, he takes mine, bringing it up to hook behind his neck as he kisses my shoulder.

"What do you need?" he asks again.

My words are stuck in my throat, I manage, "I was just going to ask you something."

Jason splays his hand across my stomach, pulling me flush against him as he peppers soft kisses up my neck. His beard tickles and I try my best to hold in my laughter. Unfortunately, clenching my stomach is making my cramps worse, and I wince.

"Hey, are you okay?" He turns me to face him. "What's wrong?"

"I think my pain meds are wearing off."

"Shit. Char, I'm so sorry. I totally misread this whole thing, didn't I? You needed me to grab your ibuprofen and here I am trying to seduce you in the shower. Fuck, I'm such an asshole. I'll go get them."

He tries to leave, but I grab his arm. "No, it's okay. I was…" While talking to Ethan, he suggested I experiment with taking control. I straighten and try to hold the same command in my voice that Jason does. "On your knees, Jay."

A small smirk tugs at his lip as he brushes the hair off my shoulder, then presses a soft kiss to my neck. "What are you doing, babygirl?" I swallow hard as he pulls me flush against him. "You said you wanted me 'growly,' as you put it earlier. I'm getting mixed signals here, sweetheart."

I have no fucking clue what I'm doing; I'm out of my element. With my eyes closed, I wrap my arms around him and press my forehead to his chest. "I'm supposed to start my period any day now so my cramps are worse than usual, but I'm horny as fuck, and I had this idea that…" I shake my head. "I'm sorry."

Jason embraces me and asks for a third time, "What do you need?" He strokes his fingers up and down my back with a firm enough pressure to soothe me and doesn't tickle.

Option 1: I test Ethan's theory again and determine, once and for all, what's going on with this kink of his; if that's what it even is. If Jason expects me to be his submissive, he won't submit to me.

Option 2: Remain sexually frustrated, but keep my promise to myself to not sex with him while we're here.

"Both options suck."

Jay tilts my chin up and kisses me softly. "What options?"

"I really wanted to take a step back from everything physical with you, but I got this idea in my head and now it's all I can think about."

Frowning, he asks, "What idea? Do you want me on my knees for you?" A sly smirk tugs at his lips as he lowers one leg at a time to the shower floor, and sits back on his heels. "Do you think I can't top you from down here?" He glides his hands up the back of my legs. "If you ask me, this view is pretty great." I quickly turn off the shower and inch backward. He takes his time standing, towering over me again. "You're mine, babygirl." He caresses my cheek and leans in, nipping at my ear as he whispers, "But I won't touch you unless you ask me to."

"I'm not a sub, Jay."

"What?" Jason pulls back, laughing. "Sweetheart, I don't want you to be. I'm not…" He shakes his head. "What's this about?"

I step out of the shower and grab a towel to dry off, keeping it wrapped around me under my arms when I'm done. *I'm a fucking idiot.*

"Char, please talk to me."

"I just thought you might be into something that I'm not and I needed to see for myself."

His jaw tics, eyes narrowed as he finishes drying off. Unlike me, he makes no effort to cover up. "You could have just asked."

"Could you put your sweatpants back on?" I avert my eyes. "You know it's a little distracting talking to you like this when all I want to do is…"

Stepping toward me, he takes my hand, placing it on his chest. "All you want to do is what?"

Finally meeting his gaze, I ask, "What do *you* want?"

"Was that fun for you? Asking me to kneel? Taking control?" I shake my head, chewing on my lip. "Then let's do something that is."

He grabs my bottle of ibuprofen and hands me two with a glass of water. "Take these and finish the glass, sweetheart." I nod. As soon as I'm done, he takes it from me and sets it on the counter. "Let me take care of you before we go to dinner."

"Take care of me?"

"You're cramping; an orgasm can help with that. I'm not just saying that because I want to bury myself inside you; you can look it up. I want you to enjoy the rest of the trip. Sure, I'm selfish, I've missed the taste of you, but I want you relaxed and feeling fucking amazing. *That* is what I want."

"It's just a kink? The whole enjoying me getting off thing? You don't want me to be a submissive?" I ask with a grimace.

"No," he chuckles. "You've read too many books, sweet-heart. Yeah, I get off on making you come, but that's it." I drop the towel and his gaze falls to my bare body. "So, is that a yes?"

"And they say I'm the one who doesn't get hints…"

33

JASON

"Are you sure the tacos in San Diego are better? These are *so* good." Charlotte lets out an adorable moan and my cock twitches at the sound.

I take another bite of my carne asada street taco and nod. "Yeah, those are better but these might be a close second. Nothing beats SoCal tacos."

As much as I wanted to touch her earlier, I couldn't do it. She set a boundary of not wanting to have sex. I pushed it in the shower. It wasn't until I had her naked and ready for me that I couldn't go through with it and had to stop everything. My dick hates me for it. Charlotte probably even hates me for it. Making it up to her with a full back massage and tacos will have to do for now.

"We have about two hours until the fireworks; enough time to grab an ice cream or a drink, and one more ride," I offer. The crowds are going to be a lot for Char.

People begin camping out for a good spot to watch the show nearly four hours before, packed in like sardines. After some research, I discovered there's a spot right outside the park to watch where she can enjoy them without feeling claustrophobic.

"Ooo, I heard there are amazing cocktails at a place in the superhero land up the way. Then, maybe we should ride something mellow. The last thing we need is you tossing your cookies, old man."

"Come here, you have something right... there." I kiss the side of her mouth. "I'm not old. I'm seasoned."

"Seasoned?" Char barks out a laugh, biting her lip as she shakes her head.

We finish our tacos and venture out to grab a drink. She orders their version of a lemon drop, and I get a vanilla stout. She was right; hers is actually pretty damn good. Since most of the lines are beginning to die down, we're able to wait in the traditional queue for one of the rides themed after her favorite cartoons from when she was a kid. The smile hasn't left her face tonight, and I intend to keep it that way.

The fireworks are about to start, so I lead us out of the park and into the esplanade. The woman from this morning is still out here, trying to scalp tickets. I'm about to guide Charlotte away from her, but she spots the woman first.

"Apple! Hi. How's the ticket biz going?"

Really, Char?

"Oh, it could be better. How was your day? Did you two have fun?"

A man approaches her. He's dressed better than Ethan typically is. Maybe he works here? "My star, what are you doing?" he growls. "Tommy's been looking everywhere for you, and don't get me started on Rachel."

"Gio, these are my new friends. Charlotte and… I'm sorry, didn't catch your name. Damn girl, if I wasn't married… *oof*."

This is officially too much for me. "We really should get going," I offer and begin leading Charlotte away. "It was nice to meet you, Apple."

"Night," she says with a wave unfazed.

Thankfully, Charlotte takes my hand and we walk away from what has to be some kind of mob or cartel couple. Who shows up to an amusement park in a suit?

"She was sweet," Char sighs. "Too bad I didn't get her social media handles."

Bang! The first firework goes off, lighting up the night sky. Charlotte covers her ears, and I stand behind her to cover them for her. We do this every Fourth of July; it's second nature for me.

"They're so beautiful," she squeals.

"Not as beautiful as you, babygirl."

Char removes my hands from her ears, and wraps them around her middle. I rest my chin on the top of her head, letting out a contented sigh. We must be far enough away that the sound doesn't bother her. I don't question it, wanting to stay present in the moment. We only have tomorrow before I'm back on the road for another week—every minute counts.

As soon as the firework show is over, she turns in my arms, her wide smile still tilting her lips. "Thank you for today. I know you don't love amusement parks as much as I do, so it means a lot to me."

I kiss her cheek and whisper, "I had a good time. I'm glad you did, too."

We're both exhausted as we make our way back to the hotel. My feet are killing me from walking the equivalent of a half marathon. Once back at the hotel, I take an incredibly quick shower and put on my sweatpants— with underwear this time. She's already asleep in bed when I slide in next to her.

Charlotte turns and snuggles into my side. I wrap my arm around her and pull her close to me. "Night, sweetheart."

"Night... I love you."

My heart swells as warmth spreads through my entire body. "I love you, too."

We have a thirty minute drive to the dog breeder and trainer. She specializes in service and emotional support animals and, based on reviews, is one of the best in the state. If nothing else, we'll walk away with a wealth of information.

"You must be Charlotte and Jason," she greets, shaking our hands. "Welcome. I'm Trina, it's a pleasure to meet you both. Come and have a seat, and let's find out a little more about what you're looking for."

"I... I'm not sure." Charlotte casts her eyes down, fidgeting. I take her hand in mine and she finds her voice again. Glancing back to Trina, she admits, "I want to be safe and not rely on someone else if I have sensory overload."

Trina nods with a kind smile. "I completely understand. Independence is so important. My oldest is nineteen. He's autistic and lives on his own with an emotional support pup. The key is to find out what your greatest needs are for us to pair you with the right animal. Do you have any self-harm or self-injurious behaviors?" Charlotte shakes her head. "Seizures?" Charlotte shakes her head again. "How large of an animal are you looking for?"

"Honestly, I don't know."

"Can you describe your sensory overload for me? Are you able to self-soothe, or do the meltdowns take over?"

Charlotte blows out a long breath, closing her eyes and squeezing my hand tighter as she describes her experiences. "They are infrequent, and I'm proactive to prevent them. When my emotions get too big, the world around me falls away. It feels like I'm in a sound-proof room that is too loud and too quiet at the same time. I can tell when it's coming on, so I usually end up rocking and scripting from some of my favorite songs to self-regulate. I guess what makes sense is having a dog or other animal that can keep me grounded and potentially get help from another person if I need it."

"My service dogs are well trained. I feel like that might be the best option for you, especially if you're living alone." Trina looks to me. "Do you live nearby?"

"I live next door to her." *Maybe I should ask her to move in? No, it's too soon.*

"I might have the perfect one for you. Her name is Besvär, which is Swedish for trouble."

I can't help but laugh. "Trouble?"

Trina chuckles. "Yes, she was fostered by a Swedish family for a year and the name sort of stuck. I hope that isn't a problem." She calls for the Golden Labrador, who comes barreling in. Besvär goes straight to Charlotte, resting her snout on Char's lap. "Well, looks like she has a new friend."

"Oh, Trina, she's beautiful," Charlotte coos. "Can I pet her?"

Trina nods and Charlotte is all too eager to pet the pup. "Besvär is trained to handle all emergencies. If there's anything that requires medical attention, she will find the closest adult and bring them to you. In case of sensory overload, she can sense elevated heart rate and will do her best to keep you safe and grounded."

Charlotte looks at me, biting her lip. "Jay, I know this is only the first place we've been to and the first service dog I've been around but... I feel a connection with her."

"Well, let's test that theory. Do you have any other dogs here we can meet? Just to make sure my wife can see for herself that Besvär is the one?" I ask, intending to rule out the possibility that she's just excited to be around animals.

Char sucks in a breath as Trina eyes me with suspicion. "I'm sorry, I thought you said you were neighbors."

Frowning, I insist, "We are."

"I must have misheard, I thought you said she was your wife." *Fuck, I let that slip.* "One moment." Trina whistles, then calls for another dog, "Daisy!"

Daisy comes in slower than Besvär did. She ignores both Charlotte and myself.

"This is Daisy, she's a Golden Retriever mix and one of the most loyal dogs I've trained."

Charlotte pats her lap for Daisy to come. She does, but there isn't the same enthusiasm Besvär had. I smile, shaking my head. "Well, sweetheart. I think you're right. Trouble is probably meant to come home with you."

Besvär looks up at Charlotte with so much hope. Even if she wasn't a service dog, we would bring her home. "There's a matter of cost. I know Charlotte's insurance doesn't cover all of it. Do you know what the remainder is?"

"Besvär is twenty-two thousand, but her insurance is covering seventy percent, leaving about sixty-six hundred out of pocket."

"Do you take cards?" I offer.

Trina nods as Charlotte fawns over Besvär. With Charlotte distracted, Trina and I settle up. I don't want Char to pay me back for it. If she tried, I would probably just rip up the check or resend her e-payment back to her account. I want to do this for her. She deserves to have the same independence that the rest of us have, and I can rest easier knowing she'll be safe.

34

CHARLOTTE

I'm bringing Besvär with us to the game today. Jason thinks I didn't overhear him paying for her, so I sent $6,600 to his account when he wasn't looking. While I love that he wanted to do this for me, it's important for me to do this on my own.

Jason and I make sure Besvär has the appropriate markings on her harness before we get to the stadium. When we arrive, Jason secures seats to the side of the away team dugout, next to one of the other coaches' wives. He's a bit overprotective, insisting he escort me to my seat. I know he wants me close during the bottom half of the inning, but it still feels a little smothering. I prefer being closer to home plate.

Besvär and I grab a few concessions and, when we return, the seat next to mine is occupied. I sit next to her, and she grins. "Hi, Charlotte? It's so great to finally meet you." She offers her hand and I take it. "I'm Kendra, Todd's wife."

"Nice to meet you."

"And who is this?"

"Oh, this is Besvär, my new service dog."

"She's beautiful," Kendra swoons. She gets settled, placing her beer in the cup holder and shrugging off her sweatshirt. "Less than a week until we're home. I can't wait. Are you staying on the road with us?"

I shake my head. "No, I'll be flying out first thing tomorrow. I have a few projects this week and need to get back home. I'm a market researcher and do various studies in Northern California." *Crap, did I word vomit on her?*

"Like surveys?"

I nod and breathe a sigh of relief. I love my job and know I can get a little excited. Doing my best to not overshare, I explain, "Among other things. I specialize in interviews and focus groups but I have an online survey to knock out later this week."

"That's amazing, I…" Her voice trails off when she spots Jason. "Man, I wish Todd still looked at me like that."

I follow her line of sight. "What do you mean?"

"That," she replies with a knowing chuckle, gesturing to Jason. Meeting his gaze, it's as if the whole stadium melts away. He's talking to another coach by third base but his eyes never leave mine. "That's my husband he's talking to." Her voice pulls me from Jason. "Todd!" she hollers, beckoning him over. Once Jason and Todd make their way to us, she introduces me. "Honey, this is Charlotte and her service dog Besvär. Charlotte, this is my husband, Todd."

"Nice to meet you." I stretch over the divider to shake his hand.

"So, you're the one putting up with this guy? Good luck to ya, he's a handful," Todd laughs as Jason smacks his arm. He then tells Kendra, "Baby, come here." He curls his finger, gesturing for her to lean over the divider. Gliding his hand into her hair, he kisses her like something out of a movie. It's a little embarrassing. Cheeks warm, I look away.

"Charlotte." Jason's deep but soft voice not using his typical pet names catches my attention. My eyes snap to him. "How are you and pup holding up?"

"We're okay," I reply, a little squeakier than normal. "Good luck today; not that you need it."

Jason claps Todd on the shoulder. "Hey, man. Save it for later."

"See you after the game," Todd chuckles as he breaks apart from his wife.

Jason and Todd head into the dugout and I turn to Kendra with a cocked eyebrow. "Doesn't look at you that way, huh?"

She laughs. "He's just showing off. Jason hasn't stopped

telling Todd about how excited he was for you to come today. How did you and Jason meet?"

I begin explaining how we're neighbors and how we met through my sister, purposefully leaving out that she's his ex. It's a little weird and I don't know how much she's already been told.

My phone dings with a text from Jason. "Excuse me. Mind if I…"

She shakes her head and takes out her own phone to busy herself.

> JAY
>
> Thank you for being here today.
>
> > Shouldn't you be focusing on the game? It starts in a few minutes.
>
> I am focused, but I also forgot to tell you today how beautiful you are. Warranted a text.

A blush creeps up my neck.

> Love you, babygirl.
>
> > I love you too.

I can't help my heart skipping a beat when he tells me he loves me. I breathe a sigh of contentment as I pocket the phone. Kendra has an unmistakable smirk. "What?"

"Nothing," she chuckles.

The national anthem starts. The performer is incredible, but it's also very loud. When it's over, I'm thankful Besvär isn't bothered by all the cheers and clapping like I am. She sits between my legs, looking on as if she is watching the game as an actor I don't recognize throws the first pitch.

Once the other team takes the field, everyone begins chanting "*Cha-vez Cha-vez*" for Robbie. He's incredibly popular, even at away games. He steps up to the plate. At the first pitch, he knocks it out to right field in a pop-fly that the outfielder misses by just an inch. It wasn't quite enough for a double, but the crowd cheers like they do when he's at home.

Harriet has been following Robbie since he joined the team and asked if I would get his autograph before I leave. She rattled off statistic after statistic, which I was barely able to keep up with. I have a feeling she has a little crush on him, and I wouldn't blame her. My walls were plastered with hot rockstars and athletes when I was her age. I snap a photo and send it to her after his base hit, along with a message about how the game is going.

The next few innings are pretty uneventful. We're up three to one, so Kendra and I stretch our legs and grab a drink. We find a small sports bar at the top of our section where she orders a vodka soda and I ask for my usual vodka martini with a twist.

"When I get back to San Francisco, we'll have to go out for a proper drink," Kendra insists.

"Do you live in the city?" I ask, sipping my drink.

"No. Todd and I actually just moved to Emeryville; I don't like the hustle and tourist traffic of San Francisco. I work from home, so I'm able to travel with the team during the regular season. It's too much stress during the playoffs, so I stay behind. What about you? I never asked Jason where you were living."

"We're in San Francisco; I'm next door to Jason in a tiny apartment where rent is ridiculous. I should really get a bigger place now that I have Besvär."

Her brows pinch. "Aren't you two married?"

Oh fuck. He told them.

"Yeah, but… um… it's complicated."

She nods and takes a long sip of her vodka soda. This whole thing with Jason is a bit of a mess and I'm grateful that Kendra's now preoccupied with the giant TV in front of us.

Besvär has been such a good girl today. I was worried she might not do well being in a busy stadium on top of being her first day with me. When I get back home, I should look into moving to give her more space—my one bedroom apartment is not going to cut it.

After a drink, we head back to our seats right as the seventh inning stretch begins. Kendra has an incoming text on her phone and excuses herself. I busy myself by singing along to "Take Me Out to the Ballgame" as I keep a hand on Besvär's back. I know it's only our first day together, but she feels like an old soul I've met before.

"Hey, babygirl." Jason startles me, my hand flying to my chest.

"Holy crap! You scared me." I look to Besvär. "A little warning next time?"

He rests his arms on the divider between the field and the stands. "Are you two having fun?"

"We are," I beam and scratch Besvär behind her ears.

"*It's that time everyone…*" Besvär's ears perk up. "*Get ready for the Kiss Cam!*"

I can't help the belly laugh that escapes me. There's a very good chance Jason planned this. If not, it's probably some crazy cosmic sign. *Or planets in retrograde.*

"Really, Jay?" I quirk an eyebrow

He chuckles and carefully reaches to pet Besvär. Our breeder mentioned people shouldn't pet service animals, except for their handler, but assured me that having a second handler is incredibly smart. I want Jason to be that person for her. "They do this every game. But…" He glances behind him, then hops over the divider and sits in Kendra's seat. Without another word, he turns his hat around and kisses me. It's warm, gentle, and I can't help my whimper. Forgetting I'm in public, I open for him and he teases with his tongue, playfully nipping at my lip.

"Looks like our rival third base coach couldn't wait for the cam..."

Shit. I try to break our kiss but he pulls me closer, making me laugh against his lips. When he finally breaks away, he admits, "I didn't plan that, but I don't regret a second of it." He straightens his hat and leans in to whisper, "I'm looking forward to having you all to myself later." He then corrects, "I just want to be able to kiss you however I want, without an audience."

I burst into laughter. "Get back to the dugout. Don't come back until you have original content."

"What are you talking about?"

"Just... ask Dylan." I can't stop laughing. Emma told me about her date with Dylan when they began seeing each other again. They attended a baseball game, just like this one, and he wanted her all to himself, instead of sharing Em with a jumbotron.

My giggles are cut off quickly when Jay slides his hand into my hair and kisses me again. It isn't ballpark appropriate, but I truly don't care.

"I don't give a fuck about Dylan or his wife. I only care about *my wife* right in front of me," he says between kisses. We're supposed to put the brakes on the marriage labels, but I can't bring myself to address it right now. When we break apart he adds, "I don't care where we are. I'll show the whole fucking world I'm yours, baby-girl." He presses a final chaste kiss to my cheek and hops back over the divider.

"Hey! Don't forget, I promised I'd get Robbie's autograph for Harriet."

His eyes narrow, brows pinched. "Don't tell him who it's for."

"Why?"

"Figure it out, sweetheart."

I whisper to Besvär, "Hear that? Trouble is brewing."

"Love you!" Jason yells, grinning ear to ear as he walks away.

"See," I continue whispering to her. "Trouble."

35

CHARLOTTE

While the game was a lot of fun, I crashed afterward. Besvär slept at the foot of the bed, whimpering. I was in a lot of pain and she must've known. I just hope she's not home-sick. Jason kept asking me if I was okay. Since she wouldn't stop bothering him to help me, he knew I was lying when I told him I was fine. I finally admitted my cramps were beyond pain meds and he ran to the store. He returned with hot pads, tampons, chocolate, and my favorite ice cream.

Jason held me all night, keeping the heating pad in place. Every time I woke, he asked if I was doing all right and checked my pain levels. I'm used to his atten-tiveness, but Besvär also checked in as well to make sure I was okay. It's comforting to know she'll be here for me when he isn't.

With Jason finally home from his three weeks away, he insisted that day one we do couples therapy. They were able to squeeze us in for a shorter appointment last minute. While I've been seeing my therapist on my own for a few weeks, I'm still a ball of nerves, unsure what to expect.

"It is so great to finally meet you, Jason," she greets. "Have a seat wherever you're comfortable."

We both sit in the chairs opposite hers. I feel incredibly self-conscious. Do we hold hands? Do we jump right in? What if we start fighting in front of her? I've read books and seen movies with couples therapy, but I have no idea what this will be like in real life.

"As you're aware, Charlotte and I have been meeting. Couples therapy is a little different. I'd like to have a better picture of what your biggest concerns are."

He glances over at me, takes my hand, then looks back to her. "I guess I'll just dive right in. I'm in love with Charlotte, but I've made some *big* mistakes. Ones that I don't know if I'll ever forgive myself for. I'm working through it with my own therapist and want to earn her trust." He goes on to explain how everything happened, all of it I've heard from him before.

"He told everyone we're married," I blurt out. My hand flies to my mouth. It startles Besvär and she rests her snout on my thigh. "Sorry, I didn't mean—"

"She's right. I've told people she's my wife. It's not conscious. For me, it's not just on paper." Jason faces me. "We agreed to not talk about it, but to me, you're my wife in every way that matters."

"Charlotte, does it bother you that he told someone you're his wife?"

I fidget with the hem of my shirt; Besvär paws at my hand. "I know, girl. I know," I whisper to Besvär. I blow out a deep breath and look at Jason, but I can't meet his eyes. "You promised until we do this the right way, I'm not your wife."

"I'll marry you right now, if that's what you want," he huffs, and I hate that he's defensive. I clench my fist, scratching my nails against my palm in response.

"The most romantic proposal of all time," I scoff, rolling my eyes. "Why, yes, I would *love* to marry you. It's every woman's dream to be proposed to during couples therapy." Even though I shouldn't attempt sarcasm right now, I can't help deflecting with humor.

"I'm trying here, sweetheart," he says softly. "I hid my feelings for you for years. I finally have the woman I've always wanted, so yeah, I want to scream it from the rooftops. It may have been an accident, but I'm married to my best friend. Do you know how rare that is? I'm kind of living my best life right now. But, unfortunately, it's not real. It's just a fantasy in my head because I'm terrified I'll be served divorce papers on January 1st."

Forcing myself to sit up straight, I want to stim or dissociate so badly, but I shove the feelings down. He needs answers, even if they hurt him. "I don't want to get divorced, Jay! I'm just not your *wife*. I'm barely your girlfriend. I'm not even going to be your neighbor for much longer."

"What do you mean you're not going to be my neighbor?" Jason growls. "What are you talking about?"

I look to our therapist, who gestures for me to answer. I keep my hand on Besvär; she can sense I'm uncomfortable. Taking several long breaths, I finally reply, "I'm looking at getting a new place; big enough for the two of us."

"You want to move in with me?" he asks, full of hope.

"Oh... I meant Besvär. She needs more space than a one bedroom, so I've been looking at places in Emeryville, where Todd and Kendra live. She mentioned at the game that you can get a decent backyard the further you move away from the city."

Jason covers my hand with his. "When were you going to tell me?"

I should have told him. It honestly slipped my mind because he wasn't here. I made the decision by myself. A combination of pride and guilt surges through me. "I don't know, probably when I found a place," I answer honestly.

"Move in with me."

I shake my head. "Isn't that a little fast?"

"We both travel a lot. It would be exactly how it is now. I have a three-bedroom and my living room is bigger."

"She needs a backyard."

Jason glances down to Besvär, then back to me. "We can buy a place… together." I'm about to counter when he adds, "Not right this minute, but let's look into it. You can even have it all in your name, I just…" He blows out a long breath. "I don't want to put any distance between us."

I chew on my lip. "My answer isn't no. But I'm freaked out by it."

Our therapist interjects, "Jason, let's table the moving discussion and take a step back to talk for a moment about communication. It's my understanding there are a few things that brought you and Charlotte to therapy in the first place."

"That's correct," Jason replies. I nod in agreement.

"Can you tell me a little bit about it, since I've only heard from Charlotte?"

Head down, he wrings his hands. "I've always felt this over-whelming need to protect Charlotte. She's so full of life and love. I don't want anything to dull that, you know? I took it too far. I didn't know how to tell her that we got married and, at first, I really hoped I could make it go away on my own. After a week or two, I didn't want to. At her friend's wedding, I knew, without a shadow of a doubt, that I want to spend the rest of my life with her. The only problem was: I didn't know how to tell her. I was scared she would want a divorce, scared she didn't love me the same way I love her."

"Jay," I breathe, placing my hand over his that won't stop fidgeting. I love him so much it hurts and I hate that he ever doubted how I feel about him.

"Will you ever be able to forgive me?" His eyes finally meet mine.

"I already did, but you want to skip straight to the happily ever after. I need more time."

He turns his hand over, bringing my knuckles to his lips. "Because *you* are my happily ever after. You're my forever, Charlotte."

My breath hitches. How can he speak so matter-of-factly? I'm the fun friend, never the forever girl. I've been in love with him for years, and sure we have a lot to work on, but when I imagine myself years from now... He's my forever.

"Purple." I shake my head, chuckling to myself.

Jason frowns. "Purple? Sorry, I'm not following."

"A couple weeks ago, I was asked to identify colors as emotions. It helps when I can't define exactly how I'm feeling. I've done it before in therapy, so it's not new to me, but I started mixing colors. Purple is red and blue. Blue is sad; I'm upset because things are moving too fast and still recovering from the hurt the secrets caused. Red is normally anger, but now..." I pet Besvär, avoiding the big emotion.

"What is red?" His voice is quiet. I meet his gaze, and

his expression is unreadable, at least to me. He repeats, "What is red, Char?"

"What do you think?"

"Say it," he pleads. "I need to know I'm not the only one."

"You know you're not."

He takes a deep breath. "I'm sorry, I need to hear it. I shouldn't need the affirmation, but I do. I spent over a decade with a woman who didn't love me. I need to know, am I about to spend another chapter of my life with someone who doesn't love me? And not just as your friend."

"I'm not her. Look at me." He doesn't. "It has *never* been about how much I love you. You weren't the only one fighting this for years. You're Emma's ex-husband. I wasn't supposed to love you, but... I do love you, more than I thought I could ever love anyone." When he finally looks up, a single tear leaves his eye. "Oh, fuck. I'm sorry, Jay! I didn't mean to make you sad."

Jason turns, takes my face in his hands and presses a chaste kiss to my lips. "I'm the furthest thing from sad, babygirl."

"Then why are you crying?" I wipe the tear away before it hits his beard.

"I almost lost you because I fucked up... *twice*. I tried to control everything and didn't treat you as my equal. I see that now and I'm so sorry it took me this long." He takes my hand, brushing a kiss to my knuckles. "I have insecurities, but I'm working on them. I promise I'll try to slow things down, but I have to admit, I'm still so fucking scared I'll lose you in January because you won't think this is worth it and walk away."

"As productive as this discussion is, our time is nearly up." *Seriously?* "Something I would like for you both to think about separately and discuss as a couple is why January is important, what a move for Charlotte would look like for you both, and how you can talk through things if one of you has a secret that comes to light. I'd love to see you both this time next week for a full-length appointment."

We leave the appointment and the car ride home is quiet. I expected as much, but I feel the need to fill the silence. No words give it justice. We've never talked about his relationship with Emma, but a lot of what's happened makes sense now that I know he's hurting. I would too if I spent years of my life in a loveless marriage, no matter how good of a friendship I have with them.

The moment we approach my front door, I tell him quietly, "I won't move. Not yet, at least. I'm not moving away from *you*. I just need to find a place that's a better fit for this pretty pup of mine."

"Why don't we do a trial run? You keep your place, but stay with me? With our schedules, we normally only have a few nights a week together, and I want you here. I was actually considering asking you to move in while we were in LA. You don't have to decide right now, but will you consider it?"

I lift onto my toes and kiss him on the cheek. "Okay."

"Take your time. We can talk about it with the boys when they're here tomorrow." He wraps his arms around me, and the moment our chests touch, he lets out a satisfied sigh, though it sounds more like a growl. Besvär paws at him.

"It's okay, girl. I'm safe," I chuckle, patting her on the head. "I wasn't saying 'okay' to considering moving in. I was saying 'okay, we can do a trial run.' But if things get weird and I move back next door, will you be okay with that?"

"If you're next door and not in a whole other city? Yes, but are you sure about this?"

"Absolutely. We should run it by your boys first, though."

He sighs deeply, and his voice shakes as he asks, "Do you want to stay tonight?"

While I'm unsure about things moving too fast, he's equally worried I'll break his heart. Our therapist is correct and I need to think about why January is so important. If things feel right, and he keeps to his word that he'll slow down, I shouldn't be putting an arbitrary end date on our accidental marriage. Moving in when I still have my own place is a good compromise.

"If I live with you now, shouldn't I be staying the night?" I tease with a smirk.

Jason slides his hand into my hair and pulls me in for a brutal kiss, but Besvär kills the mood and paws at Jason to get off me. We both laugh as we break apart.

Jason presses one last kiss to my cheek as I whisper, "I love you."

"Not as much as I love you, babygirl."

36

JASON

I have the perfect woman, but I still feel like I could lose her at any given moment. Today's therapy appointment was eye-opening; Charlotte really needs me to put on the brakes... *again*. She's said it over and over, but today it clicked for me. Her moving in isn't taking things slow, but she'll keep her apartment, and Besvär will have more space. When Charlotte's ready, I'm going to ask her to marry me, but I won't rush her into it like I have with everything else.

We spend most of the day at my place so Besvär can get used to it. I brought over her dog bed and food, so she'll be more comfortable here. She's a working dog—not a pet—but Charlotte said she wants her to be treated with the same love we'd show any other dog. I have a feeling the pup will sleep in our bed if Char has her way.

With the boys coming tomorrow, Charlotte suggested we have a lazy day at home, just the two of us... Well, three of us. We're watching one of her favorite romantic comedies, and about twenty minutes in, Charlotte surprises me by straddling my lap. She grabs the remote to pause the movie.

I grip her thighs and as much as I want my hands on her, I allow her to take the lead. Leaning in, she cups her hands behind my neck and kisses me. She tastes like the mango iced tea she had earlier and I find myself wanting to buy stock in whatever company makes it. She pulls back with a devilish grin.

"Hey, sweetheart." I tuck her hair behind her ear. "What are you up to?"

"I need you to listen to me, and really hear me."

"I'm listening."

"You said something in therapy and it's really been bothering me. We aren't on the same page when it comes to love." My stomach drops at her words. "I think we need to take one of those love language tests. You know, the ones that'll tell you how you show and receive love? We should take one."

"That's a good idea. Is there a book or…"

She immediately takes out her phone and begins typing. "Okay, question one—"

"You want to take it *now?*"

Charlotte shrugs. "Why not? No time like the present. I think it'll help me understand you better."

"I think you understand me just fine, babygirl," I chuckle. She grinds onto me, making me groan. "*Fuck. You can't be doing that if you want me to focus.*"

"Don't get a smart mouth with me and I won't rub my pussy on you." Her forwardness takes me by surprise but I can't help smiling; she's fucking adorable.

Charlotte and I finish the quiz and discover that I prefer words of affirmation and quality time. She needs physical touch and quality time. It makes sense to me, given that we spend all of our free time together, even before we got married.

"See! I knew yours would be words of affirmation." Her grin is wide. I can't help but laugh at her sincerity. She's so damn proud of her intuition. "I think it bothers you that I don't tell you how I feel. I'm not good at expressing myself, but I promise I'll work on it. You went years without someone loving you. *Fuck*, that's depressing." She mutters the last part, mostly to herself.

"It's not that it bothers me; it's just baggage I carry." It's weird talking about Emma with her, but she deserves the truth. "I love Emma." Before I can explain, Charlotte's eyes blow wide. "No, babygirl, not like that. I love her like you love Eddie or Mel. She's an important person in my life, but I don't think I was ever *in love* with her. I never woke up thinking 'I can't wait to see her.' I never wanted to do bigger things with my life because of her. I never felt an ache in my chest when she wasn't around. I feel all of that with you. I always have. You bring me so much joy. I just hope I am good enough for you that you'll feel a tenth of what I feel."

"Jason David Kelly," she groans. "You need to stop with all of these sweet, romantic speeches of yours."

"Or what? You'll fall in love with me? Should I lean against more door frames to seal the deal?"

Char lets out a hearty laugh and I feel it everywhere. "You have my permission to lean on anything you want. Oh, but don't forget your gray sweatpants *without* underwear."

I glance down at my sweatpants and playfully ask, "Should I take my boxer briefs off to complete the look for you?"

"I think you should take all of it off."

My eyebrows raise and jaw drops. "My sweet Charlotte, what have I done to you?"

"I want you." All laughter and banter stops at her words.

I snap. A man can only take so much. When the most beautiful woman I have ever known tells me she wants me, who am I to deny her? I wrap Charlotte's legs around my waist and stand to carry her to the bedroom. Her hands in my hair, these kisses aren't the sweet Charlotte I know; it's fiery and urgent.

"Slow down, babygirl. If we're doing this, I plan on

taking my time with you." I set her down on the bed and stifle a groan. *Fuck, she's so damn beautiful.*

Besvär hops up and settles at the foot of the bed—she must know something is off with Charlotte, too. While I love the enthusiasm, I'm worried after what Charlotte said in therapy that she's still feeling a combination of sadness and love.

"Baby, what's going on?"

"I feel like I'm going to explode," she admits. "My emotions are all over the place."

"Talk to me, what are you feeling?" I lie next to her and tuck her hair behind her ear.

"I don't want things to be only physical between us." She props herself up on her elbow. "But I also want *this*. So, my mind is kind of a mess right now."

"Pick a number between one and ten."

She chuckles. "I can't handle ten orgasms right now, Jay. One."

"I'm in love with you, Charlotte. I know we've talked about this, but it bears repeating. For me, nothing about what I feel for you is just physical. I've had time to wrap my mind around us being married, taking this job, and what it might mean for us. You haven't. I've thrown you curveball after curveball, but I haven't given you the time and space to be okay with any of it. By some miracle, you've forgiven me for being selfish and I don't take that for granted. If I'm completely honest with you, it might just be sex with your boyfriend for you, but for me, I'm making love to my gorgeous wife."

Okay, so I might suck at taking things slow.

Char sucks in a breath. "I thought we weren't going to talk about the whole marriage thing."

"You need to know where I'm at. There's your *one*, sweetheart. My one truth. I don't want you to think for one moment that any of this is only physical for me."

She pulls her lip between her teeth. "Pick a number between one and ten, Jay."

Unsure what to expect, I reply, "Three."

Charlotte climbs on top of me, straddling my increasingly hard cock. She strips off her shirt and tosses it to the ground. "Besvär, go lay down on the couch, please. You don't want to be here for this." Once she's gone, we both laugh. It's cut short when Charlotte unhooks her bra and tosses it to the ground. I slide my hand up between her breasts and claim her throat, bringing her in to kiss me.

"One. I love that you love with your whole heart," she mutters against my lips. "Two. I love that you take care of those who are important to you; you make me feel safe and adored. And three… I love *you*. All of you. It might not be making love to my husband for me, but it sure as hell isn't just sex with my boyfriend." She pulls back, her hair falling to one side over her shoulder. "Bonus truth? I do see myself spending the rest of my life with you. Just give me time. I feel red… *not* anger, Jay. I love you."

"What did I do to deserve you?"

"You don't," she says with zero hesitation or sarcasm. "We don't deserve each other. But that doesn't mean I love you any less."

"Come here, babygirl." She smiles and kisses me again. "Strip those pants off and sit on my face."

"Are you sure you can handle these thunder thighs as earmuffs?"

"Fuck yes, but don't you dare talk negatively about your sexy body." I never understood why women are so self-conscious about climbing onto a man's face if he asks for it. Death by pussy sounds like a great way to go.

Charlotte sits back and takes off her leggings and thong. *Shit, since when does she wear thongs? She fucking planned this.* She slowly crawls up the bed to me and tugs at my sweatpants, freeing my cock.

"Hold on there, sweetheart. You know the rules: I don't come unless you do… at least *three* times."

She doesn't listen, instead licking up my length before taking me in her mouth—never breaking eye contact. It's not just a few inches… she takes *all* of me at once. Her tongue massages in circles as she sucks hard. It feels fucking amazing, but I'm not going to come. Just as she struggles with finishing when she's in her head, I can't come if I know my partner hasn't.

"Have you had your fun?" I pull her off me and she whimpers in protest. "I was promised earmuffs." I roughly kiss her and she chuckles against my lips, then crawls up my body until she's straddling my face. "That's right, babygirl, just like that." I grip her hips. "Fuck, I missed you." She grinds onto my mouth; I swear I've died and gone to heaven. I alternate between teasing her clit and long firm strokes of my tongue, desperate for her to make a mess.

"Right there… Oh, fuck… Keep doing that."

I curl my tongue inside her as she fucks my face. When I groan, the vibration is almost enough to send her over the edge.

"Do that again," she whimpers.

I growl against her again, keeping her pressed firmly against me as I flick my tongue on her clit. It takes her by surprise and she comes fast and hard for me. I lap up every drop, tempted to coax another from her.

"That was…" she pants.

"I'm nowhere near done with you, babygirl." I lift her up enough to slide out from under her. I rummage through my bedside table and take out a pair of black fur-lined cuffs, tossing them on the bed. Her eyes wide, I explain, "I don't want you overstimulated or to feel restricted. Your choice: I can cuff you or"—I can barely control my smirk—"you can cuff me. I've dreamt about being able to do whatever I want to you as I pull orgasm after orgasm out of you. If you ever want that kind of control, I'm up for it."

Eyes alight, Charlotte bites her lip. "Cuff me. I think I can handle it, but keep the key handy just in case."

"There's no key; they release with a button. Are you sure?"

She sits up and snakes her hand behind my neck, pulling my lips to hers. "Yes."

"If at any time you need me to stop, I'll remove them, okay?"

Char grabs the handcuffs, attaches them to one wrist. She hooks them around the bedframe, then binds her other wrist. "Do your worst, Jay." She continues to surprise me.

"Careful what you wish for, babygirl." I slide my hands firmly up her legs, grip her thighs, and spread her wide for me. "I'm yours, Charlotte." I kiss up her thigh, nipping at her as I confess, "I worship at your altar, I want to give you the world. But right now? You're going to give yourself to me."

I press two fingers inside her. She's still so wet, they slide in with ease. Her head falls back as she moans, egging me on. I swirl my tongue around her clit, curling my fingers to hit right where she needs me. I want to bring her right to the brink, have her begging to come, then build her up again.

"You're mine," I groan against her.

"I think you're taking the growly book boyfriend thing a little too far, Jay."

"Fuck that. Your book boyfriends have nothing on me." I drive my fingers deeper, forcing a moan from her. "Please, send them my regards." She tugs at the handcuffs and arches her back. "I know you're close but you don't come unless I tell you to, Charlotte."

"Keep talking, Jay."

"You're so fucking beautiful, all tied up for me." I pick up my pace and press firm kisses up her body. She's clenching around me; she can't hang on much longer. "Okay, babygirl, are you ready?" She nods. "Come for me," I whisper against her lips. She cries out, pulsing around my fingers, and I roughly kiss her to help her through her orgasm, not removing my fingers. When she catches her breath, I ask, "Doing okay, sweetheart?"

"I want to touch you."

"Not yet." I break our kiss and drive my fingers deeper. "You're going to let me take at least one more from you. You feel too good, I want to play with this pretty pussy a little longer. How do you want to come?" She lifts up to kiss me but I pull back. "Tell me first."

"I like the weight of you on top of me. I want to feel you deep inside me as I come."

"Give me one more and you can have my cock."

I fuck her with my fingers and she shatters for me again. Not waiting for her to come down from her orgasm, I replace my fingers with my cock in one quick movement. Her gasps and moans fill the room and I keep my pace slow and controlled, pushing deeper inside her with each thrust. She's still tugging at her cuffs; I don't want to risk it being too much for her and reach to pop the lock on both of them. Her legs and arms wrap tightly around me, pulling me impossibly closer as her nails scratch down my back.

"Still doing okay, babygirl?"

"Yes," she whimpers.

Charlotte needs me to talk to her, to keep her out of her own head. I pull back, breaking our kiss and look deep in her eyes. I don't care if she needs to look away, but I fucking love that she doesn't. I give her all my truths between thrusts. "I love you, Charlotte. You're the most incredible woman I've ever known, and I'm the luckiest man alive to have you in my life." I lean in to whisper beside her ear, "I'm going to spend the rest of my life making sure you know how loved you are."

"Jason, I—"

"No, baby. I'm not finished." She tightens around my cock, and I continue my same pace. "I've been yours since the day you told me you wanted to move next door." I kiss her neck, careful not to suck too hard or accidentally mark her, no matter how much I want to. "You're my everything." A small tear leaves her eye and I slow, wiping it from her cheek. "Purple?"

Charlotte chuckles. "No... red. Just red." She lifts her hips to meet my thrusts. "I love you," she whispers and grips my back. "I'm close, just a little harder... Yes, just like that. Will you come with me?"

I nod and insist, "Only if you let me make love to you again tonight to finish what I started." I fuck her harder, the bedframe knocking against the wall. She shatters, coming for me with my name on her lips. My own release follows, and my lips never leave hers as I settle inside her, relishing the feeling of her beneath me.

"What do you mean finish what you started?"

"Guess you'll just have to find out, won't you?"

37

CHARLOTTE

After what has to be the best sex of my life, Jason and I need to eat. Or, rather, I do. Tacos are always a great choice, even if they aren't as good as the ones we had in Southern California. "What time are the boys coming tomorrow? Do you need me to bring them to the game?"

Jason wipes his mouth with his napkin after taking an entirely too big of a bite of his taco. "I can have Dylan bring them."

Does he not want me to? Does he not trust me?

"Oh, okay." I'm probably in my head about this but it bothers me.

He stills, then asks, "Hey, what's wrong?"

Shit.

"Nothing's wrong." I offer a tight-lipped smile.

"You think I can't tell when you're faking it?"

My cheeks heat. "If you don't want me to bring them, I understand."

"It's not that. I don't want you to feel you have to take care of the boys when I'm not around. I'm not about to turn you into a housewife," he insists.

I nod and distract myself with my plate in front of me. "I don't want to be a housewife, but your boys are my nephews. I don't mind."

"Our family is complicated. When Dylan wanted to marry Emma, I told him there's no such thing as too much love and I like the fact that my boys have a bonus father. You're their aunt, but I never want to assume or ask you to step into a parental role for them." He takes my hand and kisses my palm before placing it on his cheek, covering my hand with his hand. "I'm trying to slow things down. So, no, I don't *need* you to take them. But, if you want to, that's something completely different."

"Do you trust me with them?"

He frowns. "Of course. Why wouldn't I?"

"I have a service pup, I have meltdowns, I—"

"You haven't had a meltdown since Delasnia—which I was the cause of. I don't think I'll ever forgive myself for it. Besvär is here to make sure you're safe, but even without her, I trust you with my life. Why wouldn't I trust you with my boys? That's rhetorical, by the way." He smirks and huffs a small laugh. "I love you, sweetheart. I never want you to feel like I'm taking advantage of you. If you want to bring them, I want it to be because you want to, not because you feel like you have to."

Dylan is dropping off the girls, since Harriet insists on coming. I was already bringing them, so a few more in tow isn't an inconvenience. Poor Harriet is still obsessed with Robbie. I think it's hilarious but Jason and my brother-in-law think otherwise.

"Are Dylan or Em coming?"

"No."

"If they're okay with it, I can take everyone."

After shoving the rest of the taco in his mouth, Jason takes out his phone, types something and shows me his phone a minute or so later.

> Since Char is bringing Harriet and Lizzy, want her to bring the boys?

DYLAN

> Lizzy is sick, so she's staying home. I'll have Harriet come with the boys in the morning, if that's okay?

> Sure thing. Still on for Sunday?

> Only if you bring Char. We haven't seen her in forever.

> I'll check with her, but otherwise, we'll be there.

As I'm reading, there's a message on my own phone.

DYLAN

Please come Sunday. My kids won't shut up about when they'll get to see you again. Some shit about waffles and Taylor Swift. Please?

> Okay, I'll be there with Besvär after my focus group at noon.

Also, Harriet is only going to the game because she has a crush on Robbie.

> Oh, to be 16 again.

She's almost 17, but maybe you can talk some sense into her?

> I'll do my best, but there's no harm in having an innocent crush on a baseball player who doesn't know she exists.

That's the problem. Jason seems to think he does.

> I'll keep an eye on them.

> See you Sunday.

Eyes wide, I slide my phone over to Jason. "Looks like me bringing everyone is the least of our worries."

———

We arrive at the ballpark and Jason was able to get us my favorite seats right behind home plate. We were going to be near third base, so the boys could see their dad in action, but Jason's hoping giving Harriet a little space from third will help lessen her crush. I know better. He could put us in the nosebleeds and she would still be entirely too excited to be here and only cheer when Robbie's at bat, or when he tags someone out.

"I need to use the restroom, can you keep an eye on the boys while I'm gone?" I ask Harriet. "I'll grab snacks for everyone too."

Harriet nods but is otherwise focused on the game. I get everyone's snack order before Besvär and I head up the stairs. After using the restroom, I stop at the concession stand and, hands full, return to our seats.

Halfway down, a man stops me. "Can I see your ticket?"

"It's in my back pocket." I try to juggle everything and can't manage it. "Could you follow me to my seat? My family is down there and I can't grab it right now."

"Miss, I need to see your ticket or you're not going down there."

Are you fucking kidding me?

My heart rate must be elevated because Besvär is nuzzling into me. "Then, get my husband; he's the third base coach. I'm sure the crowd would love you pausing the game for this." My eyes narrow and Besvär whimpers. I glance to third base and Jason's eyes are on me. I don't need him distracted, so I shake my head at him. He returns his attention to the game, glancing back a few times.

"Ma'am, I am going to need you to go back the way you came."

Defeated, I begin walking back up the stairs so I can set everything down and show him my ticket. Over the man's walkie-talkie, there's garbled words and "*a Ms. Wentworth escorted to her seat.*"

I stop in my tracks. "That's me. Answer that."

"What? You said you're Mrs. Kelly. All of a sudden you're Ms. Wentworth? Nice try."

This is getting ridiculous. I let out a sigh and continue up the steps to the top, pausing when I hear loud shouts and clapping behind me. When I turn, a man is barreling up the aisle.

Robbie? What the fuck?

"Miss Charlotte, what are you doing?"

The attendant tries to put space between us. "Mr. Chavez, what are you doing up here? A rogue attendee doesn't concern you."

"He wants to see my ticket, but it's in my back pocket and my hands are full," I explain to Robbie.

Robbie takes the snacks, which allows me to pull out my ticket. "Rogue, huh?" I wave it at the attendant defiantly.

Unfortunately, the whole interaction made the jumbotron. Robbie offers me his arm and leads us down to my seat. "I'm sorry," he whispers. "Coach wasn't acting like himself. When I looked out from the dugout and saw that it was you… Are you okay?"

"Yes, I'm fine, thank you. You shouldn't have come to my rescue."

"He would have done it for me," he insists with a wide smile. When we reach my seat, he asks the boys, "Okay, who ordered the nachos that will make the eleven o'clock news?"

38

ROBBIE

"Fuck, *mi cielo*, you're stunning."

"Um... Robbie, please don't take offense to this, but you totally said that out loud," Charlotte whispers, and I'm suddenly acutely aware of how inappropriate all of this is.

"Sorry, uh, who had a hotdog?" The little kid waves and I hand it to him. "And the cotton candy?"

The announcer drowns us out. *"Our very own Robbie Chavez is helping a few fans behind home plate..."*

Fuck! "Sorry, Miss Charlotte, I need to get back before I'm fined. Are you good?"

Charlotte laughs and glances at Harriet whose cheeks are a rosy pink. "Yeah, we're all right, Robbie. Thank you." She leans in so only I can hear, "Stay away from Harriet though. Give her a year or her dad and Jason will probably murder you." Sitting down with her service dog at her side, she winks at me.

I make my way toward the dugout and hop over the divider. I still have two players before I'm on-deck, so no one should care…

Harriet's dad won't murder me, but Coach definitely will.

I glance back at Harriet and Jason glares at me.

Worth it.

We only have one out when Tony is up. I'm in the hole, and from here I have the perfect view of the goddess I can't have. Charlotte's right. I need to bide my time.

What am I saying? I know nothing about this girl.

The buzzkill announcer chimes in, "*Next up, we have third baseman, Robert Chavez.*"

Before I step in the box, I steal a glance of Harriet. She has an ereader in one hand but is otherwise at the edge of her seat. The flirt in me can't help kissing my fingers and pointing to her before I step into the batter's box.

Swing. Strike one. *Crack.* I pop one to far left field; it's foul. *Damn it.*

I'm being cocky right now, showing off for some underage chick I can't have. I look to third base and Coach is *pissed.* He knows damn well I'm not playing with everything I have; I need to get my head in the game.

The ball comes fast and low, the perfect opportunity for me. I swing hard at an angle and *crack*. She flies deep right field. Being a switch hitter with a leftie pitcher worked to my advantage today.

"It's going, it's going… It's gone. Robbie Chaaavez home run!"

Fuck yes. That one was for you, mi cielo.

When I round third, Coach is proud of me, but he can't hide his concern over everything that just happened. As I approach home, all of Coach's family are on their feet yelling and cheering. The rest of the stadium fades away because I can't keep my eyes off the one person who could be trouble for me.

At the post-game press conference, the cameras are flashing and I can't focus. No less than twenty questions are being thrown at me at the same time.

"GNN, you're up," Jason chimes in, surprising me as he claps me on the back and sits beside me.

"The woman in the stands today, what is your relationship with her?"

Damn, it. Saw this shit coming.

"That was Miss Charlotte," I reply. "She's…" I whisper to Jason, "Do I tell them she's your wife?"

He chuckles and says into the microphone. "Charlotte

has nothing to do with Robbie's performance today. Next question."

"The woman next to her. You all but dedicated your home run to her. Can you tell us more about the mystery woman?"

Fuck.

I look to Coach for an answer, but he looks back at me like my dad would. "*Mi cielo?*" Jason's eyes narrow and mine widen. "What I meant to say was I dedicated my home run to Coach's *whole* family. He's the reason I'm here."

That was a close one.

"If you're not going to ask questions regarding Robbie's performance, we're done here," Jason growls, looking like he is two steps from murdering me and hiring someone to clean up the body.

I answer five or so questions about the game. Once we leave and are out of earshot, I begin apologizing, "Shit, I am so sorry, Coach. I didn't mean anything by it, I promise."

"My wife and kids are off-limits in interviews," he calmly explains. "While Harriet's not my daughter, that means her too. Also, even when she's eighteen, you would have to get through me, Charlotte, Dylan, *and* Emma before you even considered what you're thinking about. I took Spanish in high school, Robbie, and know damn well what you called her."

I'm about to deny it when his family comes down the hallway. His youngest son wraps his arms around Jason. "Dad, your team is doing... okay."

All of us laugh and Jason admits, "Yeah, we barely skated by today, but Robbie brought in three runs, which made the game."

One of the older boys chimes in, "Maybe Aunt Charlotte was good luck?"

"Or Harriet," the other one says with a smirk. Harriet blushes and looks away.

Fuck.

"No, it was the hard work and determination of the team," Charlotte insists with an expectant head nod for me to agree.

"Yes, absolutely. Hard work. Determination." *And being into a girl I have no business even looking at for over a year...*

"Right, well, I'll take Harriet home, and the boys will see you later," Charlotte offers, seemingly unsure of herself.

"Damn it," Coach says under his breath. I feel like I shouldn't be here for whatever this is, but I can't help wanting to be in Harriet's space as long as possible. I can't take my eyes off her and I'm pretty sure I'm going straight to hell for it. "Boys, um... What are your thoughts on Charlotte and Besvär moving in?"

Fuck, I was right and it's a family discussion.

The older kids shrug, seemingly not caring either way. The youngest beams, "I love Aunt Charlotte! Can we get our own dog, since Besvär isn't a pet?"

"I probably shouldn't be here for this conversation," Charlotte says, slowly backing away.

"Me, either," I quickly agree.

"I'll go too," Harriet offers.

"Actually, Harriet, can you stay with me and the boys?" Coach asks and she nods.

Charlotte and I both turn to leave and she tells him, "Text me when you're ready to head out." As we walk away, she gives me a side eye. "You're not getting her number, kid. *Mi cielo?* Really? Think Dylan or Jason didn't catch that in the interview?" She gives me a knowing look. "Give it a year before you profess your undying love for someone who isn't legal yet."

"I didn't."

"Yes you did, Robbie."

"Okay," I sigh. "It won't happen again, Miss Charlotte."

She stops in her tracks. "Oh, no. Don't you dare try to 'Miss Charlotte' me. I'm barely a decade older than you. But I'm serious, give your *cielo* a year, Robbie. She's leaving for Oxford next summer. Don't fuck up two lives, okay?"

"You're right," I sigh. "Maybe you should take over for Coach Kelly with your inspirational speeches."

Charlotte chuckles. "Maybe I should."

One year… I can wait one year for Harriet.

39

JASON

While I wanted Char here for this conversation, now that I'm in the thick of it, I understand why she's giving me privacy. Emma and Dylan were made aware of Charlotte moving in and both agreed that I needed to have a chat with the boys solo. I don't think they'll have any issue with it, but I need to talk to them about it all the same.

Harriet is busy texting, and since Robbie stepped away, she's now ignoring us. I don't care if she listens in, but I need to talk to Noah, Aiden, and Charlie about Charlotte. Hopefully Char will give Robbie the same speech I did earlier.

"We can definitely discuss getting a dog," I answer Aiden. "You all know I'm dating Charlotte, but I need to be honest with you. I don't only want to ask her to move in, I want to ask her to marry me."

"That's cool," Charlie offers with a shrug.

Noah doesn't seem to care either way, agreeing, "Yeah." I expected a little more from them, but they're teens now, and I'm lucky to get more than grunt replies at this point.

Aiden is hung up on wanting another dog, asking, "What about a Dachshund?"

"If we get another dog, it has to get along with Besvär. She's the priority because she's a working dog. Understood?" They nod and I add, "We might look at moving somewhere that has more space, too."

Noah chews on his lip. "Do we still get to see Mom and Dad as often if we move?"

"Of course. Why wouldn't you? I love both of them, and what have I always told you boys?"

"There is no such thing as too much love," Charlie grumbles with a roll of his eyes.

"Exactly." I take Aiden under one arm and Noah under my other. Charlie reluctantly finishes the circle. "You can see them as often as you want. You can also see Charlotte and me just as much. All of us are a phone call away, no matter where we move to, or what house you're at that week. We all love you."

The boys seem okay with everything, but only time will tell.

40

CHARLOTTE
ONE MONTH LATER

We're basically on top of each other when the boys are here. A few nights a week, I end up staying at my place next door because the commotion at Jason's is too much for me and Besvär. Jason hates it, I hate it, the boys hate it. We need a new place.

Unfortunately, the real estate market isn't on our side and we've been outbid on no less than two dozen properties. Ethan found a listing that's not on the market yet; I'm hoping this is the one. Jason is on the road, so the boys and I are headed there and will video call him when we arrive.

"All right, you know the drill. If you don't like this one, that's okay. We need to find the *right* house, not just *a* house," I tell the boys as we pull up. Jason insists we get a new place as soon as possible, but I'm pretty sure it's mostly that he wants me home with him all the time. We get out of the car and I give Aiden my phone to video call Jason.

"Hey, Dad. We're headed in." Aiden flips the camera so Jason can see everything. He begins reciting home facts and walking around the house giving him a tour. The twins and I check out the rest of the house.

There are five bedrooms, three bathrooms, and there's a lot of natural light. We could easily convert the extra room into a small library or guest bedroom. The kitchen is small, but larger than Jason's current apartment. I let Besvär investigate the backyard and she does a quick lap before returning to my side.

A few minutes later, Aiden joins us. "Here's Charlotte."

He hands me the phone and Jason's smile is wide. "Hey, babygirl. What do you think?"

"I love that this one has a huge backyard." Aiden wanders inside and I lower my voice. "We'll be able to get a second dog here for Aiden." Returning my voice to normal volume, I ask, "What do you think?"

"Ethan said to put in a bid twenty-thousand over asking and, if they don't budge, we can go from there. I really like this one, but what do you and the boys think?"

"I love it but I'll let them tell you themselves."

I walk in and hand the phone to Charlie, who is indifferent. He passes it to Noah, who is positive it's the best house we've seen yet. Aiden wants us to move in tomorrow. If we're lucky, this will be the one.

Jason comes into the kitchen and announces, "We got the house, sweetheart," with a stack of paperwork to sign. "They expedited everything and we should be able to move in a month." He tosses them on the kitchen table then wraps his arms around me from behind while I'm browning ground beef for tacos. "What do you think you're doing? It's Tuesday, I make tacos."

"You make *over-seasoned* tacos. I thought the cooking class last week would have rubbed off, but instead you're still spice happy."

He kisses my neck and whispers against me, "Oh, I'll show you spicy, babygirl."

"Come on, that's cheesy, even for you. Go sit down, everyone will be here in ten." I school my expression, holding in a smile as best I can.

"Everyone?"

"It's a big day."

He looks away, deep in thought. "We don't have an anniversary. Your birthday is in February. The boys just had a birthday... Fuck, it's one of the girls' birthdays, isn't it?"

"Yeah, Harriet's. She texted me today that she wanted to come by with everyone for tacos and cake. I invited Robbie, I hope that's okay?"

Jason groans. "Not a good idea, sweetheart. I know he has a thing for Harriet and Dylan would kill me if something happened."

"He's only, what, two years older than her? Let them be friends for a year. When she's eighteen, she can live her best sports romance book life," I offer with a shrug.

"Life isn't a romance book, Char."

"Really? Last time I checked, I accidentally married a book boyfriend."

"That you did, babygirl." He pulls me in for a searing kiss and I can't help chuckling against his lips.

Ten minutes later, Jason's apartment is full of family and friends. This might be the last big get together we have here before we move. I'll miss our little apartment, but I can't wait for more space. The boys are just as excited, since they will get their own rooms and the twins won't need to share anymore.

"Hey, doll, I just heard the news that you got the place! Look at you, all grown up, and owning your own home," Ethan teases as he brings me in for a tight hug.

"Oh, shut up, ol' man. How's Mel feeling?" I glance over to see she's taken over my reading chair, propping her feet up on the table.

He follows my gaze and there's so much love in his eyes. "She's great. Pregnancy looks good on her."

"Another kiddo for me to love on. I can't wait to meet the little one."

"You sure that's not in the cards for you?" he asks with a frown, and I reach up to rub the lines away.

"Absolutely. I'm the perfect auntie."

"That you are." Ethan squeezes my arm and joins Mel. He's the brother I never had, and while I appreciate that he's worried about me, I have no desire to have kids of my own. Jason has hinted that he would want to have one of our own, but only if I did. I'm grateful he accepts that I'm more comfortable being Aunt Charlotte to everyone, at least for the foreseeable future.

Robbie knocks on the door as he comes in. "Hey, everyone."

"Robbie! Thanks for coming," I greet, giving him a side hug. "Come on in. Can I get you something to drink? Soda or tea?" I gesture for him to follow me into the kitchen. Harriet spots him and her cheeks turn bright pink. Ethan would say 'a little chaos never hurt anyone,' and while chaos is the last thing those two need, there's no harm in them getting to know each other as friends.

"Water would be great. Thank you, Miss Charlotte."

"Will you please stop with the 'Miss Charlotte' bit?" I chuckle.

"Sorry, it's how my parents raised me. Plus, you're Coach's wife. I don't think he would be okay with me only calling you Charlotte either."

"Jason," I call. He's talking with Dylan and excuses himself when he hears me. "Please tell Robbie it's okay to call me Char or Charlotte."

"Robbie, there are no formalities in my house. If she wants you to call her Charlotte, go for it." Jason kisses my temple and grabs a beer from the fridge before adding, "Just stay away from the birthday girl."

I lean in and whisper to Robbie, "Okay, so maybe call her dad 'Mr. Alexander.' I doubt he'd be cool with you calling him Dylan if you date his daughter next year."

"Shit, am I that obvious?" I wince.

"Yeah, sorry dude." I pat him on the shoulder. "One year, not a day before, do you hear me?"

"Yes, ma'am."

I groan. "That's worse than Miss Charlotte." We both laugh and he heads over to talk to Harriet, Lizzy, and the boys.

I refresh the taco toppings that are quickly depleting when a deep voice startles me. "Hey, babygirl."

"Shit, you scared me." I glance behind me and Jason's leaning against the doorframe of the kitchen. *Damn he looks good.*

"Dylan and Em are taking the boys tonight. What do you say, once everyone leaves we head out? Maybe grab a drink or something?"

I consider it, then shake my head. "I think I'd rather stay in, if that's okay?"

"Whatever you want."

Checking to make sure no one can hear me, I keep my voice low. "I distinctly remember a pair of furry handcuffs that haven't been used in a while, *Sir*."

"Fuck. That's it, everyone out."

I wrap my arms around him. "Not yet. Good things come to those who wait."

"What are you talking about? You hate waiting." He leans in and kisses below my ear. "But you're always worth the wait, sweetheart."

JASON

THREE MONTHS LATER — WORLD SERIES GAME 7

"What if she says no?" Edmund chuckles with his whiskey halfway to his lips.

"You think I haven't thought about that, Eddie?" I groan. "The last few months have been a little too perfect." I rub my hand down my face and I wish I could have a beer right now. The guys thought it would be a good idea to grab a drink as an early celebration, but I need to stay sharp before the big game.

These assholes think I haven't considered every possible negative outcome. Not only am I about to coach one of the biggest games of my life, but I'm also proposing to Charlotte. I could walk away losing on all fronts... Fuck, I don't even want to think about that.

"If she says no, what's the plan?" Ethan asks, expectantly.

"Then, she says no." I shrug. "I'll hate it, but I'll ask again in a few months."

"You're really going to be okay with her saying no?" Dylan blows out an exaggerated breath. His eyes are wide with shock.

I take a few quick gulps of my water. "Yeah, wouldn't you?"

Dylan huffs a laugh. "Honestly, no. It's okay to be nervous, I was a fucking wreck when I proposed to Emma. This is game seven. If your team wins today, are you willing to walk away after what could be the biggest game of your life, and potentially have it all shattered by a no from her?" Dylan's far more worried about this than I am.

I finish my water and set it down roughly on the bar counter. "You're missing the point. I'm spending the rest of my life with Charlotte. If she says yes today, great. If she says yes in a year, fine. It doesn't matter. She wanted to wait until January, but I don't want to wait on an arbitrary date. I just wanted you all here for it." I check the time. "Fuck, I should get going."

"Speaking of which, we better get down to our suite. No matter how comfortable we make her, Mel isn't a big baseball fan and is probably done listening to Emma rattle off stats to her," Ethan chuckles as he tosses back the remainder of his Old Fashioned.

"Good call," Edmund agrees. "Sage and I don't do kids, I'm sure your crotch gremlins are being less than pleasant, even if most of them are teenagers. I should get back to her." He finishes his whiskey and signals for two to take back to the suite, then chuckles to himself. "You know what I told Sage the other day? I'm the only one of the four of us who hasn't shagged Emma. The lot of you are bonded for life."

Shit. He's right. Ethan and I look at each other, wide eyed. I hope no one clues Charlotte or Emma in on that unfun fact.

"Fuck you, Eddie," Dylan growls. "That's my wife you're talking about." He pats me on the shoulder. "Good luck with Charlotte." He takes his gin and tonic and joins the other two as they head to their suite.

Fuck, what if she says no?

We're up six to two and it should be in the bag. It's the seventh inning stretch and I hate that I can't be up in the suite with my family and friends. Luckily, everyone is in on what's happening to ensure Char doesn't leave to take my call.

The song "Paper Rings" by Taylor Swift blares through the stadium and I video call Charlotte. She picks up on the second ring. "Jay! I think you're going to win this!"

"Hey, babygirl, I don't have much time. Look in your bag."

Charlotte hands Emma her phone so she can look in her purse. When she finds the box, she slowly pulls it out and Emma whispers in her ear. She looks around and I see the moment it hits her, she gasps, "Is this…"

"Open it."

Charlotte cautiously opens the box to find two braided paper rings that the boys made. A few months ago, we told the boys about our wedding we don't remember, and Noah suggested we get married for real. I wanted to give Charlotte time, and if she's not ready, I'll wait until I'm on my death bed until she is.

Her hand flies to her mouth as Aiden clings to her side. He tells her to listen to the song playing and she looks to Emma, then back to the phone. "Jason," she breathes, "is this… are you…"

"Yeah, babygirl. Will you marry me, not by accident this time? I have a real ring but—"

"How do I get to the dugout?" she shrieks.

With impeccable timing, Robbie approaches her from behind. "Miss Charlotte, will you come with me?"

"What the fuck? Robbie, you're supposed to be on the field or the dugout or literally anywhere but here! What's going on? And what have I said about calling me that? I'm not some kind of governance or Regency heroine."

"Coach couldn't be up here right now, but they let me do what I want." Robbie shrugs. "There's no time, we've gotta go. Here's your VIP pass." He places the lanyard over her head. "No one should question me, but I grabbed one, just in case they give you and Besvär trouble."

Charlotte looks back at everyone with wide eyes. Eddie suggests, "Hang up, love. Go give him your answer."

She doesn't say goodbye before she hangs up the phone. I'm left in limbo. With less than ten minutes to get to me, I'm suddenly worried she won't make it, or worse, say no.

I watch the clock tick down, waiting for her to make it to me. They won't start the game without Robbie, who insisted on being part of the proposal so he could boost his social media presence if she said yes.

Five minutes.

She's still not here, but neither is Robbie.

Three minutes.

Fuck, is this a no?

Two minutes before we start the bottom half of the inning, Charlotte makes it to the dugout with Besvär and Robbie. "I'm sorry, Coach, there was a new guy who kept saying I wasn't who I said I was. What's the point in having a multi-million dollar contract if you can't even bypass security?" He lifts his hands in front of him in surrender. "Oh, right... Do your thing."

Unfortunately, because of Robbie's PR stunt, we're on the jumbotron. I stuff down my nerves and drop down to one knee anyway, cracking open the box to the real engagement ring—which is a princess-cut solitaire in a white gold setting, *not* made of paper. "Charlotte Anne Wentworth, will you do me the honor of being my wife?"

She leans in so that only I can hear, "You could have just proposed with the paper rings. My answer was already yes."

"Are you ready to spend forever with me, sweetheart?"

"Are you? I'm a lot of fun, you know," she teases, a call back the day Dylan proposed to Emma. I can't help but laugh.

"Or a whole lotta trouble." I stand and take her face in my hands as I kiss her. She sighs against my lips and the whole damn stadium erupts in cheers. "I love you, babygirl."

"I love you, too."

"I now pronounce you man and wife."

Jason dips me, and even through his kisses, the grin hasn't left his face. There are claps and cheers from our family and friends. He brings me upright and whispers against my lips, "No longer just on paper, sweetheart."

Baseball season is in full swing again and Jason's team is favored for the playoffs. We decided the easiest way to get married would be to squeeze it in between games. When he suggested we get married at my favorite amusement park, I was beyond excited. It's truly a fairy-tale wedding that puts all epilogue weddings to shame, but only because I'm marrying my own real life book boyfriend.

Jay still rolls up his sleeves and leans against door frames to get me all hot and bothered. He even went to more cooking classes and, thankfully, no longer over-seasons our food. We take trips—sometimes just the two of us and other times with the boys. Therapy is still weekly; it's helped us get to know each other better, since I'm horrible at expressing myself and he wants to overstep from time to time. Gray sweatpants are a must whenever the boys aren't home, and he still asks me to pick between one and ten... I usually pick ten.

Through it all, I fall deeper in love with him every single day. After everything that's happened, I make sure to tell him every opportunity I get. Most of the time, he beats me to it. Waking up with a man who has made it his personal mission to make me feel loved and adored, I never in a million years would have thought this would be my life.

The reception is beautiful. Sage did an incredible job making sure everything was just as we wanted it. There are splashes of red roses everywhere, and our center-pieces are stacks of our favorite books. I don't remember the last time I felt "purple," so showering today in red felt right. I have the love and support of one of the most incredible men I have ever known, and all of our family.

Eddie is my Man of Honor and insisted on giving a speech. "About a year ago, most of you were at my own wedding. You know, the one where I wasn't actually married. Today, we celebrate my favorite friend who has been secretly married this whole damn time. The last few years, I've watched you two fight how you felt about one another. It's about damn time you got your act together so you can spend the rest of your life with your best friend. Am I bitter that you asked my Sage to plan your wedding? Maybe. But, she's better than me in every way, so I'll let it slide. Anyway, wishing you a lifetime of love and happiness. Love you both. Cheers." He raises his glass.

Dylan is about to make a speech when Robbie whispers something to him, and Dylan hands him the microphone. "I'm sorry to steal the attention on your big day, but I have an important question to ask someone. Harriet, *mi cielo*, I know we've only been dating for a month but I know in my heart that you're the woman for me. Would you do me the honor of being my wife?"

While I'm shocked, I'm nowhere near as shocked as Harriet is. All of our eyes are wide, and nearly everyone gasps. Emma and Dylan exchange a look. He gets a little growly when it comes to all the women in his life, so I hope he goes easy on Robbie.

Harriet glances around, then whispers to him…

Harriet and Robbie's story continues in Wine About It.

LOVED TROUBLE WITH A TWIST?

I hope you loved reading Charlotte and Jason's story as much as I loved writing it!

Wherever you feel most comfortable, please consider leaving a review on Goodreads, Amazon, or social media! Your honest review means the world to me.

To keep up with all of my upcoming releases, be sure to follow me over on Amazon!

xoxo,
Irene

ACKNOWLEDGMENTS

First, I would like to thank my amazing alpha readers — Whisper, Lakshmi, Jessica, and Amanda. You ladies are amazing! I'm so grateful for all of your help with this book.

To my beta readers Emily and Hayley — Thank you so much for your feedback! I couldn't have done this without you.

To my neurospicy sensitivity readers — Thank you for being on this journey with me and making sure Charlotte was given the perfect story.

To my ARC readers — Thanks for taking a chance on me! I know I'm known for my spicy romcoms, so thank you for jumping in with two feet with this sweet as fuck novella. I am so blessed to have all of you reading and reviewing my work before launch.

To my amazing graphic designer friend Robert Boord — Thank you for creating Charlotte and putting up with my rapid release schedule.

To my incredible line editor H.M. Darling — Another one bites the dust! Thank you for putting up with my comma confetti.

Finally, thank you to all of my author friends for not letting my imposter syndrome take over, my "real life" friends for believing in me, and my family for putting up with my silly little dream of becoming a published author.

ABOUT IRENE

Irene Bahrd is a feisty Capricorn and one of the most avid readers you will ever meet. Her favorite genres to read or write include romantic comedies, political romance, romantasy, and the occasional contemporary or dark romance.

She started her writing journey as a dare from a friend, after recounting dating stories from her early twenties. They inspired her to write spicy romantic comedies and parodies that feature a variety of book boyfriends—though most are cinnamon roll golden retrievers. Many of her stories contain LGBTQIA+, disabled, and neurodivergent characters.

Irene can be found on most social media platforms under @irenebahrdauthor

ALSO BY IRENE BAHRD

Top Shelf Romances Series

Mine with Extra Lime

Falling the Old Fashioned Way

Royally on the Rocks

Trouble with a Twist

Top Shelf Novellas

Wine About It

Rosé to the Occasion

Mule Tide Cheer

Love at all Cost Series

A Voice Without Reason

Not Her Villain

Maybe in Fifty *(Prequel Novella to Unexpectedly Ruined)*

Unexpectedly Ruined

Sip Happens *(Novella)*

Sapphire Lake Series

Never Yours

Always Heated

Needing to Score Series

Kick Out of It

There is No Try

One Goal in Mind

Ready to Snap

<u>Love & Politics Series</u>

Arranged Vacancy

Absolute Majority

Accepted Precedent

<u>Stand Alone ErotiComs</u>

Flexible Standards

Royally Cuffed

Hard to Swallow

<u>Holiday ErotiCom Novella Series</u>

Merry in Spite

ForNever Mine

Summer of the Switch

Haunted Happenstance

Save a Horse

<u>Stand Alone Parodies</u>

Divorce of Convenience

<u>Expect the Unexpected Parody Novella Duet</u>

Undeclared Heir

Undecided Heiress

<u>Pelligini Crime Daddies Parody Novella Duet</u>

Running from the Garden with Eden

Not My Bodyguard's Keeper

<u>Magical Mischief Parody Novella Series</u>

Unshifted

Uncharmed

Thirst Trap Book Boyfriends Satire Series

Trapp Temptations: Vol. 1

Trapp Temptations: Vol. 2